A portion of the proceeds from sales of
Retirement Can Be Murder *will be donated to the*
Breast Cancer Survival Center (breastcancersurvival.org),
a non-profit organization which provides
post-treatment education and support for
breast cancer survivors and their families.

Chapter 1

The hardest years of a marriage are the ones following the wedding.

Here's an amazing weight-loss tip for all the women in America: an out-of-body experience makes you look thinner. Forget about vertical vs. horizontal stripes. I'm telling you, an out-of-body occurrence does the trick. Plus, it can be quite a pleasant sensation to look down and see a movie starring...you. What's not to like?

Of course, there's a down side to my weight-loss tip. Out-of-body experiences are triggered by a traumatic event, like the panicky phone call I'd just gotten from Jim, My Beloved Husband of 36 years, telling me he'd found his retirement coach, Davis Rhodes, dead at his kitchen table. When Jim said that the police were grilling him like he was a prime suspect in a crime, rather than an innocent person who happened to be at the wrong place at the wrong time, I could feel my mind and body separate. This was immediately followed by an overwhelming sense of guilt.

Because the whole rotten mess Jim found himself in was my fault.

Don't get me wrong. I didn't murder Rhodes, although I will admit I'd often harbored dark thoughts about the guy because of the havoc he caused in our lives. However, I was responsible for hooking up My Beloved and Davis Rhodes in the first place. Well, to be honest, I manipulated Jim into consulting Rhodes about his impending retirement. The thought of having my dear husband around the house 24/7, with little to do except sit in his recliner with the television remote clutched in his fist, appealed to me as much as a root canal without Novocain. On second thought, I'd definitely take the root canal.

I made the decision to stall Jim's retirement as long as I could. By whatever means I could come up with. I admit I was pretty desperate, but I told myself I was doing it for his own good. Jim was too young to retire and have his mind turn to mush from lack of use. Any other well-meaning, loving, slightly devious wife would do the same thing. Right?

How was I to know that the chain of events I'd innocently set in motion a few weeks ago would end up this way?

Four Weeks Earlier

"I'm really getting worried about Jim."

There was no response from my luncheon buddies, who also happened to be my three best friends.

I figured they hadn't heard me, so I raised my voice to be heard above the lunchtime din. The patrons at Maria's Trattoria were extra loud today.

"I said..."

Before I had a chance to finish my sentence, Mary Alice interrupted me. "I don't know why we came here for lunch. It's always so noisy. You can't even carry on a decent conversation. And the food is so high in cholesterol and calories, it can't be good for us."

I rolled my eyes at Claire and Nancy, silently telegraphing, "There she goes again." Mary Alice, being a nurse, often went into graphic detail about high cholesterol, osteoporosis, cancer risk, high blood pressure, hot flashes, menopause, the benefits and risks of soy, and other assorted topics that are part of the natural aging process we're all going through. Guaranteed to kill the appetite, although I doubt that was her intention.

"Why don't you pick the place for next month then, Mary Alice?" snapped Claire. "You always complain when I pick it. And you know we like to come to Maria's because she taught all our children before she retired and opened this restaurant." She rummaged in her purse for her glasses so she could read the menu. "Damn it. I always leave the reading ones at home." She held the menu out as far as her arm could reach and squinted. "Are there any specials today?"

"Oh, for heaven's sake." My very best friend Nancy waved her perfectly manicured hand to get the attention of a passing waitress, who ignored her. "You know we're all going to get salads anyway. We always get salads. I think I'll have the Caesar salad this time.

"Did you hear about the new facelift technique?" Nancy continued, changing the subject as usual. "It's called a contour thread lift. Supposedly it's the ideal procedure for forty-to-fifty-five-year olds with premature sagging of the upper neck and jowl area."

She checked her face in a small mirrored compact that cost as much as one week's worth of groceries for the average family. "It's being touted as a way to look younger without the risk and recovery period of traditional face lifts. And it can be adjusted when the face starts to sag so the results are constant. I'm thinking of going for a consultation. Anybody want to come with me?"

"Can we forget about face lifts for just a second?" I pleaded. "I'm really worried about Jim, and you're the only ones I can talk to about it. I need help. I think he's losing his mind."

"You're always complaining about Jim," Claire said. "Every time we get together, you have something new to add to his ongoing list of sins. What's he doing now? Still getting up at five in the morning to watch The Weather Channel and obsess about when the next major storm will disrupt his commute to the city?"

"Let me guess," said Mary Alice. "I bet he's into his manic coupon-clipping phase again. What was it you called it, Carol? Obsessive Coupon Disorder?"

"Very funny." I was getting more and more aggravated. "This time it's serious. Jim's behavior is becoming weirder and weirder. He's impossible to deal with." I paused, then raised my voice again to be sure they heard me.

"He's driving me nuts. I think he needs to see a shrink."

Unfortunately, when the word "shrink" popped out of my mouth, it was at one of those quiet times that can happen in very noisy places. Now, everyone in the restaurant was staring at our table.

"Don't look now," said Nancy, "but Linda Burns just walked in the door."

Great. The one person in town who loved to lord it over everyone about her perfect life, her perfect family and her perfect career as a college professor.

"Oh, God, do you think she heard what I said about Jim? That's all I need."

"Well, she's seen us all sitting here so we have to be nice," replied Claire, always the Goody Two Shoes in our group. She gave Linda a friendly wave, and the rest of us pasted false smiles on our faces.

"I haven't seen you in ages, Linda," Claire said. "Can you join us for lunch?"

Nancy's mouth dropped open in shock.

"Thanks, but I can't. I have just enough time to pick up a takeout meal in between classes. Plus, I have office hours this afternoon. So many students depend on me for advice. Even some who don't take my classes."

Linda checked her watch. "I must get back to campus. Enjoy your leisurely lunch. You're fortunate to have so much spare time. Ta for now."

"She is such a pain in the you-know-what," said Mary Alice, once Linda was mercifully gone. "'Enjoy your leisurely lunch!' She just couldn't resist a chance to stick it to us. Claire, don't you ever invite her to have lunch with us again."

"You know" Nancy said, "the only time Linda was even remotely human was when her cocker spaniel was sick a few years ago. She and Bruce nursed that dog for months before they had to have it put down. It was like the dog was their child."

"That's because they had that nutty idea about starting a new dog breed," Mary Alice reminded us. "They were going to breed their cocker spaniel to a poodle, and call it a 'cockerdoodle.' Then Bruce found out there already was a cocker spaniel/poodle mix, the cockapoo, so they gave up on that idea. You know it's all about money with them. Money and status."

"I heard a rumor that Linda's going to be named chairman of the college history department this fall," added Claire. "I hate to say it, but if we think she's obnoxious now, she'll be even more unbearable then."

"Look," I said desperately, "can we get back to Jim, please? Nobody else but people our age can understand what I'm going through."

"Actually," teased Nancy, "I believe I'm almost a year younger than you are, Carol."

It's true that Nancy is nine months younger than I am, but because of the arbitrary cutoff dates which determined when a child was eligible to start school back in the 50s, we had ended up in the same class. I had other things on my mind today, however, so I let her comment pass.

"Well, you certainly have our attention now," said Nancy with a laugh. "Anytime I remind you that I'm younger than you are, you never let me get away with it. What's going on?"

"Ok," I whispered. "Come a little closer to me. I don't want to have to say this too loud." And have everybody in the restaurant staring at us again.

"Jim's obsessed about retirement. He talks about it all the time. He even bought himself a retirement countdown clock. He's figured out the earliest date he can retire, and programmed the clock to keep track of the time remaining until his big day. It's on our nightstand, ticking away like a time bomb.

"I guess what I'm looking for from all of you is a reality check," I continued. "Have your husbands ever been as consumed as Jim is with retirement? Do they obsess about it, even during those intimate moments we all have? Oh, God, I'm sorry, Mary Alice." My friend Mary Alice had been a widow for more than fifteen years. "I didn't mean to offend you."

"You didn't offend me, Carol," responded Mary Alice. "I'm actually starting to think about taking early retirement myself."

"You're kidding!" said Nancy. "What would you do if you stopped nursing? Wouldn't you be bored?"

In response to the "empty nest" syndrome Nancy went through after her children left for college, she'd begun a career as a local Realtor. I think her success in business surprised even her. I know it surprised the rest of us.

"Well, I'd still need to make some money," admitted Mary Alice. "I couldn't completely retire from nursing. But the everyday hospital stress is really beginning to get to me. And the hours are so long. I went into nursing years ago because I wanted to help people. Nowadays, I seem to spend most of my time at the hospital doing mounds of paperwork. The time I get to spend with patients is very limited. It's so frustrating. I was thinking I could sign on with a nurses' registry and maybe do some private duty cases."

"That's a great idea, Mary Alice," I said supportively. "But could we get back to Jim for a second?"

"Hi, I'm Sally. I'll be your waitress for today. May I take your order?"

Our waitress had finally arrived, and the lunchtime crowd was starting to thin out. "Sorry it took me so long to get to you."

"I'll order for everybody," I said. "We'll all have the Caesar salad with chicken, no anchovies, dressing on the side. And iced tea with extra lemon. Be sure the lemons are cut in wedges, not slices. Ok with everybody? Fine. Now, can we get back to Jim?"

"Carol, you really do have our undivided attention now and thanks for placing the order. Does that mean you're picking up the check, too?"

"Very funny, Nancy. All right. Claire, you're our role model in this," I said. "When Larry was first thinking about retirement, did he get, well, nutty about the idea? It's been three years for you guys, right?"

"Larry is so easy-going," said Claire with a smile. "He doesn't stress about anything. We've always been pretty much in sync with one another.

Not that we haven't had our share of arguments over the years. But when it comes to the really important stuff, we usually agree. I don't remember him getting worried about retirement. But remember, I left my teaching job a year before he started thinking about retiring himself. I sometimes kid him that he retired because he saw how much fun I was having. And he still has a license to practice law, so he keeps busy taking on a few cases every now and then."

"You know, Carol, this restaurant is a perfect example of someone who re-invented her life when she retired," said Nancy. "Remember when Maria was Miss Lesco, and she taught all our kids in sixth grade? When she retired from teaching, she re-did her kitchen and started offering take-out meals from her home. We all thought that she'd never make a go of it. But one thing led to another and she eventually opened this restaurant. It's been a huge success for her. Retirement doesn't have to mean you stop being productive. Maybe it means you finally get to do the things you really want to do. It sure worked for Maria."

"Yeah, Carol," added Claire. "Remember all those back-to-school nights and parent-teacher conferences we went to over the years? I used to be petrified of Maria back then. She seemed so demanding and cold. Never tried to coddle the kids, that's for sure. But she was a damn good teacher. Who could know that underneath that starched exterior was an artistic soul yearning to express itself through food?"

She turned in her chair and managed to catch Maria's eye. As usual, Maria was front and center in her open kitchen, a huge area which had been expanded during the restaurant's renovations a few years ago so guests could watch the food being prepped and cooked. Food prep was a major source of entertainment these days, and Maria, smart enough to sense the trend, had positioned her work area so she was the visible star of her own show.

"So what exactly are you worried about, Carol?" asked Mary Alice, returning to what was, I felt, the main subject of our luncheon conversation.

"You all know how Jim's hated his job at the agency ever since the new boss was brought in, right?" Jim was a senior account executive at Gibson Gillespie Public Relations Agency in New York City, an easy train ride from our home in Fairport, Connecticut. The agency founder had died last year and his widow, Cherie, who had inherited ownership of the agency along with everything else in the estate, had brought in a 36-year-old whiz kid, Mack Whitman, to run the operation.

"Every night Jim comes home with more complaints about Mack," I continued. "How he conducts staff meetings and does yoga exercises at the same time. Or how he has no real vision for the agency. Jim says that all Mack's doing is pumping up his personal expense account while the agency is floundering. I think what really scares him, though, is that everybody who's been hired since Mack came on board is under thirty-five. Jim's beginning to feel like an old man, and he talks about leaving his job all the time. But then I ask him what he'd do if he left, and he has no answer. You know that his whole life has been that job. He has no hobbies or interests at all. What's he going to do if he retires, stay home all day and drive me crazy?"

"Bingo," said Nancy, aiming an imaginary gun at my head. "That's the real problem. You've got this nice little life here in Fairport, with a home office setup you can use to do occasional freelance work. Your kids are grown and out of the house, and you have a few volunteer activities to make you feel worthwhile. You get to go out to lunch with friends, and go shopping whenever you feel like it. Between seven a.m. when Jim leaves for New York and seven p.m. when he comes home, you're free as a bird to do whatever you want. Your only real responsibility is to be sure to let the dogs out a couple of times a day. You don't want Jim underfoot rocking your boat."

I sat back in my chair. I was stunned that Nancy could be so harsh.

"Did anybody read the Sunday *Times Magazine* last weekend?" asked Mary Alice. "It had a huge feature on retirement, because so many baby boomers are retiring now. There's a whole new industry to deal with it.

Not the financial stuff, the lifestyle change stuff. Retirement coaching, I think it's called. It was really interesting. "

"Hey, Carol," Nancy said. "Maybe that's what you and Jim need. A retirement coach."

"Don't be ridiculous," I said, still smarting from Nancy's comments. "You know Jim would never go to see someone like that."

"Oh, come on," Claire retorted. "You know you can get Jim to do anything you want. All you have to do is make him think it was his idea. Remember how you wanted to take that trip to Europe, and you knew Jim would never go for it because he wouldn't want to spend the money? You never directly brought the subject up with him. You called me and told me all about it, knowing full well that he was in the next room and would overhear our conversation. Next thing you know, he was starting to think about it, too. Why don't you go home after lunch and go online and see what you can find about retirement coaches? It's worth a shot.

"Oh, great, here's our food at last. I'm starving."

I don't remember what else we talked about at lunch. I was itching to get home, turn on my computer and Google retirement coaches.

Chapter 2

Q: When is a retiree's bedtime?
A: Three hours after he falls asleep on the couch.

We didn't leave the restaurant until about 2:45. It took forever to get the check from our waitress, and nobody wanted to split the bill evenly since Mary Alice hadn't ordered dessert. When Claire pulled out her calculator to figure out what each one of us owed, I snatched up the bill and said, "My treat." Jeez. My whole life was a stake here. Who cared about a few measly dollars one way or the other?

Usually, I love driving around our town, especially on our street, Old Fairport Turnpike, a graceful road filled with stately homes, many of which date back to the American Revolution. Fairport, Connecticut, is a very old town, and Jim and I live in the historic district, where several of the houses were burned by the British in a brief visit during that war. To have burn marks on the floor of an antique home like ours is considered a primo selling point, according to Nancy.

When I'd left for lunch more than three hours before, I'd closed and latched the gate on the picket fence that surrounds our property. Old Fairport Turnpike is a busy street in town, and some people have actually had the nerve to use our driveway as a turn-around. I hate that, so I always lock the gate.

Of course, because the gate was old, like our white colonial house, and I was in such a hurry to get inside, I had trouble getting it open. Ditto the kitchen door, which sticks no matter what the weather is. Part of the "charm" of an antique house. That and crooked door frames, low ceilings and uneven floors.

My two English cocker spaniels, Lucy and Ethel, raced up to greet me.

"Hi girls." I reached down to give them each a quick pat. "You'll never guess what happened at lunch today. I may have discovered a solution to our latest problems with Jim. I'll tell you all about it after you go outside for a quick run."

I admit it's crazy to talk to my dogs all the time the way I do, but they're good listeners and I can trust them to keep a secret. They always agree with me, too. Too bad a handful of kibble, fresh water and some dog biscuits weren't enough to produce unconditional love from humans.

The red light on my telephone blinked at me accusingly. I had one message and, of course, it was from My Beloved. I could tell by the tone of his voice that something was up. "Carol," he barked into the phone, "why are you never home when I want to talk to you? I was going to leave a message on your cell phone, but then I figured you didn't have the damn thing on."

He had me there. I thought my cell phone was a nuisance, and I rarely turned it on. Those folks who drove their cars or walked down the street or did their grocery shopping with a phone plastered to their head, like every call was a life-and-death situation, were ridiculous, as far as I was concerned.

I heard the sound of Jim shifting some papers in the background.

"I didn't mean to yell," he continued. "I've got exciting news to tell you. It'll have to wait until I get home tonight, since I don't know where you are. Don't try to call me back. I'll be in meetings for the rest of the afternoon. See you later."

Exciting news, huh? That could mean anything. But he did sound upbeat, once he got over the fact that I wasn't home. I'd told Jim this morning, before he flew out the door to catch his train, that I was going out for lunch today, but of course, he didn't listen. I refused to speculate about Jim's news. I'd find out soon enough.

"Come on, girls," I said to the dogs, back from performing their necessary outdoor duties, "we've got work to do." I tossed them each a dog biscuit to reward them for a job well done. They followed me into my home office and flopped at my feet. When the cheery computer voice said, "Welcome! You've got mail," for once I didn't immediately rush to check my e-mail messages.

I looked at my blank computer screen and tried to remember exactly what phrase Mary Alice had used. My short-term memory, sadly, isn't what it used to be. Neither is most of my body, but let's not get into that now.

I typed in "Retirement" and got more than 2,000 possible web sites I could check out. Then I tried "Retirement Planning" and got web sites that were all about financial planning issues. Not what I was looking for. I cursed myself for not writing the phrase down.

"How about 'Baby Boomers and Retirement'?" I asked Lucy and Ethel. They wagged their tails in agreement. Nope, no help there either. I didn't need to know the number of baby boomers there were in the U.S., nor did I need any more sites about financial planning.

I looked at the clock on my desk. It was already close to 4:00 and Jim was usually home by 5:30 these days. Sometimes, even earlier. I had no time to waste, and I certainly didn't want him coming in while I was online and asking me what I was looking for. When he was around, I had no privacy at all.

"Wait a minute," I said to the dogs. "I think Mary Alice said the key words are retirement coaches. Let's try that one and see what happens. Bingo!"

In no time I had web sites on healthy aging (an oxymoron if I ever heard one), lifestyle changes, retirement lifestyle coaching, lifelong learning, and on and on. How could I choose the right one and check out it out before Jim got home?

Then I scrolled down to a site which read: "Re-tirement Survival Center, dedicated to helping Baby Boomers make the transition to the best part of their lives." Hmm, I liked the sound of that one, though I didn't understand why "retirement" was hyphenated. A double click of my mouse and I was gazing into the face of Dr. Davis Rhodes, founder and director of the Center.

Briefly I scanned his bio. A Ph.D. in lifestyle counseling, whatever that meant. Originally from California. Author of the book, *Re-tirement's Not For Sissies: A Baby Boomer's Guide To Making The Most of The Best of Your Life.* There was that hyphen again.

I clicked on "Mission." His approach certainly was unique. "In my book, I break down the word 'retire' into re-tire, just like rotating tires on a car. If your tires are a little worn, you don't throw them away, you rotate them to get the most out of them," he explained. "When you re-tire, you are rotating your personal tires and looking at your own life differently, determining how to get the most out of what promises to be the very best part of your life." Interesting. I wondered if Jim would go for it.

I clicked on "About the Center" and got "This Site Is Under Construction." I tried "Key Services." Again, "Under Construction." Impatiently, I clicked on others: "Re-tirement Lifestyle Coaching," "Private Consultations," "Individual and Couples Counseling," "Re-tirement Lifestyle Seminars." Each time, I kept getting the prompt, "Under Construction."

Very frustrating. I checked the clock again. It was now 4:45. Not much more time left to fool around with this.

One more try and then I had to get off-line and start dinner.

I clicked on the only heading I hadn't tried, "R.A.T.", which turned out to stand for "Re-tirement Aptitude Test." This time I got a list of questions which were to be answered and then e-mailed to Dr. Rhodes for evaluation. "Pretend you are being interviewed for a new job," he suggested. "But this time you are interviewing yourself. You now have the opportunity to hire yourself to do something you really want to do.

"How do you adjust to change? How do you measure your self-worth? What is your idea of time well-spent? What is your definition of success? How do you see yourself in the next ten years?

"On a scale of one-to-ten, with one being the highest, rank the following as being important in your life: Financial security, a solid family life, social interaction, giving back to the community, professional satisfaction, living independently, good health, spousal interaction, being in charge of a situation, positive feedback."

I scrolled down a little further and found a separate test for spouses whose husbands were facing retirement, the Re-tirement Aptitude Test for Spouses (R.A.T.S.).

"This is great," I said to the girls. "He gets the fact that wives could have problems when their husbands are suddenly around the house all the time with nothing to do."

I was ready to fill in the R.A.T.S. questions when I realized there was a catch to all this. If I e-mailed my test to Dr. Rhodes for his feedback, I had to pay an up-front non-refundable $85 registration fee (via credit card) to have him evaluate my answers.

Jim would never go for that. He was forever lecturing me on the dangers of cyberspace and credit fraud.

I was about to log off when I realized there was a "Contact Me" icon with an office address and phone number. I couldn't believe my luck. Dr. Davis Rhodes had an office in Westfield, only five miles from here.

I needed to think this through. Maybe when I was cooking dinner, I'd come up with a strategy to entice Jim to make an appointment with Rhodes. One way or another, I wanted Jim to check out this web site.

"Honest to God, a brownie troop is run better than that place."

Jim burst through the kitchen door and slammed his briefcase on the black granite counter. "You won't believe what that idiot did today!"

My Beloved was home from the office, and even more agitated than usual. Obviously, something had happened after Jim's "exciting news" phone call.

I took a deep breath and considered a variety of responses. None of them seemed likely to diffuse the situation, so I fell back on the tried and true method I used whenever our kids, Mike and Jenny, came home from school upset about something that happened on the playground—a food diversion.

Instead of offering Oreos and milk, however, I pulled out some grownup guns.

"I just finished cutting up fresh vegetables, Jim, and there's ranch dip in the refrigerator. I also warmed up some homemade clam chowder. Why don't you fix yourself a snack and have a glass of that nice merlot while I finish grilling the salmon?"

"Don't you want to hear what happened today?" Jim asked testily.

"Of course I do, dear." As if there were a way I could avoid it. "But why don't you tell me when we're sitting down at the table and I can give you my full attention? Right now, I really need to keep an eye on this salmon. You know you don't like it too well-done."

"I'm going to wash my face and change. But just let me tell you this—I don't know how much more of this I can take! I've decided to go to the human resources office tomorrow and look at my retirement options!"

With that dramatic announcement, Jim stormed out of the room and headed upstairs.

Oh, boy. This was even more serious than I thought. He had never threatened to go to the human resources office before, no matter how much he complained about the agency.

That meant I only had tonight to put my plan into action.

Quietly, so Jim wouldn't hear me, I called Nancy on her cell phone.

"Thank God I got you," I whispered.

"I was just about to go out and show a client a house. Some people are so inconsiderate. They think Realtors are at their disposal twenty-four hours a day. This is some young yuppie with big bucks who..."

I cut her off before she could get into one of her familiar tirades about the trials and tribulations of being a real estate agent.

"Nancy," I whispered again.

"Carol, I can hardly hear you. Why are you talking so softly?"

"I can't talk any louder," I hissed. "And I have to make this quick. Jim just got home and he's threatening to go to the human resources office tomorrow to look at his retirement options."

"Oh, God, that's awful. What are you going to do?"

"I've been thinking about what Mary Alice said at lunch. Maybe a retirement coach would help Jim and me. I found someone I think would be perfect. But I need to get Jim to look at his web site tonight, and I need him to think it was his idea. Can you help me?"

"Sure I'll help you. What do you want me to do?"

"Can you call me here in about an hour?" I asked. "Will you be through with your client by then?"

"I'd better be. And if I'm not, I'll just go out to my car and use my cell for a minute. What do you want me to say?"

"Nothing. All I want you to do is listen to me. I'm going to tell you all about this retirement counselor's web site I found, and talk loud enough so Jim will hear me."

I thought fast. "Maybe I'll pretend that you're calling me about the web site. I don't know. I'll figure out something. The important thing is that I'll sound so excited that it will pique his curiosity. Hopefully. All you need is to call me in an hour and let me babble away. Ok?"

"Consider it done," said Nancy. "It's five-forty-five now. I'll call you at six-forty-five sharp."

"Thanks. You're terrific."

Well, I had a plan, sort of. But whether it would work with My Beloved in such a foul mood was anybody's guess.

Jim stomped into the kitchen, dressed in his favorite baggy gray sweater and a pair of paint-stained sweat pants. Ordinarily, I would have been prompted to make a snappy comment about his clothing of choice, but tonight I had more important things on my mind.

"So tell me what happened at the office today, dear," I asked as I poured Jim a glass of wine.

"You know, if we're having salmon tonight, we really should be drinking a white wine." Jim took a sip from the glass I had put in front of him.

"Hmm, this is pretty good. Did Mike recommend it?"

Our 25-year-old son Mike had become the family authority on all things relating to wine choices as well as the latest in mixed drinks. No, he wasn't a recovering alcoholic. He was a budding entrepreneur.

Right after he graduated from college three years ago, Mike took off for the warm weather and bright lights of South Beach, Florida. He'd taken a bartending course over the summer of his junior year, and supported himself with a variety of bartending jobs for a few years. Jim and I used to joke privately that Mike's bartending degree had turned out to be more useful to him than his four-year diploma from college.

Then Mike had the opportunity to buy into a new martini bar in South Beach. Jim and I talked it over, and agreed to lend him the $50,000 he needed to become a partner. But we made it clear, in writing, that this was just a loan, and drew up a contract, which we all signed, detailing the terms of repayment.

The bar was re-named Cosmo's by Mike and his partners. They added cosmopolitans to their drinks menu, and completely redecorated the bar with a *Cosmopolitan* magazine theme. The walls were now adorned with covers from magazines going back to the mid-1960s, when Helen Gurley Brown had taken over the editor's job, to the present. It was incredible to see how the publication had changed over the years.

I especially got a kick out of Cosmo's as the choice of the bar's name because in 1974, for one year, I had worked at *Cosmopolitan* magazine in the copy department as a fact checker. I still have all the old magazines with my name on the masthead—in very small type, of course.

Mike claims the bar name is just a coincidence, but I secretly believe the name was chosen in my honor. A mother can have fantasies, right?

Jim was proud as punch that Cosmo's had become such a success, and when the time came that Mike had enough money to start paying back the $50,000 loan, we decided to keep some of our money in the bar and be "silent partners." Mike and his partners were now thinking of expanding Cosmo's to another site in the New York metropolitan area.

"I haven't heard from Mike this week, have you?" I said, my hackles rising ever so slightly at Jim's obvious lack of faith in my wine choice. My Beloved Husband drank jug wine from a jelly glass for years. And I can't count the number of dinner parties we'd hosted where he poured cheap wine into a Waterford decanter and put it on the dining room table, so guests wouldn't realize what they were really drinking. Lots of puckered lips in those days.

I took a sip of the wine myself and swirled it around in my mouth. "This merlot is pretty smooth, isn't it? I saw it advertised on The Food Channel. It was only twelve dollars a bottle. We can switch to a white wine with the fish if you want to."

I plated the fish, added some steamed asparagus and a baked potato, and set the repast in front of my husband. He seemed to be slightly mellower than when he'd come home from the agency, which I took as a hopeful sign.

"Now," I asked with wifely concern as I joined him at the kitchen table, "what happened at the office today to get you so upset? You sounded so upbeat on the phone." When you weren't giving me grief about being out of the house when you called.

Bad mistake. I'd just calmed him down, and now he was even more agitated than before.

"That was then. And if I'd been able to reach you, Carol, you'd already know the first part of this." Jim attacked a piece of asparagus on his plate.

"Do you remember two years ago, when Gibson Gillespie was honored by the Public Relations Society of America with the Silver Anvil Award for Excellence?" he asked me. "Of course, Jack Gibson was still alive then, which is why we got it, I'm sure."

I nodded my head. The award had been presented at a fancy formal dinner in New York at the Waldorf Astoria, and Jim and I had both gone.

Naturally I wore black, the official color of New York parties. I remember I dieted for a month to get into the dress. And I haven't worn it since.

"Well," Jim went on, gesturing with his fork for emphasis, "those days are gone forever. And it just makes me so angry. Mack is running the agency into the ground.

"Today we got a new client." He paused to take a sip of wine, then slammed the glass on the table. I winced as some of the wine spilled onto the place mat.

"That's why I called you," Jim said. He glared at me. "But you weren't here."

He waited a minute to see if I'd respond, but I didn't. I'd learned in over thirty years of marriage that some battles weren't worth fighting.

"I wanted to tell you that we were hired by Reynolds Consulting Group to do a big campaign about their selection by *Fortune* magazine as one of the top hundred companies to work for in the country. Our whole agency staff sat in a meeting for hours and listened to Mack list all the reasons why Reynolds was singled out for *Fortune's* top one hundred list. The company offers its employees compressed workweeks, telecommuting opportunities, free lunches in the company restaurant, on-site day care, a whole list of things designed to build employee loyalty. Very impressive. Reynolds thinks of its employees as friends who look out for each other, and the company's thriving under that approach, even in this weak economy when other corporations are cutting back."

"It sounds like a wonderful place to work," I offered, not really sure where he was heading with this.

"Of course it's a wonderful place to work," he exploded at me. "That's why *Fortune* selected them. But Mack had the nerve to compare their corporate culture to the current one at Gibson Gillespie. He actually had the gall to say that it isn't the nature of the business that makes a company great. It's the management. That excellence starts at the top and then trickles down. He went on and on about how things have only changed for the better at the agency since he took it over; how he trusts employees to do their best and doesn't micro-manage; and how he always tells the employees they're doing a great job. What a crock! All the young flunkies at the meeting clapped and clapped for him. I thought I'd throw up!"

The veins in Jim's forehead were pulsating now.

"But you haven't heard the best part. You won't believe this. Guess where Mack was in the conference room while he was conducting the staff meeting."

"Why, Jim, I would assume he was in his usual seat at the head of the conference room table."

"Wrong! Mack was lying flat on his back in the middle of the conference room table. He'd hurt his back in a parasailing accident over the weekend and had to either lie completely flat or wear a back brace. He looked like a damn centerpiece. All he needed was an apple stuck in his mouth and he could have been a stuffed pig. It was absolutely ludicrous.

"And that's when I made up my mind to go to the human resources office tomorrow and discuss my options. I can't continue to work in a place that's run by a jerk like that."

Uh oh.

Chapter 3

Q: Why do little boys whine?
A: They're practicing to be men.

Jim was so preoccupied with the goings-on in his office that the rest of the dinner conversation required no response at all from me. Just a few sympathetic nods of the head now and then. And an occasional "Oh, Jim."

By 6:30 My Beloved was in his favorite place, sprawled in front of the flat screen television in the family room, remote control in hand. He was switching back and forth between *The NewsHour* on public television and The Weather Channel. No network news shows for him.

I had already booted up the computer in my office to make it easy to access Dr. Rhodes's web page. Subtle, right?

Promptly at 6:45 the phone rang.

"Jim," I called from the kitchen, "can you turn the television volume down a little bit, please? It's Nancy."

"What?"

"I said, please turn down the volume on the television. Nancy's on the phone. I can't hear her with the television blaring."

"Ok, ok. But don't be too long."

"Nancy, can you hear me?" I whispered.

"Yes. The client's already left. Do you want me to respond at all?"

"No, I don't think so. Let's just play it by ear. Here goes.

"Nancy, what's up?" I said in my normal voice. "You sound upset. Oh, you're not upset? You're excited?"

Pause.

"What? Yes, I've been thinking about lunch today, too. All that talk about retirement coaches sure was interesting."

Pause.

Nancy giggled. "It's fun hearing you conduct a monologue, Carol."

"Oh, you went online to do some research about retirement coaches?" I asked, my voice getting louder. "I didn't realize that you and Bob were talking about retirement. What did you find?"

Pause.

"Really? There's a retirement coach right here? Oh, in Westfield. What's his name?"

Pause.

"Dr. Davis Rhodes? Does he have a web page? It's called what? Re-tirement Survival Center? Catchy name. Are you going to tell Bob about it?"

"Is Jim buying any of this?" Nancy whispered.

"I can't tell," I whispered back. "But it's very quiet in the family room.

"Why, Nancy, no wonder you're excited," I said in a more normal tone of voice.

Pause.

"Yes, I guess if you plan ahead, retirement really isn't such a scary thing after all. Let me know if you and Bob decide to go see this Dr. Rhodes."

Pause.

"I have to go now," Nancy said. "I hope this worked. Let me know, ok?"

"Yes. I'll talk to you tomorrow. Bye, Nancy."

I hung up the phone. My palms were sweating. I certainly was no actress. I was sure that Jim saw right through my whole performance and ignored the conversation entirely.

I waited for a few minutes, and rinsed a few dishes to put in the dishwasher. The suspense was killing me. Then I decided there was only one way to find out.

"Jim," I called, "where are you?"

"In your office. I'm on the computer. Come on in. There's something I want to show you."

Play it cool, I told myself. I tried to keep my face expressionless when I walked into the office.

"I couldn't help overhearing your conversation with Nancy." Jim gave me a knowing look. "Which, I suspect, is exactly what you wanted, right?"

I started to deny it, then glanced down at the computer and saw the Re-tirement Survival Center web page on the screen.

"Jim, I..."

"After all these years, I still don't understand why you always use such underhanded methods when you want me to do something. Just ask me. You know I'm always open to what you have to say."

"Honestly, it's not what you..."

"You could be onto something here with this retirement coach," My Beloved said, switching subjects rapidly. "This guy is a genius. Do you have any idea how many baby boomers are hitting retirement age every year? About seventy-eight million people were born from nineteen-forty-six to nineteen-sixty-four. Millions of them have already turned 60. What a concept he's got! What a huge potential service market!"

"You really think so?" I asked excitedly. "Is he someone you'd talk to about retirement?"

"You bet. I already took the test and e-mailed it to him. Didn't take me more than three minutes to fill in the answers."

I could hardly believe it. This was more enthusiasm from Jim than I ever dreamed of.

"This was one of your best ideas ever, Carol. Of course, I don't need any help personally, but I think Rhodes has a great idea with this re-tirement concept, plus a book that needs to be marketed. I know I'm just the guy to help him, and he could be the answer to my career slump at the agency. I'm going to make him a media star. And I'm very impressed with his immediate follow-up. We have an appointment to see him on Thursday when I get home from the city."

He got up and kissed me. "Thanks, honey. I'm going downstairs to throw in a load of laundry. I'm out of clean socks."

"Jim, please don't touch any of my clothes. You know that you don't separate colors right."

Then I stopped myself. Was I crazy? Who cared about ink marks on my undies when my life was in major crisis. How could this have gone so wrong?

On second thought, maybe if Jim could land Rhodes as a client, he'd decide to delay his own retirement. Unless Jim brought Rhodes into the agency and Mack gave the account to one of the young rising stars instead. That'd send Jim to the human resources office for sure.

I dashed off a quick e-mail to Nancy. I knew she must be dying of curiosity about how things had gone.

Good News, Bad News.
You won't believe this. The good news is, we were so convincing that Jim and I have an appointment with Davis Rhodes on Thursday evening. The bad news is that the only reason Jim's going is because he thinks Rhodes would make a great client for his P.R. agency. I'll tell you more as things develop.

I pushed the "Send" icon, logged off, and decided to calm down by reading a favorite mystery for a while. I was deep in concentration when the phone rang.

I was very tempted to ignore that call. It was the time of night when we're bombarded by telemarketers, even though we're on the "No Call" list, which drives me crazy. Something made me check our caller I.D., and I realized it was our daughter Jenny.

"Hi, honey. How are things? You wouldn't believe how hot it is here at home."

"Hi, Mom," said my first-born child. Then she burst into tears.

Oh, boy. No wonder she was calling. More trouble in paradise, no doubt, with her live-in significant other, Jeff.

Jenny had left for Los Angeles two years ago, to pursue a Master's degree in American literature at UCLA. We hadn't wanted to let her go, but at the age of 24, no parent really "lets" a child go. The child just leaves home. Period.

It wasn't long after her arrival in L.A. that she got involved in a variety of (highly unsuitable—Jim's words) relationships with, among others, an unemployed actor, another unemployed actor, an unemployed scriptwriter, a waiter (at least he was employed), a nightclub manager and, finally, Jeff.

Jeff was a lawyer in his late twenties, on the fast track to success in his firm, and Jim adored him. I wasn't so sure. He seemed a little controlling of our sweet Jenny, but then, I was her mother and tended to be overprotective. They had been living together (no, we weren't thrilled about the arrangement but kept our opinions to ourselves) for almost a year.

"Sweetheart, what's wrong? Why are you crying?"

"Oh, Mom, it's Jeff. I just can't take his trying to control my life any more."

"Jenny, what do you mean?" I asked, silently thinking that a mother always knows.

"He picks at me all the time. Nothing I do is good enough. He thinks I should leave school and just spend my time taking care of him. He says he's making enough money to support both of us. Mom, I can't leave school. I am so close to getting my Master's, and then I want to go for a Ph.D. It's important to me. But what I want isn't important. It's only what he wants!"

"Honey, listen to me," I said. "All relationships go through some rough times. And most men think they know more about what's best for a woman than the woman does. It even happens with Dad and me sometimes."

Whoops. Probably shouldn't have said that. Not that Jenny heard me anyway. She was still crying.

"Mom, I have a tremendous favor to ask. I want to come home."

I stared at the phone. Stupidly. I repeated, "Home? You want to come home?"

Hold it, Carol. She'll think you don't want her. I took a deep breath, then chose my words very carefully.

"Honey, if you want to come home for a few days or a week to get yourself together, you just come. This is your home too, you know. We're always glad to see you."

"Um, Mom, what I had in mind was a little longer than that."

Jenny seemed to be calmer now.

"What did you have in mind? A month?"

"Actually, Mom, I should have given you and Daddy a head's up about this before, but I want to come home for good. Or at least until the summer semester ends. I've transferred all my graduate credits to Fairport College. I'm going to be a teaching assistant there through the summer."

There was a long pause. I didn't know what to say.

Then, Jenny spoke again. "Mom, can you go get Daddy please? I'm at LaGuardia Airport. Can he come and pick me up right away?"

And she burst into tears again.

Chapter 4

Q: What is the best way to describe retirement?
A: The never-ending coffee break.

"You know, I really like having Jenny home."

It was Thursday morning. Jim and I had had two days to adjust to having our daughter back in the house.

Nancy, Claire and I were having coffee in my kitchen while I brought them up to date on all that had happened to the Andrews family. Both women had known Jenny since she was born, and loved her almost as much as Jim and I did.

"It's funny," I said. "When I heard some television pundit use the words 'boomerang baby' to describe an adult child who moves back home, I never thought it would apply to one of my kids. But now that Jenny's here, it's turning out to be great. At least, it is for me. I'm glad she finally figured out what a jerk Jeff is."

"I never liked him," Nancy admitted. "When Jenny brought him home for Christmas last year, I thought there was something about him that wasn't quite right. He was so up tight, for one thing."

"I never said anything to you at the time," added Claire. "But I could tell you had reservations about him too. Jenny didn't seem natural and relaxed around him. I remember her jumping up several times during your holiday open house to re-fill his wine glass. I mean, who needs a guy who has to be waited on all the time?"

"Yeah," said Nancy. "That kind of behavior comes out after the wedding, not before."

"As it turns out, Jeff's relentless attempt to control Jenny's life was the final straw," I said. "He actually had the nerve to tell her she shouldn't finish her graduate studies. He wanted her to quit school and stay home and tend to his needs all the time, like what she wanted to do with her life wasn't important at all."

I took deep breaths. The idea that Jeff had the gall to suggest that to a bright young woman like Jenny really upset me.

"How is she doing?" Nancy asked sympathetically? "Oh, gosh, she's not upstairs where she can hear us talking about her, is she?"

"Relax," I answered. "She's hit the ground running with the Fairport College teaching assistant job. Started yesterday. She's there three mornings and one afternoon a week as of now. Hopefully she'll be able to get her Master's thesis done, then start on her Ph.D. She was out of the house before Jim this morning and won't be home until at least four."

"Speaking of Jim," asked Claire, "how's he adjusting to having his daughter home? He must have freaked when he had to go to the airport Monday night and pick her up."

"It could be more of an adjustment for him than for either Jenny or me." I giggled at a recent memory. "For one thing, he may have to stop doing laundry. He picked up a pile of dirty clothes from the hamper and brought them downstairs to wash last night.

"All of a sudden, I heard a yell. I ran downstairs and he was holding—you won't believe this—a thong bikini in his hand! I don't think he's ever seen one before. His eyes were bugging out of his head. Apparently Jenny had thrown her underwear in the hamper with ours."

"You mean you don't wear a thong bikini, Carol?" Nancy's eyes were wide with feigned innocence.

"Very funny." I gave her head an affectionate swat. "I'll wear one when you do, too."

"Isn't today the big day for you and Jim?" asked Nancy, searching for another subject.

"What big day?" Claire broke off a piece of blueberry muffin and popped it into her mouth.

"Oops, I think I spoke out of turn," said Nancy.

"That's ok. It's not a secret, certainly not from Claire. Jim and I are going to see a retirement coach tonight for a consultation. His name is Davis Rhodes. Remember how we talked about this at lunch on Monday?"

"Wow, I'm impressed," said Claire. "How'd you trick him into going?"

"Well, to tell you the truth, Jim thinks he's going to size Rhodes up and see if he'd make a good client for the P.R. agency," I confessed. "Nancy and I put on this great act on the phone Monday night to get him interested, and he completely misunderstood the point of it. He thinks signing Davis Rhodes as a client will rescue his career, if you can believe it."

"Hey, Carol, you know how men can be. Jim's probably telling himself that's why he's seeing this coach, but deep down inside he's hoping to get some insight from Rhodes about his own retirement. He just can't admit that part of it to you." Trust Claire to put a positive spin on the situation for me.

"You know," I said with a tiny flicker of hope, "you just may be right. At least he's going to meet Rhodes. I'll let you both know what happens."

"Now, I've got to go." Nancy pushed back her kitchen chair and picked up her designer purse. "Realtors' open houses today that I have to check out."

"I have to go too," said Claire. "Good luck tonight! Take good notes."

"Oh, I will," I answered. "I have a feeling it's going to be a memorable experience."

"Now, Carol, you have to let me do the talking."

Jim had picked me up on Thursday evening at 5:30 and we were on our way to Westfield for our initial meeting with Davis Rhodes.

"You know how you have this tendency to interrupt me when I'm speaking," Jim added.

I bit my lip. It seemed to me that he was the one who did most of the interrupting in our relationship, but I decided, just for once, to let his comment go.

"He's probably going to ask us a lot of questions based on the test I e-mailed him, so let me answer most of them. After all, I'm the one who's supposed to be considering retirement," he said. "Though I don't know if he'll buy that from me, since I obviously still have so many productive working years ahead of me. The important thing is to put him at ease. He thinks he'll be interviewing us, but actually I'll be interviewing him. Got it?"

Huh? This speech came from the same person who just a few nights ago had threatened to check out his own retirement options? I was having a little trouble keeping up.

"Got it," I replied. "You lead and I'll follow." Just this once.

"Perfect. I knew I could count on you. But I do remember that this was all your idea." He took his right hand off the steering wheel and gave my hand a quick squeeze. "Don't think I'm not grateful. Oh, here we are."

Jim swung the car into the driveway of a white Victorian house off the Post Road in Westfield.

"Are you sure this is the right address?" I asked. "I don't know what I was expecting, but it certainly wasn't this."

"What did you think his office would look like, Carol? A tire store?"

Jim laughed at his own joke.

I didn't.

We weren't even in the door yet, and already there was some tension between us.

Keep your eye on the goal, I told myself silently. At least he's here.

Jim must have realized I was a little miffed, because he opened the car door for me, something he hadn't done for years.

No one answered our knock, so we let ourselves in. And found ourselves in one of the loveliest living rooms I'd ever seen. Not a reception room, a living room.

Decorated in traditional furnishings in subdued tones of blues, wines and creams, the room could have been pretentious, but somehow it wasn't. Instead, there was an atmosphere of comfort in the leather wing chairs (carefully placed flanking a beautiful marble fireplace) and striped camel back sofa. Each seat had a slight indentation in them, as though someone had recently sat there. Silver-framed photos were carefully arranged on the mantel. The effect was enhanced by an open book, turned face down on the mahogany coffee table. It looked like someone had just left the room to get a snack.

"What do we do now?" I whispered to Jim. "There's nobody here."

At that moment, a door to what I assumed was the dining room opened, revealing a stunning woman, about 45 years old, dressed in crisp navy slacks and a white blouse. Her blonde hair was loosely tied in a pony tail.

"Hello, I'm Sheila Carney, Dr. Rhodes's associate," she said, coming forward and offering us her hand to shake. "And you must be Carol and Jim Andrews. Please, sit down. Dr. Rhodes will be right with you."

She was carrying a plate of cookies, which she placed on the coffee table in front of us.

"Help yourselves," Sheila said, gesturing to the cookies. "Would you like some coffee or tea to go along with them? Or a soft drink? Bottled water? Wine?"

Jim reached for a cookie (you can always count on him when food is around), but I could tell he was getting a little annoyed. He does not like to wait—for anyone or anything.

Sheila must have sensed his mood, because she laughed and said, "I'm sorry Dr. Rhodes is keeping you waiting, but he's such a stickler for his baking. When he has a batch of cookies in the oven, he doesn't trust anyone else to watch them, even me."

I looked at Jim. Jim looked at me.

The guru of the Re-tirement Survival Center baked these cookies? What kind of a place was this, anyway?

Jim began to fidget in his chair, a sure sign he wanted to leave now.

I sent him The Look I have perfected over the years and use only when I really need it. Stay put and chill out, it said.

Then the door opened again, and the tantalizing smell of freshly baked chocolate chip cookies wafted into the living room.

A man walked in, wearing an apron and carrying a spatula in his hand.

The great man himself, Dr. Davis Rhodes, had made his entrance at last.

Chapter 5

Q: What's the biggest advantage of going back to school as a retiree?
A: If you cut classes, no one calls your parents.

"Bet I'm not what you expected," Rhodes said, putting out his hand to Jim and giving it a hearty shake. He turned to me and enveloped my hand with both of his, not easy when you're also holding a spatula.

Davis Rhodes was immaculately dressed in knife-creased chino pants, a starched blue oxford cloth shirt and shiny tasseled penny loafers. No socks. His face, though tanned, was unlined and smooth, so it was difficult to guess his age. His salt and pepper hair was cut short, and I couldn't help but notice how shiny it was. He was of average height, a little taller than Jim, who's 5 feet 10 inches.

His cobalt blue eyes were his most riveting feature. I'd never seen eyes so blue. Probably contacts, I thought to myself, although I had to admit that the guy exuded charisma. He hadn't looked this good on his web page. I mentally slapped myself. Get a grip, Carol. You're here for Jim, remember?

The one thing I found extremely disconcerting was Rhodes's apron. I'd never heard of anyone greeting clients dressed that way, unless he was a professional chef, of course. I tried not to stare, but the apron had writing on it which proclaimed, "In the game of life, friends are the chocolate chips." Had we happened into a cookie exchange by mistake?

"I'm Davis Rhodes, but please, both of you, call me Dave," said Rhodes, releasing my hand. "Come on, let's all go into the kitchen for a chat and get to know each other."

The three of us started to follow him.

"No, not you, Sheila. You stay out here to answer the phone. Tell anyone who calls that I'm in conference."

A brief flicker of annoyance crossed Sheila's face, but she recovered herself quickly and flashed a brilliant smile.

"Sure, Dave. No problem."

I couldn't look at Jim's reaction to all this. He was probably going to read me the riot act all the way home about wasting his time setting up an interview with a pastry cook.

I admit that I thought it was kind of funny, though. Ok, well, odd. But we were here and what else could we do besides follow Rhodes into the kitchen?

"I always suggest new clients have their first meeting with me around the kitchen table. It puts everybody at ease," Rhodes explained. "Please, have a seat."

He pulled out two ladder back chairs from a highly polished cherry tavern table and motioned us to sit down.

Our chairs were positioned side by side.

He sat opposite us.

Hmm, interesting. That way he can gauge both of our reactions at the same time, I thought.

"I can see you're both put off a bit by my apron," Rhodes said with a laugh. "And by our meeting in the kitchen rather than an office setting.

"But, as I said before, I always meet my new clients here first. After all, you've come to visit me, and we're developing a relationship here, right? And where do most people spend their time when they come for a visit? In the kitchen, right?"

I had to admit the guy did have a point. How many parties had I given over the years where most of the guests congregated in the kitchen, not in my carefully arranged and artfully decorated living room?

I snuck a look at Jim. He wasn't buying it. I had to say something quick to save the situation.

"Dr. Rhodes, Dave, I have to ask you something, but I don't want to appear rude." I paused, not really sure how to go on.

"I bet you want to know about the baking, right?"

"Well, I..."

"That's ok. Here, have a cookie." He pushed a plate of warm chocolate chip cookies toward us. They looked heavenly.

"When I first came up with the concept of the Re-tirement Survival Center, I have to admit I was at a crossroads in my own life," Rhodes explained. "I had been a lifestyle counselor for many years out on the West Coast, but the challenge just wasn't there for me any more. I realized that I needed to change direction somehow, but I still wanted to use the professional skills I had perfected over the years.

"Maybe you know what I'm talking about." Rhodes shifted his gaze from me to Jim. "Have you ever gotten up in the morning and wondered what you were doing it all for? And wanted a way to recapture the excitement and passion you once had about your job? Heck, even about your whole life?"

Jim relaxed a little in his chair. "Well, Dave, I guess everyone feels like that at one time or another."

"Exactly. So I began to wonder what I really wanted to do with my life. I thought how interesting it would be to go on a job interview, but this time to interview myself. You know, ask myself a series of questions, the kind most job applicants still have to answer, to find out what my interests really were. I realized that people's focus, priorities, and choices change as we mature. But that doesn't mean we're ready for a rocking chair. Just a new challenge or two to keep the juices flowing. Do you see where I'm going with this, Jim?"

Jim nodded his head in agreement. I munched on a cookie. Clearly, I was no longer part of this discussion.

"At the time, I hadn't even thought of retirement for myself," Rhodes continued. "Just restructuring my professional life. Like you, Jim, I'm really too young to retire."

That did it. Jim was now bobbing his head up and down so hard I thought he'd lose it. In an agency dominated by men under 35, nobody had told him he was too young for anything for years.

"So, I wrote a series of questions for myself to answer. And you'll never guess what I figured out."

He paused dramatically and looked at both of us. "I discovered that what I've always wanted to do is bake. Maybe it takes me back to my childhood when I'd come home from school and my mother would be in the kitchen with a snack for me. I don't know. But I started to do some baking, and realized how much fun I was having. And how much satisfaction it gave me to do it.

"Now, I knew that I wasn't going to leave my clients to become the next Mrs. Fields."

Rhodes laughed.

"But I also realized that many men, particularly in their fifties, begin to experience what I had been experiencing. I like to think of the next phase of life as a tune-up, physically, mentally, and professionally. Kind of like taking your car in for routine maintenance, changing the filters and rotating the tires, to get as much mileage out of the vehicle as possible. Do you see where I'm headed here, Jim?

"So that's how the Re-tirement Survival Center started. I'm really the first client. And I never let myself forget it."

My eyes glazed over. All this focus on cars was not doing it for me.

But it sure was doing it for Jim. I looked at My Beloved Husband to see his reaction to all this, and I swear, the guy was so excited I thought he'd jump out of his chair.

"You know," Jim said, "I don't think I've ever admitted this to anyone before, but..." and then he was off and running. Babbling about things at work that he hadn't even told me.

I sat in that kitchen for the next half hour and I might as well have been invisible. There was so much testosterone flying around the room that I thought I might gag.

They traded stories, laughed at each other's jokes, and all the while I just sat there with a smile pasted on my face. The kind of smile I'd mastered from years of going to boring corporate cocktail parties, not really listening to all that inane chatter but appearing to. Believe me, it's an art form.

"So, Jim," Rhodes finally said, "what can I do for you? Your online test was one of the most interesting and insightful ones I've ever seen. It would be an honor, and a challenge, to work with you."

Needless to say, Jim preened at this flattery.

"I think," I started to say, but was interrupted by Rhodes. "Jim, what I think you need, and what we are going to come up with together, is a retreading strategy for your life. What do you say?"

Rhodes pushed the plate of cookies toward Jim. "Here, have another."

What? I couldn't believe my eyes.

My hard-headed, stubborn, "I-don't-need-any-help-from-anyone, I-can-do-it-all-myself" husband was now shaking hands with Rhodes and making an appointment to see him again next Tuesday night.

What the heck was in those cookies anyway?

During the ride home from the meeting with Davis Rhodes, Jim was strangely quiet.

I was bursting with questions, but the first time I tried to start a conversation, Jim stopped me cold. "Not now, honey. I'm thinking."

I waited a few minutes, then tried again.

"I don't really want to talk right now, Carol. I need to mull over what happened tonight. Dave has given me a lot of serious things to consider."

"Ok," I said, throwing up my hands in mock surrender. "Let's go home and have a nice dinner. We can talk later."

But when we got home, Jim surprised me by saying he didn't want any food.

"You go ahead and get yourself something to eat," he said, giving me a peck on the cheek. "I'm going to work on the computer for a while. I may stay up late, so don't wait up. If you get tired, just go on up to bed."

I tried not to take Jim's desire for solitude personally. It was hard not to be frustrated, though. I was dying to talk, but had no one to talk to.

The message light on the phone was blinking. I pressed Play and heard Jenny's voice: "Hi parents. Just wanted you to know that I'll be at school late tonight. Don't wait up. Hope all went well with Davis Rhodes. I'll see you in the morning. Love you. Bye."

I considered calling Nancy, but decided against it. I couldn't even unburden myself to the dogs without Jim overhearing me. I nuked a Weight Watchers dinner, had a glass of wine (small), and went to bed at 9.

I don't know what time Jim came to bed, or Jenny came home.

But I had dreams of chocolate chip cookies all night.

Chapter 6

Q: How do you keep your husband from reading your e-mail?
A: Rename your mail folder "Living With Menopause."

By the time I got up at 7 the next morning, Jim was already gone. This was very unusual behavior for My Beloved. For the last four months, he hadn't been leaving for the office before 8:30. And he claimed that, even if he didn't get into the office until 10, he still was the first one in. This was one of Jim's many ongoing complaints about the agency these days—staff people came to the office late and left early. And, to hear him tell it, none of them did much work while they were there, either.

I didn't know if it was bad or good that Jim had left so early. I was very worried that he was still going to make an appointment with the human resources office about his retirement options, despite our meeting with Davis Rhodes last night.

Jenny was still sleeping (at least I assumed she was), so I tiptoed down the stairs.

The dogs greeted me and followed me into my office, their nails clicking like tap shoes on the hardwood floor.

I went online to check my e-mail.

Of course, there was one from Nancy, wanting a full report on what happened last night.

I quickly e-mailed her back.

Guru Update

Meeting went pretty well. Believe it or not, Jim seemed really interested in what

Rhodes had to say. If this guy can really help him, I'd be thrilled. I didn't connect with Rhodes at all. Too much macho talk. I kind of zoned out. But I got a great recipe for chocolate chip cookies. I'll explain when I see you.

No need to share with her that I'd been (briefly) attracted to Rhodes.

I smiled to myself and pressed Send. That message would certainly pique Nancy's well-known curiosity.

I was just about to log off the computer when I was "Instant Messaged." The new e-mail was from Jim.

Hi Carol.
Didn't want to wake you when I left this morning. Thought last night went great. Davis Rhodes is some guy, and I know you're as excited as I am that he seems interested in having me put together a proposal to have our agency represent him.

Huh? This was news to me. Guess I had really zoned out last night.

So when I came home, I wanted to get on the computer and make notes on what we talked about while everything was still fresh in my mind. Dave and I are going to meet again next week so I can show him some P.R. concepts. He may even come into the agency some day soon to meet more of our staff. Wanted to let you know that I'll probably work later for a few nights to get this proposal done. Even Mack was impressed when I announced at this morning's staff meeting that I'd landed this new client. I haven't felt this energized in years!"

Oh, dear.

"Girls," I announced to Lucy and Ethel, "I may have accidentally created another problem."

They both wagged their tails and looked sympathetic. I reached down to give them each a quick scratch. "Thanks for the vote of confidence."

Sighing, I closed my e-mail and sat staring at the blank computer screen. None of this sounded good to me.

"Did Davis Rhodes really agree to have Jim do a proposal for marketing his book and his Center?" I asked the dogs. "How could I not have heard that last night? Is Jim reading things into our meeting that didn't happen?"

I shook my head to clear my muddled brain.

"No," I told the dogs. "Jim is a professional. He'd never do that. He has good judgment when it comes to his work."

But Jim was also desperate. I knew that better than anyone.

Was he grasping at straws to reinvent his job? Should I be happy that he was fixated on landing a new client now, rather than on early retirement? How could Jim have told his boss he'd signed Davis Rhodes as a client for the agency before he'd even given the guy a proposal?

I needed to think hard about this.

And worry.

And feel guilty, because if it hadn't been for me, Jim would never have met Davis Rhodes in the first place.

What would happen if Jim wasn't able to sign Rhodes, and Mack found out My Beloved Husband had been lying about it being a done deal?

I had a momentary vision of us being forced to sell our beautiful home because we couldn't keep up with the property taxes. Jim was now worse than unemployed—no one wanted to hire him since word of his shameful behavior and lack of professional ethics had swept the public relations world. We'd end up living in a small bungalow at the Connecticut shore, and I'd take a part-time job as a check-out clerk at the local food store just to make ends meet. Jim would take the only job he could find, driving around neighborhoods delivering newspapers at 5 a.m. He'd lie and tell all our friends he'd taken early retirement and was in "media relations."

We'd shop at thrift stores for our clothes, and buy day-old bread, dented canned goods and perishable food items whose "use-by" dates had long since expired.

Our children would send us money to live on, instead of the other way around.

Well, maybe there was a bright side to this after all.

"Hi, Mom."

"Sweetheart. You startled me."

Jenny came into my office. Her short blonde hair was sticking up endearingly on one side of her head, and she was wearing a pair of old pink pajamas with red hearts on them. She looked like she was about ten years old.

I got up and hugged her, smoothing down her hair.

I felt a little tremor go through her body. Was she crying in my arms? So far neither Jim nor I had asked Jenny for any details of what had made her come back from the West Coast. We knew she would tell us what she wanted us to know when she was ready for us to know it.

Then she pulled away and said, "Sorry Mom. I didn't realize you were on the computer. I'll go into the kitchen and grab some breakfast."

"I'm never too busy for you, honey. Come on. There's coffee already made. And I'll make you some eggs, ok?"

"No eggs for me. Cholesterol, you know? But I'll have some coffee with you and maybe some fruit or granola and yogurt if you have some? I can get it myself. You don't have to wait on me."

"I want to wait on you," I protested. "Maybe the reason you ended up coming home wasn't the most positive one, but I'll admit that it's a treat for me to have you here. If that's kind of selfish, well, I guess I'm guilty. So let me get your breakfast."

The dogs raced ahead of me and then stopped by their food bowls.

"I get it, girls. You need some food, too."

Jenny laughed and settled herself in a kitchen chair.

After giving the dogs fresh water and a few handfuls of dry dog food, I pulled out a mug from the kitchen cabinet. It had a picture of a ballerina on it.

"Are you too grown-up to have your coffee in this?"

"Oh, Mom, I can't believe you still have this," Jenny exclaimed.

"Using this mug for chocolate milk was my special reward when I finished all my vegetables."

I was rummaging in the refrigerator for yogurt. "Jenny, I'm afraid that we don't have any yogurt right now. I need to get to the food store sometime today. How about some cold cereal and a banana?"

"Sure, Mom, thanks. Living in California for a while has changed my eating habits. I've become much more conscious of sugar and sodium in food. Jeff used to say…"

She stopped and her eyes filled with tears.

I wasn't sure how to react. I'm an impulsive person, and in the old days I would have crossed the kitchen in two steps, tissues in hand, kissed her and told her that whatever was wrong, Mom and Dad would make it better. But she was all grown up now, and in charge of her own life. My job was to be there for support when she wanted it.

I sat down at the table beside her and covered her hand with mine.

"Jenny, honey. I hate to see you so upset. Dad and I both wish we could do something to help you."

I paused.

Careful, said my brain to my mouth. Don't say exactly what you're thinking, that Jeff is a jerk and you're much too good for him. Some of my friends had said negative things about their offspring's partner after the couple broke up. Then the pair reconciled, and their harsh criticism had alienated their child, in one case for a whole year. I didn't want to take that chance with my daughter.

"We don't want to pry or intrude on your space," I continued cautiously. "You know we're glad to have you home, and if you want to talk about your issues with Jeff, that's fine. I'll just listen. If you don't, that's ok too. It's your call."

Jenny sat there moist-eyed. "It's kind of hard to talk about this with your mother. It's just so personal. I suppose that sounds stupid. Of course it's personal. Oh, I'm just so mixed up!" She covered her eyes and began to cry again.

To give her some time to get control of herself, I decided to share a little of my relationship with my own mother. "Sweetie, you know that I never had these kinds of intimate talks with your grandmother. I admit that Grandma and I had our problems over the years. There were times that I really wanted to talk to her about personal things, especially when I was a new bride. The few times I tried, she got very upset, embarrassed, defensive, whatever. Of course, you have to remember that your grandfather died before I was born, so her experience with married life was pretty brief. Anyway, I certainly didn't want to upset her, so I just backed off.

"But I'd like to think that you and I have a different, more open relationship than Grandma and I had," I went on.

Dramatically I put my hand over my heart. "I hereby promise that whenever you want to talk, I'll just listen and won't say a word. You know how hard that will be for me. I'll even put it in writing."

Jenny smiled, just a little.

I got up from the table and kissed her on top of her head.

"Whenever you're ready, I'm here. Now, let's change the subject. How are things going at Fairport College? Tell me about your classes and your students. I have to admit I've been bragging just a little to Nancy and Claire about your being a teaching assistant there."

"T.A., Mom."

"What?"

"The job is called a T.A."

Jenny ate a bite of her cereal and drank a few sips of her coffee. Nourishment: balm for a mother's soul.

"The students are an interesting cross-section of people. All ages, all ethnic groups. I was kind of intimidated the first day by the fact that so many of my students are older than I am. But Dr. Burns said not to let that bother me."

"Dr. Burns?" I repeated. "You mean Linda Burns?"

"Yes. Even though she's in the history department and I'm in American literature, she made a point of stopping by my department office to welcome me."

"That was nice of her," I said slowly. "I don't see her that often any more." Thank God. And I think she's a royal pain. But if she was nice to my daughter, she went up a notch in my estimation.

"I used to baby-sit for her two sons, remember? They were real terrors. I called her Mrs. Burns then. But when I called her that at school, she oh-so-gently reminded me that she's Dr. Burns. What's up with that?"

"Well, Jenny, I guess she's just proud of having her Ph.D. Maybe when you get yours, you'll be the same way."

Did I want to tell Jenny that I thought Linda Burns was incredibly pretentious? I was sorely tempted. But Linda Burns was also in a position to help my daughter, and besides, as my mother used to tell me, "If you can't say something nice about someone, say nothing."

So, I clamped my lips together, and said nothing.

Chapter 7

Marriage is a relationship in which one person is always right and the other is a husband.

I decided to be supportive about the Jim-Davis Rhodes situation. For the next few weeks I was an empathetic sounding board to many of My Beloved's ideas for making the retirement coach a household word. I was happy to see Jim so enthused about his career again, but I couldn't ignore the fact that he had bragged to his boss about landing a client before the deal was set.

There was also something niggling at me about the great Dr. Rhodes. I remembered sitting there in his kitchen with that blasted plate of chocolate chip cookies in front of me, listening to him go on and on about his re-treading strategy. He almost seemed like he was reciting from a prepared script. Not that I ever would have said that to Jim.

Or, maybe—to be completely honest—I was a little jealous of Jim's continuing infatuation with him.

Anyway, between Jenny's living at home and keeping an erratic schedule because of her classes, and Jim's life revolving entirely (at least that's how it seemed to me) around Davis Rhodes's availability, I began to feel like a short-order cook. We never ate meals together and talked, the way I'd fantasized we would when Jenny came home from California. Either she was leaving when Jim was coming in or vice versa. Diners passing in the night, so to speak.

Jim became more and more obsessed with his campaign to make Davis Rhodes a media star. It was all he talked about.

Then it all came crashing down, like the stock market on a very bad day.

Four weeks had passed since our meeting with Davis Rhodes. The day started like any other; Jim dashed into the kitchen and grabbed a quick cup of coffee and a bagel to take with him to the train. I remember that it was a cinnamon raisin bagel, his favorite. It's funny, the stupid things that stick in your mind.

"Don't expect me for dinner tonight," he said over his shoulder on his way out the kitchen door. "Dave and I will be working late. I think he's as enthused about this whole project as I am, and we're almost through with an initial media presentation and a press kit."

"Jim, just one thing before you go."

He turned around and looked at me, clearly annoyed. "Don't make me miss my train, Carol. What is it?"

"Well, I just wondered if Dave has given you any kind of retainer for all the work you're doing for him? I mean, you did sign a contract with him, right?"

"Don't be ridiculous," Jim snapped. "We shook hands. That's enough for me. You don't understand how business is done these days. I'll be late tonight. I'm going to Dave's directly from the train, so don't wait dinner for me."

He aimed a quick air kiss at my cheek and was out the door.

I tried hard not to overreact to Jim's words. I certainly did know how business was done these days, thank you very much. Maybe I hadn't gained most of my professional experience in corporate America, but I knew that a handshake wasn't necessarily a binding contract.

I turned to the dogs and said, "Well, girls, our day isn't starting out so great. Let's chill out with *Wake Up New England* for a little while. You know how you love that show."

They wagged their stubby tails in agreement, and we all headed into the family room to turn on the television. I kept the volume low because Jenny was still asleep upstairs.

I must admit I was only half-listening to the television while, multitasker that I am, I was sorting through a week's worth of newspapers to put out for recycling.

And then I heard Dan ("The Morning Man") Smith, the show's co-host, say, "Since January one, two thousand and six, eight thousand baby boomers are turning sixty every day. Boomers currently make up forty-six percent of this country's work force. The oldest members of this generation will be eligible for retirement soon, precipitating what some economists have called a boomer retirement revolution. Tomorrow on *Wake Up New England,* join us as we meet Dr. Davis Rhodes, a retirement guru and lifestyle coach whose unique approach is guaranteed to help these potential retirees achieve complete satisfaction in the next phase of their lives."

I screamed. I couldn't help it. Jim had actually done it. This time I was glad I was wrong. What a coup! Davis Rhodes on *Wake Up New England*! And Jim never said a word to me about it.

I knew My Beloved wouldn't be in the office yet, but I just had to call and leave him a message on his voice mail.

"Hi, it's me. I am so proud of you! Congratulations on getting Davis Rhodes on *Wake Up New England* tomorrow. How did you do it? Why didn't you tell me? This is so wonderful. Call me when you get a chance. I'll be here all morning."

I took a quick shower and, when I was drying myself off, the phone rang. I ran to get it, wrapped in a towel, and it was Jim.

"Carol, are you crazy?" he yelled at me. "What the hell are you talking about? I didn't get Davis Rhodes on *Wake Up New England.*"

I wrapped the towel tighter around me, trying hard not to drip on the floor.

"I know what I heard," I answered defensively. "Dan Smith announced a special feature on baby boomers and retirement that's going to be on tomorrow's show, and Davis Rhodes is the guest."

"You must have heard wrong," Jim barked at me. "I haven't even sent out a press release about the guy yet. You absolutely misunderstood, and it's not the first time you've called me at work with some ridiculous news that turned out to be completely wrong. Are you trying to get me upset? Do you want me to lose my job? Why are you doing this to me? I have to go."

He slammed down the phone in my ear.

I lost it. I really did. I've never been able to deal with it when Jim yelled at me. He was a prime example of the "Shoot the messenger first, and then ask questions" school of communication. As a result, over the past few years, I began to rely more and more on e-mail when I had something to tell him that I suspected would make him blow his top. Sadly, I've learned that it's often easier to interact with My Beloved via the computer than in person.

But this time I was truly caught off guard.

"Oh, my God," I said. Tears sprang to my eyes. I couldn't help it. What was going on? And how dare Jim take it out on me if Davis Rhodes was turning out to be an undependable liar and a jerk.

Ok, calm down, I told myself. You know how Jim operates. Once he thinks this through, he'll call back and apologize for yelling and taking out his frustrations on you. He always does, eventually. And you always, always overreact, Carol. Don't be such a cry baby. And don't let Jenny see you like this.

I toweled myself dry and threw on a pair of jeans and a hooded sweatshirt.

What you need, I told myself, is to treat yourself very nicely today while the situation—which you can do absolutely nothing about—works itself out.

Frowning, I studied myself in the bathroom mirror. In addition to my pink puffy eyes, was that some gray hair I saw peeking out around my temples? Now, that was something I could do something about, assuming I could get an appointment today at Crimpers, our local hair salon.

I reached for the phone and, for once, I got lucky. Deanna, my favorite stylist, had just gotten a cancellation. She would work me in for a color and cut if I didn't mind coming over right away.

I tiptoed downstairs, let the dogs out for a quick run around the back yard, left a note for Jenny, and then I was on my way to get coddled, colored and pampered.

And I deserved it.

Chapter 8

Q: What do retirees call a long lunch?
A: Normal.

Perhaps there are some women out there who don't have a special relationship with their hair stylist. But believe me, they are few and far between.

Hair salons are to American women what local pubs are to European men: a place to relax, laugh and talk. To take and give advice on a wide variety of subjects. A sisterhood. And, if you're really lucky, like I am, a place to share secrets with your hair stylist while the other patrons are under the dryer and can't hear.

Deanna knows more about me and my life than most members of my family and some of my closest friends do. A petite brunette (this month) with spiky hair and a pale complexion, she favors ruby red lipstick and matching nail polish. She's forever trying to lose weight—though she certainly doesn't need to—and she can read my face and body language like an open book.

So it was no surprise that, when I walked in the door of Crimpers that morning, she gave me a big smile and waved with her scissors, then frowned and looked at me questioningly. "What's up with you?" she was asking me in her private shorthand.

"Thanks for squeezing me in, Deanna," I said brightly. "I'll have a cup of coffee and look through the latest magazines until you're ready for me."

She nodded and turned back to the client in her chair. "I'll just be a few more minutes. You can go and put on a smock now if you want to."

"Hi, Carol," said my friend Mary Alice, who turned out to be the client Deanna was working on.

Thank you, God. Mary Alice was the most sensible of our group, and just the person to put things in perspective for me.

I immediately started to babble. "You won't believe what's happened. And, I swear, I never thought Jim would be so angry at me. I only called him at the office this morning because..."

"Hi, Carol."

I stopped in mid-sentence and peered under the nearest dryer. Good grief. Just the person I most needed *not* to see, Linda Burns. But for Jenny's sake, I was cordial. Charming, even.

"Linda, it's wonderful to see you," I gushed. "I've been meaning to call you and thank you so much for taking Jenny under your wing at the college."

Mary Alice rolled her eyes at Deanna.

Linda waved her hand dismissively. "I'm glad to do it. Jenny is a lovely girl. So bright. So determined to succeed. She reminds me a lot of myself when I was just finishing up my graduate degree and starting out. And after all, I've known her forever, since she was babysitting for the boys. She and I used to sit in the kitchen when I came home from teaching and talk and talk about all kinds of things. Who knows," she added with a laugh, "maybe she wants to teach at the college level to emulate me."

She paused, then said, "I always wondered, Carol, did you graduate from college?"

There it was, the famous Burns zinger. As if I didn't have enough to be upset about today.

I smiled at Linda and pretended I hadn't heard her. Bitch, I thought.

"Jenny couldn't have a better role model than you, Linda," I assured her as sincerely as I could. And I thanked my lucky stars that she had said hello to me before I unloaded the entire Davis Rhodes story onto Mary Alice and Deanna.

Linda turned off the dryer and asked Deanna, "Do you think I'm dry now? I really have to get back to class. I have students depending on me for tutorials today."

She took off her smock and handed it to Deanna, just as the door to the salon flew open, revealing Nancy, looking like she was going to explode with excitement. She saw me and rushed over to give me a huge hug.

"I'm so excited, I can't stand it," she gushed. "I'm so glad I found you. I figured you'd be here celebrating! How did Jim do it? I heard that Davis Rhodes is going to be on *Wake Up New England* tomorrow morning. That's fantastic. Aren't you thrilled?"

I grabbed her arm and tried to propel her toward the changing room, but she was in full roll and there was no stopping her.

"Oh, Mary Alice," Nancy shrieked, "did you hear about Davis Rhodes, the retirement coach? Carol got Jim to go and talk to him about retirement options, and Jim took him on as a client to promote him and his book, and he's gotten him on *Wake Up New England.* Everybody will see it."

Nancy turned and noticed Linda for the first time.

Linda said dryly, "Oh, I doubt everyone will see the show, Nancy. Some of us have to work and don't have time for morning television." She turned to me. "And I, unlike other people, am much too young and have far too many important things to accomplish to think about retirement.

"I really have to leave now, Deanna. I'll see you in four weeks."

She dropped a check on the counter, spritzed her hair with a little hairspray, and walked out the door.

Linda's rudeness momentarily diverted me.

I had actually forgotten (briefly) that My Beloved had absolutely nothing to do with Davis Rhodes's television appearance tomorrow morning, as well as the fact that Jim was probably losing his job at this very minute.

Or, at the very least, that he was humiliating himself in front of his boss and confessing that Rhodes had never been a real client of the agency, and now apparently never would be. And, in the process, Jim was blaming me for the entire fiasco and we would probably be divorced before the end of the year.

"Carol," Nancy said, shaking me by the arm. "what's the matter with you?"

"What's the matter with me?" I repeated. "The matter is that you've made things even worse. How could you be so stupid, flying into the salon screaming about Davis Rhodes being on television tomorrow? Do you ever think before you speak?"

Nancy looked stricken, and I felt terrible. It wasn't her fault, not really. She had no way of knowing what was going on with Jim.

"Nancy, I'm sorry. I shouldn't have talked to you that way."

"Hey, everybody," Deanna suggested, "let's calm down. I want to hear what this is all about." She glanced around the salon, which was now blissfully quiet.

"It's just the four of us now, but I don't know how long that'll last. I have other clients coming in soon. So what is going on, Carol? I could tell something was up with you when you walked in the door."

"Here, Carol," said Mary Alice, always the nurse. "You don't look so good. Sit down. Nancy, get her a glass of ice water. Now, take some deep breaths and tell us what's wrong. It's more than Linda goading you, isn't it? Aren't you happy about this television appearance?"

I took a sip from the glass Nancy handed me.

"Ok," I answered shakily. "Here goes. You know that I sort of tricked Jim into going to Davis Rhodes in the first place, and that he's been working with Rhodes for the last few weeks on a big media campaign to promote Rhodes's re-tirement strategy and his book?"

"Of course we know, Carol." Clearly, Nancy was getting impatient. "I helped you do it, remember? And now Jim's gotten Rhodes on *Wake Up New England.* That's fabulous."

"No, it's not fabulous. It's terrible. I heard Dan Smith announce Rhodes's appearance on *Wake Up New England* too, and I left a message on Jim's office voice mail to congratulate him. But Jim called me back and was livid. He accused me of deliberately misunderstanding what I heard. Jim had nothing to do with Rhodes's television appearance tomorrow.

"In fact," I admitted, "Rhodes was never a client of the agency, although Jim lied and told everybody, including his boss, that he was. It looks like Rhodes was just stringing him along, and already had been working with another P.R. firm. Jim never got a retainer from him, either. He'll probably lose his job over this."

Nobody said a word for a few moments. My purse began to chirp. I realized it was my cell phone which, for once, I'd actually charged and turned on. I checked my caller I.D. It was Jim.

"That's him now," I said. "I don't think I can talk to him right now. I'm too upset. And I can't take him yelling at me again."

"Let the voice mail pick it up," Deanna advised. "Fortify yourself with a cup of coffee, and then play back the message."

The phone rang once more, and then went into my voice mail.

"I'll go into the changing room to listen to Jim's message alone. Forget about the coffee. It'll probably make me jumpier than I already am."

"I'll make a fresh pot anyway," Nancy offered, "in case you change your mind."

"And I'll continue making Mary Alice look beautiful," said Deanna. "Come out when you're ready, Carol. If you don't want to tell us what Jim said, that's entirely up to you."

I closed the changing room door for some privacy, then punched in the voice mail. I noticed my hands were shaking.

"Carol," Jim said, "I shouldn't have yelled at you before, but I was shocked by your call. I'm sorry, honey. I've been trying to get Dave on the phone, but Sheila keeps saying he's with a client and can't be disturbed. I haven't said anything around the office about this fiasco, and I'd appreciate your keeping it quiet too. You know this could mean my job. I'm going to leave work early and go directly to Dave's office and have it out with him. I can't believe he'd double-cross me like this. I told Sheila I'd be there by four o'clock. I'll let you know what happens."

I sat down on a hamper filled with used smocks. Unfortunately, I had already told Nancy, Mary Alice and Deanna about the Jim-Davis Rhodes *Wake Up New England* fiasco. Another demerit for Carol and her big mouth. But I was sure I could trust them not to say anything to anyone else.

Look on the bright side, Carol, I told myself. Maybe Jim would be able to straighten things out with Rhodes. Maybe it was a simple misunderstanding.

Maybe pigs really do fly.

I groaned and put my head between my hands.

I had to accept the fact this mess was in Jim's hands, and he had to deal with it. I repeated to myself, out loud, "There is nothing you can do. There is nothing you can do. There is nothing you can do."

What I could do was to cheer myself up and get my hair done. And wait for Jim to come home and tell me what happened. I realized I'd better take advantage of this opportunity with Deanna. If Jim really did lose his job, this might be the last time I could afford to come to the hair salon for a long time. Sigh.

Chapter 9

Q: Why does a retiree often say he doesn't miss his job, but he misses the people he used to work with?
A: He's too polite to tell the whole truth.

Deanna really performed a miracle on me that day. When I left Crimpers, not only were my highlights a little blonder—always guaranteed to lift my spirits—but Deanna had a new brand of cosmetics that she tried out on me, and when she was through, my eyes looked bluer, my skin looked rosier, and all that combined with my newly blonde shiny hair made me look pretty damn good.

The ego boost alone, to say nothing of the support of good friends, had done wonders to lift my spirits.

But when I got home and let the dogs out, I checked the home voice mail and there was no message from Jim. The afternoon wore on and he still hadn't called.

By 5:30, I was going a little crazy. Jenny had left a note that she would be home by 6:30, so I decided to start dinner. I needed something to do with my hands, and hopefully cooking would keep my eyes from constantly straying to the clock. And worrying about what was happening with Jim and Rhodes. I had the phone in my pocket so there was no way I would miss a call.

I remember I had just started to wash greens for a salad when the phone finally rang.

"Carol." Jim's voice was very high, a sure sign that he was upset.

"Where are you? What's going on? I've been so worried."

"Carol. Please, don't talk. There's been a terrible accident."

"Accident! Jim, are you hurt?"

"It's not me. It's Dave. He's dead."

"Dead!" I screamed into the phone. "How could he be dead?"

"He's dead because he's not alive, Carol," said My Beloved. "What a stupid thing to ask."

Jim is upset, I told myself. Shut up. Let him talk. It's not important that he's taking things out on you.

I waited a beat, and then Jim continued. "When I got to the Center late this afternoon, the front door was locked and the only car in the parking lot was Dave's. So I went around to the kitchen door and let myself in that way. At the time, I wasn't thinking clearly, but I should have realized it was strange that the front door was locked."

Jim's voice quavered. "I found Dave slumped in a chair at the kitchen table. I touched him to see if he was sick or something, and he fell onto the floor. I felt for a pulse, but there wasn't any. It was pretty horrible."

"Oh, God! What did you do then?"

"I called nine-one-one immediately. Thank God the police and the emergency squad came right away. The police are still here. They've been taking my statement."

He choked back a little sob.

"The way they've been questioning me, it sounds like they think I had something to do with Dave's death."

"That's ridiculous," I started to say. "You'd never…"

But Jim interrupted me.

"I think I need a lawyer here. Can you call Larry right away? Please."

Then, for the second time that day, he hung up on me.

I stared at the phone, willing myself not to cry. This was a nightmare.

Then, I started to giggle. I just couldn't help myself.

All I could think of was, do the producers at *Wake Up New England* know they're going to be minus one guest for tomorrow morning's show?

I forced myself to calm down and call Larry at home. Fortunately, Larry, not Claire, answered the phone and I managed to give him a fairly coherent account of what had happened. He asked me a few questions, very gently. I guess he was used to dealing with clients who don't make a whole lot of sense.

Larry assured me that the police's questioning of Jim was standard procedure, since Jim was the one who had found Rhodes's body and reported it. He also assured me that Jim was unlikely to be arrested, but that he was smart to ask for a lawyer to be present during the questioning. I gave him Jim's cell phone number—I hoped he had it on—and Larry, after repeatedly assuring me that everything would be fine, said he would contact Jim immediately. And that one of them would get back to me as soon as they knew something more.

I felt a little better. But not much.

I was still hanging onto the phone when Jenny came home about a half hour later. She was in a very good mood, almost like her old self. I, of course, was about to ruin that.

"Hi, Mom," she said, planting a kiss on my cheek. "Let me just drop my stuff upstairs and I'll be right back to help you with supper."

Then she looked at me more closely. "Mom? Why are you holding the phone like that? Is something wrong? Did you get bad news? Is someone sick? Mom! Talk to me!"

I moistened my lips. Deep breaths, Carol. Try not to get her upset, too.

"Jenny, honey, there's been an accident. Well, actually, it's a misunderstanding. Your father…"

"Mom, was Daddy in an accident? Is he all right?"

"No, honey." I rushed to reassure her. "It's not your father. Davis Rhodes has had a terrible accident. Your father called me from Rhodes's office about half an hour ago. When Dad got to the office, he found Rhodes dead at his kitchen table."

"Poor man," said Jenny. I wasn't sure if she meant her father or Rhodes, not that it mattered. "He probably had a heart attack. How awful for Dad, finding him."

A heart attack. Of course, that must have been what happened. Why didn't I think of that?

"You know, you're probably right," I said. "But when your father found Rhodes, he called the police, and they came right over. They started questioning him, and Dad got very upset. He called and asked me to get a lawyer for him. He sounded like he thought he was going to be arrested."

"I'm sure Dad freaked, Mom. No wonder. Imagine going to an innocent business meeting with a client and finding him dead. Anyone would freak. Did you call Larry McGee?"

I decided not to clarify the fact that Jim's appointment with Rhodes was not the innocent business meeting Jenny had described. The less she knew about that, the better.

"I called Larry right away. He said not to worry, and that questioning Dad was just standard police procedure because he found Rhodes. I hope he's right."

Jenny gave me a big bear hug.

"Mom, I know you must be worried sick, but I really think the best thing we both can do right now is to put something together for supper, so Dad will have something to eat when he gets home."

"Honestly, Jenny, sometimes you remind me of my mother, thinking food can solve almost anything." I laughed to take any sting out of my words, and then we both set to work.

About a million hours later—though it was only an hour and a half since Jim's frantic phone call—My Beloved finally arrived home.

I handed him a glass of merlot. "Don't say a word yet. Just take off your coat, sit down, and sip."

To say that Jim looked distraught would be an understatement. The man had aged ten years since he'd left for work this morning.

"This has been the worst day of my life."

I tried not to rush him, but part of me wanted to just shake him and scream, "Tell me what happened! Tell me what happened!"

I've never been a patient person. When I get a new mystery to read, I always peek at the end first. Just can't stand the suspense. I know, I know. That's what mysteries are supposed to be about—suspense. But this was real life and the suspense was killing me.

"I told you on the phone how I found Dave. It was horrible. I've never touched a dead body before." Jim shuddered. "Of course, at the time, I didn't know he was dead. I thought he was just sick. But when I put my hand on his shoulder, he rolled off the chair onto the floor. I felt for a pulse, but there wasn't any."

He covered his face with his hands. "Oh, God, what a day."

"Dad, it was a worse day for Rhodes, after all," Jenny pointed out sensibly. "I mean, you just found him. Rhodes is the one who's dead."

At first I thought Jim would snap at Jenny for her remark. But instead, he smiled for the first time since he got home.

"You know, honey, you're absolutely right. But the police kept asking me more and more questions, so I felt I needed to have a lawyer with me. They eased up when Larry got there. Both Larry and the police assured me that, in the case of a sudden death, they always question the person who finds the deceased pretty thoroughly. Oh, Jenny, you'll get a kick out of this. One of the police who questioned me was Mark Anderson, remember him?"

"Dad, no kidding!" Jenny exclaimed. "Of course I remember Mark. When we were in grammar school, the teachers always sat us next to each other. Guess it was easier for them to keep track of us kids if we were all in alphabetical order. He's a policeman now? I'd completely lost track of him."

Before they both started going too far down memory lane, I interrupted them. I still had lots of questions that I wanted answered, and, as I have already admitted, I am not a patient person.

"Jim, what kind of questions did the police ask you? Did they want to know why you were at Rhodes's office? Did they ask what your relationship was with him?"

"I told the police that Rhodes and I had a client relationship, Carol. He was a retirement coach, after all."

"But Jim," I persisted, "did you clarify that Rhodes was your client, not the other way around?"

"I didn't feel it was necessary to go into details," Jim said impatiently. "The police didn't ask me for any clarification, and I didn't give them any."

"That amounts to lying to police," I screamed at him. "Are you crazy?"

"Now who's overreacting?" Jim shot back at me.

Some of his old bravado was coming back. I think I liked him better when he was less sure of himself.

"Larry says the police have to do an autopsy on Rhodes because no doctor was present to certify cause of death, but it was probably a heart attack or stroke or something like that," Jim continued, ignoring my outburst. "He told me to come home and not worry. Good advice for all of us, Carol."

I swear, I wanted to grab him by his shoulders and shake him until his teeth rattled. How can men be so stupid?

Chapter 10

Q: What do you call an intelligent, good-looking, sensitive man?
A: A rumor.

Jim lay next to me in our dark bedroom, snoring away without a care in the world. Between his snoring and that damn retirement clock, ticking away like a time bomb, I lay there so wired and wide awake I felt like I'd drunk an entire pot of black coffee. Maybe two pots.

I tried counting sheep. No dice.

For some obscure reason, I remembered an old Bing Crosby song, when he promised you'd fall asleep if you counted your blessings. Bing was wrong this time. I counted a lot of blessings, and I still couldn't fall asleep.

I knew I was going to be bleary-eyed and the bags under my eyes were going to be suitcases in the morning if I didn't get to sleep soon. After you reach a certain age, no amount of cover-up can mask those dark circles or puffiness.

What I finally ended up doing to get to sleep was to count our problems. I had enough of those to choose from, God knows.

Hmm, let's see.

In the past 12 hours Jim had been betrayed by a "client" he never really had. The "client" was set to go on a major television show and do a live interview which would probably make him a household name. Jim had no idea the interview was scheduled until I told him. It was a pretty safe bet that his boss would find out Jim had lied about his relationship with said "client." Jim could lose his job. At the very least, Jim would lose a huge amount of credibility at the agency. So, in a desperate attempt to save his bogus "client relationship" and his job, as well as his ego, My Beloved Husband went to the "client's" office. And found his "client" dead. The police were called, and Jim lied to them.

Did I leave anything out? Could things get worse?

Sure, I felt sorry for Jim. But he was handling the situation all wrong, damn him. The more I thought about that, the madder I got.

I imagined Jim coming home tomorrow night, a broken man, and confessing that he'd lost his job. Oh, that's harsh, Carol. But, fantasies are harmless, right?

Let's continue. How about Jim coming home, a broken man, confessing he's lost his job, and the police arrive on our doorstep wanting to talk to him again. Ooh, even better.

The snoring beside me continued mercilessly. As did the ticking of that blasted clock. But so did my fantasizing.

How about this one? Jim is questioned again and again by the police because they are suspicious of his story. It turns out that—oh, yes!—Rhodes was murdered! Oh, boy, this was getting really good now.

Jim breaks down and confesses he's lied. Against his lawyer's advice, he tells the police the whole ugly story. And promptly gets himself arrested for murder, the big jerk!

When I visit him in his jail cell, he begs me through his tears to help him. "Carol, you're the only one who can save me now! Please, honey, help me!"

God, I was so loving this fantasy!

I was deciding what to wear to Jim's arraignment when I must have fallen asleep.

Jim left for the office the next morning before I had a chance to talk to him again. He was probably afraid I was going to try and talk some sense into him, and didn't want to deal with me.

Jenny left for school early, too. But at least we had time for a quick mother-daughter bonding session over cups of tea and bowls of cold cereal, where we assured each other that there was really nothing to worry about, blah blah blah.

I don't think she believed me any more than I believed her, but at least we were there for each other. And for Jim, of course. Needless to say, I didn't share my late-night fantasy with Jenny. She probably would have a pretty low opinion of her mother if she knew I was fantasizing about her father going to jail. And the fun of having him beg me to save him.

I tried very hard to avoid turning on the television. I was afraid of what I might hear on the news. But finally, I couldn't stand the suspense any longer and I clicked on the television remote. I just couldn't help myself.

I surfed through channels, trying to control my curiosity. Then, I gave in—well, I hadn't really tried so hard to resist, to be honest—and there they were: Dan Smith and his co-host, Marni Barker, outside the *Wake Up New England* studio with hundreds of screaming fans jumping up and down behind them.

I checked my watch. It was 7:50 a.m. Almost time for them to cut away for the regional weather, then to local stations for a brief update. But this was also the time to give viewers a little teaser about what was coming up in the next hour on the show, to entice folks to stay tuned. Had they acknowledged Rhodes's death? Had I missed it?

Then I heard Marni say, "Before we get to the weather, I want to tell viewers about an exclusive story we're following."

She gazed solemnly into the camera.

"You may remember that Dr. Davis Rhodes, pioneering retirement guru for the baby boomer generation, was scheduled to be a guest on this broadcast this morning. Dr. Rhodes was going to discuss his revolutionary approach for making the best out of the third portion of life."

She paused dramatically.

Dan stepped in to assist. "That's right, Marni, and we were all looking forward to his appearance. But tragically, last night Dr. Rhodes died, under mysterious circumstances, at his office in Westfield, Connecticut. Police are investigating."

A picture of Rhodes, taken from the dust jacket of his book, flashed onto the screen.

"However," Dan continued, "we are very grateful that Sheila Carney, Dr. Rhodes's trusted associate, has graciously agreed to be interviewed. We'll be talking to Sheila live from her office at the Re-tirement Survival Center, and getting her unique perspective, both on the great Dr. Rhodes as a person and as a pioneer in his field, coming at fifteen minutes past the hour. Don't miss it. Now, here's the weather."

I pressed the mute button. I had hoped that the media would ignore Davis Rhodes's death. Now I realized how ridiculous that idea was. In death, Rhodes was being transformed by the media into a legend. No, more than that, an icon. The New Elvis!

I took a sip of coffee and grimaced. Ugh. Cold. Time to replenish the cup, or better yet, throw out the old stuff, which tasted like paint remover now, and make a fresh pot. Activity always soothes me and this was certainly mindless enough.

Have I mentioned how much I love throwing out things like ketchup or shampoo bottles that have just a little bit left in the bottom? It may sound silly, but it's one of the guilty pleasures I give myself when My Beloved isn't around. He's forever going into the recycling bin and saying, "Carol, why did you throw away this bottle of hair conditioner? There's plenty left in the bottom. I'll use it up. I'm not made of money, you know." I just had to be sure I rinsed the bottles thoroughly when I got rid of them, so he wouldn't catch on.

Oh, how I missed those week-long business junkets to the West Coast he used to take back in the 80s. It was the only time I got to clean out the refrigerator.

I didn't want to miss a single word of Sheila Carney's interview, so I set the timer on the microwave for five minutes, then tossed out the old coffee and put together a fresh pot to brew. Half decaf, half regular coffee. I've read some studies that say decaf is healthier, and seen others which claim regular coffee and all that caffeine won't hurt you. I figured I'd cover myself either way.

While I was at it, I let Lucy and Ethel out for a quick run so they wouldn't interrupt me with doggie needs, and filled their bowls with fresh water. Then, I poured steaming coffee into my favorite mug, the one that shows an elderly couple in wedding attire with a caption underneath that reads, "Daddy always said the first fifty years are the hardest."

I settled myself into the family room couch again and the dogs hopped up beside me. I let them snuggle in close. What the heck, I could always vacuum off the dog hairs later, and right now I needed all the empathetic company I could get. I even had a ballpoint pen and lined pad handy, in case I decided to make a few notes during the interview. Contrary to other people's opinions, I can be organized, when I set my mind to it.

I was especially curious to see if *Wake Up New England* had sent a reporter out to interview Sheila, which would make Rhodes and his death a really important story. No, when the story began, it was obvious a local camera crew was at the Center with Sheila, and the interview was going to be conducted via remote.

I strained to see where the conversation was taking place, and realized Sheila was in the elegant living room of the Center. Dressed impeccably in a basic black dress (widow's weeds?) with the obligatory pearl choker at her throat and tiny pearl stud earrings, her blonde hair was flowing over her shoulders. She looked very fragile.

"Ms. Carney, first of all," said Dan, "please accept the condolences of all of us on Dr. Rhodes's tragic passing. We were looking forward to our interview with him this morning so much." Marni nodded her head in agreement.

"Thank you," replied Sheila, graciously accepting their condolences. "And it's Dr. Carney, not Ms. Carney." Her hands fluttered to her pearls. "But you both may call me Sheila." She smirked, just a little, into the camera.

Whoa, I thought. I was surprised Sheila was acting so bitchy to Dan and Marni. Didn't she care how she came across on camera? This prima donna wasn't the professional woman I'd met when I visited the Center with Jim for that first meeting. I wondered what the relationship had been between Sheila and Davis Rhodes. Professional? Personal? A little bit of both?

I made a note on my pad to check that question out.

Both Dan and Marni looked startled at Sheila's response, but quickly recovered, pros that they are.

"Well, Sheila," Marni put just a little emphasis on the name, "I'm sure this has been a terrible shock to you. Dr. Rhodes's re-treading approach to retirement was certainly revolutionary, and I'm sure millions of baby boomers would have benefited from his wise counsel. It's very premature, I'm sure, but has the staff of the Center given any thought as to how, and by whom, his great work will be carried on?"

Sheila smiled insincerely into the camera, revealing a dazzling set of teeth in a shade so white that it couldn't possibly be natural.

"Why, Marni, of course the work of the Re-tirement Survival Center will go on. How could we not go on? The Center will be a lasting tribute to Dr. Rhodes and his pioneering work, a memorial, if you will. And as far as someone to lead the Center, why," her blues eyes widened, "since I worked so closely with Dr. Rhodes in developing the re-treading method, of course I will now be the Center's director."

Her eyes widened even further, if possible, and she stared directly into the camera. Her lip quivered slightly.

"It's the least I can do to honor a genius whose work will impact the lives of millions of baby boomers in the coming years."

Sheila was certainly giving an Academy-Award-winning performance. How well I remembered the interaction Jim and I had witnessed, when Rhodes treated Sheila like a flunky in front of us, not a professional colleague. Hmm. I made another note on my pad.

"That's truly wonderful news to all Dr. Rhodes's clients," said Dan. "How selfless of you to devote your life to such a noble cause. Now tell us...." He leaned forward in his chair. "Has there been any progress in determining the cause of Dr. Rhodes's death? Are the police still on the premises doing some investigating? Will any public memorial service be scheduled, and if so, when?"

Sheila leaned back in her chair, as if to ward off this new line of questioning.

"Dan, as you know, Dr. Rhodes only died last night. We're waiting for the final determination of the cause of his tragic death, pending the autopsy results. This will take several days, I'm told by the police. Of course, we will have a public memorial service to honor his memory when the time is right, but in the meantime, the Re-tirement Survival Center is open and ready to serve our clients. That, of course, is the most significant memorial of all to the important work Dr. Rhodes and I pioneered together."

The interview ended on that note.

I flicked off the television and my imagination went into overdrive. Probably as a result of reading too many mysteries. But what if it turned out that Rhodes really was murdered? And that Sheila had murdered him to gain control of the Center?

Now, that would really be something.

Chapter 11

Q: Why do retirees count pennies?
A: They're the only ones who have the time.

I had just begun to scribble a few more notes to myself when the phone rang.

I checked the caller I.D. It was Jim. Probably calling to tell me he'd either been fired or arrested.

I took a few deep cleansing breaths to calm myself, then answered the phone. "Hi dear. How's everything?" Are you being measured for a prison jumpsuit? I didn't say that last part, of course.

"So far, so good," he assured me. "Did you see Sheila Carney's interview on *Wake Up New England* just now? Wasn't she great? I think it's fabulous that she plans to keep the Re-tirement Center open as a tribute to Dave. I'm wondering if I should give her a quick call and express my condolences. And also congratulate her on how well she handled herself on the air. What do you think?"

I was completely flabbergasted. In our 36 years of marriage, My Beloved had never asked my advice about anything work-related.

"Well, Jim," I said, hedging my response, "that could be a kind thing for you to do. I'm sure Sheila is feeling very upset and emotional right now over Rhodes's death. It must be horrible for her." Not that she seemed all that heartbroken in the interview. More like she couldn't wait to get on with her role as new director of the Center.

"But maybe it's not a good idea for you to contact her so quickly," I cautioned. "After all, you found Rhodes's body, and the police haven't released the cause of his death. You may still be under some suspicion."

"Carol, you're exaggerating my involvement. After all, I just happened to be in the wrong place at the wrong time. It could have been anybody who discovered Dave's body. It was just a fluke that it was me," Jim said defensively.

"I don't think I'm overreacting to this. The police may want to question you again. What if they find out that he was supposed to be your client, not the other way around? And how angry you were about Rhodes doing a major television appearance behind your back? Jim, don't you get it? The fact that you went to his office to have it out with him makes it look like you could have killed him."

There, I'd said it. My deepest fear was that Rhodes had been murdered, and the police would think Jim was responsible.

"That's just ridiculous," said Jim, his voice rising slightly. "Leave it to you to over-dramatize the situation. That's why I asked you to call Larry last night. He assured me that all those questions were standard police operating procedure, because I found the body. And I don't see why calling Sheila to express my condolences is going to raise any suspicions with the police about me. Your imagination is really working overtime again, Carol."

"But Jim," I persisted, "what if Sheila had something to do with his death? Who would have had a better opportunity to harm Rhodes than Sheila? And he treated her like a secretary, not a partner, from what we observed, remember? I saw her on television this morning too, and she sure didn't seem that broken up about Rhodes's death to me."

"That's a horrible thing to say."

He paused, then said more gently, "Honey, I know you're worried about me, and I appreciate that, even though I don't think it's necessary. I have to go. I'll keep you posted."

Well, maybe My Beloved Husband had deluded himself into thinking everything was hunky dory, but I certainly had my doubts. I remember when we were first married. One of the reasons I was so attracted to Jim was that nothing seemed to throw him. No matter how trivial or how important the problem, Jim always seemed to know exactly what to do to make things right.

I admit that I have panicked in certain situations, especially ones involving the kids. There was that time when Mike was three and fell off his tricycle in the driveway and hit his head. God, the blood! I was absolutely paralyzed. Then I started screaming. Jim came running out of the house, took one look at the situation and immediately ran inside for a cold cloth to stop the bleeding. He picked Mike up and pressed the compress to his head for a good five minutes, all the while comforting him, and me. When the bleeding stopped, it turned out to be just a small cut on Mike's forehead. Only needed two stitches to close the wound, and Mike doesn't even have a scar today.

Yes, My Beloved was great at emergencies like that.

But over the years, I've realized that there are lots of things that Jim can't fix, whether he thinks he can or not. Nobody makes terrific choices all the time, but as Jim became more and more disillusioned with his job at the agency, he didn't seem to care whether the choices he made, especially in his professional life, were good ones or not.

And the way he was handling Davis Rhodes's death was unfathomable to me.

On the other hand, I'd never found a dead body. How did I know if he was reacting normally? Maybe Jim was just protecting himself from what had to be a horrible scene, one that would give most people nightmares for months.

My mother always told me, "Don't borrow trouble, Carol. It'll find you soon enough."

I sighed, then said to the dogs, "It's shower time. I'm going upstairs and wash away all my troubles down the bathroom drain."

There's a meditation I do sometimes when I'm in the shower, which helps center me for the day. In the meditation, as the water rushes over me, I let go of any negative feelings that may be in my head. When I turn off the water, I will them all to be gone, and to stay gone for the remainder of the day.

If there ever was a day when I needed to practice that meditation, it was today. Even if I stayed in the shower until I wrinkled up like a prune.

Predictably, three people had called and left messages while I was washing away my troubles: Nancy, Mary Alice and Claire.

Nancy was the first. "I've got to talk to you!" she shouted into the phone. "I was reading the morning paper before I left to go to Realtor open houses, and there's a small article on the bottom of page one that says Davis Rhodes was found dead at the Re-tirement Center last night. The police aren't releasing any more information right now. All I could think of was Jim going over there to have it out with him. God, did Jim actually see him yesterday? What's going on? Call me on my pager or my cell as soon as you get this message." She rattled off a series of numbers and hung up.

Oh, boy. It had never occurred to me that there would be something in the local paper about Rhodes's death. At least, not this soon. But that's stupid, Carol, I chided myself. It was announced on television an hour ago. What made you think it wouldn't be in the paper too?

I dressed hurriedly and ran downstairs. Our hometown paper was still sitting on our front porch, beside the blue plastic bag containing *The New York Times.* It was raining slightly, so the local paper was wet and the pages were stuck together.

Normally, I would spread the paper out all over the kitchen so the pages would dry before I read it, but today I was in too much of a hurry to bother. I scanned the front page and didn't see anything about Rhodes. What was Nancy talking about?

I skipped to the second section, which featured regional news, and there it was, a small news item at the bottom right corner.

Local Retirement Coach Found Dead

Davis Rhodes, Ph.D., founder of the Re-tirement Survival Center and author of the recently published book, *Re-tirement's Not For Sissies: A Baby Boomer's Guide To Making The Most Of The Best Of Your Life,* was found dead at his office in Westfield last night. As of press time, police were releasing no information as to cause of death, but one source, who asked not to be identified, termed Dr. Rhodes's death 'suspicious.' An autopsy has been ordered.

Well, I consoled myself, it could have been a lot worse. At least Jim wasn't identified as being the person who found Rhodes's body.

But the police were terming the death "suspicious." That wasn't good.

I resisted the urge to call or e-mail Jim about this. He'd probably seen the story already.

Instead, I listened to my other voice mail messages. The next one was from Mary Alice.

"I just saw the paper and I'm checking to be sure everything is all right. I'm not working today, so if you want to talk, I'm at home. What can I do to help?" That message was typical of Mary Alice. Ever the caregiver, she was such an ideal nurse. I wished with all my heart that there was something she could do to help, but I was at a loss about what that could be. Except listen to me and hand me tissues when I cried. Or give me drugs to calm me down. Which was probably illegal.

The last call was from Claire.

"Carol," she said, "it's nine-forty-five and I'm checking in to see how you and Jim are doing today. Did he go to work? When Larry got home last night, he assured me that there was nothing to worry about. But finding a dead body must have been awful for Jim, especially when it was someone he knew. And there was a little squib in today's paper about

Rhodes's death. Did you see it? Thank God it didn't mention who found the body. Call me whenever you can talk. I'll come over if you want me to, but I don't want to intrude in case Jim is still home."

"End of messages," the automated voice mail said. For now, that's the end of our messages, I thought. Once word got out about Jim being the person who found Rhodes, everybody in town will be calling here to offer advice, sympathy, or pump us for information.

I ran my hands through my hair. God, what an awful mess.

Then the dogs started to bark uncontrollably. And the front doorbell rang.

I peeked out through the dining room drapes and gasped. There was a police car parked in front of the house, and I could make out the silhouettes of two uniformed patrolmen standing on my front steps.

Chapter 12

Re-tire: verb; to go away or withdraw to a private, sheltered, or secluded place.
— Webster's Dictionary

I don't think I've ever been so scared in my life. I felt like I was going to be sick to my stomach, like I'd taken a body blow which had knocked the air out of me.

I deluded myself into thinking that the police couldn't tell I was home. Maybe, if I crept up the stairs to the bedroom with my back pressed against the wall, they wouldn't see me.

The dogs, of course, continued to bark wildly and jump at the front door. I knew I couldn't shush them without giving my presence away.

Suddenly I realized that if I hid from the police, it would look suspicious. My cowardly behavior could make things worse for Jim. That was the last thing I wanted to do.

I pasted a false smile on my face and opened the door.

Lucy and Ethel, sensing an opportunity for unexpected freedom, immediately tried to make a break for the front yard. I grabbed each of them by their collars and said, "Easy, girls."

One of the officers, the younger one, flashed a badge and said, "Mrs. Andrews? Hi, I don't know if you remember me, but I'm Mark Anderson. I went to school with Jenny."

"Mark?" I repeated. "You're Mark Anderson?"

I tried not to react, but if this was really Mark, he'd come a long way from the pimply-faced boy I remembered. In fact, he was downright handsome, reminding me of a younger Brad Pitt. He smiled, and I saw just a flash of that young boy who used to tell jokes at the kitchen table when he and Jenny were supposed to be doing their homework. I remember they seemed to spend more time laughing together than actually studying.

"Yes, Mrs. Andrews. I guess I've changed a little since you saw me last."

"Why, Mark," I said, "I never would have recognized you. It's so nice to see you again."

Then I clapped my hands over my mouth. "Well, it's not nice to see you. Oh, damn. You know what I mean."

Mark laughed and shook my hand. At that exact moment, the dogs took advantage of my lack of vigilance and made a beeline out the door.

"Oh!" I screamed. "Stop them! The gate's not closed and if they get out on the street, they could get hit by a car!"

In less than a second—I swear—Mark had turned and raced after Lucy and Ethel. "Gotcha," he said, collaring each of the offending canines. "Back inside with you two." He led them gently back to me.

"Would you mind if we all went inside for a minute?" Mark asked, handing the dogs off to me.

Gesturing to the other policeman, he said, "This is my partner, Paul Wheeler, Mrs. Andrews. He was with me last night when we answered your husband's emergency call at Dr. Rhodes's office."

Paul Wheeler had to be just about the shortest adult male I'd ever seen. He seemed no more than five-feet tall, was bald, and sported a thin moustache. Rather than say hello like Mark had done, he simply gave me a hard, level stare. I disliked him on the spot. Like a lot of very short men, he overcompensated for his size by trying to appear macho. Nancy calls this behavior Short Stature Syndrome. I decided to ignore him as much as possible during my interview, and concentrate on talking to Mark instead.

"I'd shake your hand, Paul," I said with a little laugh, "but you saw what happened the last time I let go of the dogs' collars. Come on into the kitchen. It's more comfortable in there."

I was feeling less nervous now. After all, I'd known Mark since he was a little boy. Someone can only intimidate you if you let them, I reminded myself.

We all sat down around the kitchen table, and the dogs settled themselves at my feet.

"Anyone want coffee?" I asked brightly, ever the perfect hostess. "I can make a fresh pot in just a few minutes."

"That's ok, Mrs. Andrews," Mark replied, looking around the room. "Boy, being here again really brings back memories. Jenny and I sure spent a lot of time doing math at this table. Well, she was tutoring me, trying to knock some smarts into my thick skull."

I laughed. I suspected Mark knew I was nervous and was trying to put me at ease.

Paul the policeman frowned and cleared his throat. "Can we get to the reason we're here, please?"

He flipped open his notebook. "Now, Mrs. Andrews, we'd like to ask you a few questions about your relationship with the deceased. How well did you know Davis Rhodes?"

I leaned back in the kitchen chair and tried to appear thoughtful. I wasn't sure how to answer this question, because I wasn't sure what Jim had told them last night. An image of Joe Friday in the old television show *Dragnet* flashed into my mind. "Just the facts, ma'am," he would say in every episode.

I had to be sure that what I said didn't implicate My Beloved, so I chose my words as carefully as possible.

"It seems that everyone Jim and I know is talking about retirement these days," I began. "It's the favorite topic of conversation with all our friends. Jim and I have talked about it, too. We've discussed his taking early retirement from his job at Gibson Gillespie, while we're both still relatively young and in good health, so we could do some of the things we've always talked about, like traveling to Europe, driving cross-country, things like that."

I looked at Mark across the table, and he nodded encouragingly at me.

"So one day, just for the heck of it, I went online and did a web search for retirement coaches. Davis Rhodes's was the most user-friendly, and he had an office in Westfield. Jim checked out the web site, too, and he was intrigued as much as I was. We decided to make an appointment with Dr. Rhodes for retirement counseling."

So far, I thought, everything I've said has been absolutely true. Even though I wasn't exactly telling the whole truth.

Paul Wheeler was writing down every word.

"Then what happened?" Mark asked.

"Jim and I went to see Dr. Rhodes for an initial consultation."

"When exactly was that, Mrs. Andrews? Can you give me the date?" Paul Wheeler held his pen in mid-air, waiting for my response.

"It was the fourth week of June. I'm sorry I can't remember the exact date, but I know it was in the very late afternoon. I think we were Dr. Rhodes's last appointment of the day, because when we got there, the place looked deserted. When we went inside, we met Sheila Carney, Dr. Rhodes's assistant, and then we met Dr. Rhodes himself."

"What did you talk about?" Mark wanted to know. Really, I thought, these questions were getting a little ridiculous.

"We talked about retirement possibilities, Mark," I shot back. "That's what we were there for, after all." I tried not to appear defensive.

"Did either you or Mr. Andrews see Dr. Rhodes again after that initial consultation?"

Careful, Carol, I warned myself. This is where you could get Jim into trouble.

"I didn't see Dr. Rhodes again. But Jim had a few more follow-up appointments with him."

"How many?" asked Paul Wheeler.

"I couldn't say how many times Jim and Dr. Rhodes met. You'd have to ask Jim that. I only met the man at the initial consultation.

"You know," I continued, "it was just bad luck that Jim had an appointment with him last night and was the person who found him dead. It could have happened to any of Rhodes's clients."

Oops. I suddenly realized that if the police checked Rhodes's client list for yesterday, Jim's name wouldn't be in it. But it was too late to backpeddle now.

Paul Wheeler snapped his notebook shut. "We're probably going to question your husband again about last night's events," he told me in a not-too-friendly tone. "Some of the information we've received from other sources has been contradictory. We may also want to question you again."

I was not going to let this little twerp get to me. I stood up and looked directly at Mark. "It was good to see you again. I'll tell Jenny you were here. Anything Jim and I can do to help you in your investigation, we'll be glad to do."

I gave him a little hug—probably not allowed, but what the heck—and opened the kitchen door to show them both out.

"We'll be in touch," were Paul Wheeler's last words.

Great. Just great. At least he didn't say, "Don't leave town."

Chapter 13

Q: How many retirees does it take to change a light bulb?
A: Only one, but it might take all day.

I was in dire need of my friends that morning after the police left. And maybe a stiff drink too, but it was a little early for that.

Time to return all their phone calls.

I started by phoning Claire, because I also wanted Larry to know that the police had been here to ask me questions.

Claire answered on the second ring. "I was sitting here waiting for you to call me back. How're you doing? How's Jim? Did he go to work today?"

"I am literally shaking right now. The police just left here."

"Oh, Carol! How awful."

"I guess it could have been worse. One of the policemen was Mark Anderson, remember him? He went to school with our kids and now he's on the Westfield police force."

"Just like his father," Claire reminded me. "I think his dad is chief of detectives now. Unless he's already retired. At least Mark was someone you felt comfortable with. But it still must have been awfully scary for you."

"Is Larry home? I need to talk to him. I don't know if I handled myself all right with their questions. I wasn't sure if I should even have talked to them without Larry there, but I didn't want to make it look like I had something to hide. Am I making any sense? If I'm saying stupid things, just tell me."

"You're making perfect sense," Claire responded. "But you just missed Larry. He's gone to the gym to work out. I don't think he'll be home for at least two hours."

I started to cry. The stress was really starting to get to me.

"Carol, please don't cry."

I continued to sob. I couldn't seem to help myself.

"I'll tell you what." Claire said. "How about if I call Nancy and Mary Alice and we all come over and bring you lunch? We can have a council of war about how to handle all this. I can get takeout from Maria's Trattoria. And I'll leave a note for Larry to call you as soon as he gets home. I'll also leave a message on his cell phone. You shouldn't be alone right now."

I was pathetically grateful.

"That would be wonderful. I can't stop my imagination from working overtime, and the police visit really freaked me out."

"I'll call Nancy and Mary Alice, and be over with lunch in less than an hour. Meantime, do something to take your mind off your worries. Clean out a closet or something."

I pressed the "off" button on the portable phone. The cavalry was on its way, with food, yet. And Claire was absolutely right. I needed to do something mindless so I could put the brakes on my overactive imagination.

Cleaning out a closet held no appeal whatsoever for me. In my opinion, doors were invented to throw stuff behind them and then close quickly before the stuff could fall out all over the floor. How many times had Jim opened the front hall coat closet to hang up a guest's coat and had tennis racquets, hats, and other assorted junk come crashing down on his head?

Thinking of My Beloved made me wonder what he was doing right now. Had he called Sheila Carney at the Re-tirement Survival Center? God, I hoped not.

I wasn't sure if I should let him know the police had been here this morning. There was nothing he could do about it from New York City, and the news would just upset him. No, it was much better to wait and tell him in person when he came home.

I decided to kill a little time by organizing the drawers in my desk. The bottom two were so full that I had trouble opening and closing them. It wasn't that long ago that I used my desk and computer every day, when I was doing freelance editing for local magazines. But I had to admit that I spent more time on the computer these days looking for web sites on retirement planning than I did doing editing. I hadn't received an assignment from my usual sources in over a month. Not that I'd solicited any, either. I needed to send out some e-mails soon reminding editors of my availability. But not today.

I tugged on the bottom desk drawer, but it was really stuck. In my frustration I pulled the damn thing so hard that it finally gave way and dropped on my foot. Ouch! That's what I needed, some physical pain to go along with my emotional angst. When I decide to suffer, I really suffer.

Gingerly rubbing my toes, I dumped the entire contents of the offending drawer on the office floor. But when I saw what had been making the drawer stick, I had to smile. It was a treasure trove of memorabilia from Mike and Jenny's school days—old report cards, art projects, even a few hand-lettered Mother's Day and Father's Day cards. Going through these family treasures was just the thing I needed to calm my nerves.

There was also a shoe box filled with old photographs. Boy, I thought, I bet Claire, Mary Alice and Nancy will get a kick out of seeing this stuff. There are probably pictures of their kids in here, too.

I laughed as I found a photo of Jenny taken the day she had her braces put on, scowling at the camera with her mouth closed, refusing to smile.

And there was a classic one of Mike and Jim taken at least twenty years ago during one of our vacations on Nantucket. In it they are proudly displaying a fish they caught, which looked like it weighed no more than a pound. But from the smiles on both their faces, you'd have thought they'd caught a whale.

Oh, here was another picture of Jenny, all dressed up for her eighth-grade prom. The braces were still on her teeth, but this time she was actually smiling at the camera. I squinted to identify her nervous-looking escort, and realized it was Mark Anderson. Hmm. Interesting. I didn't remember that he and Jenny had dated. Just that they were good friends who did homework together. I kept that one aside to show to Nancy. She'd probably remember every detail.

I glanced at my watch and realized an hour had gone by since I started this project. The group would be here any minute. That's why you never get anything accomplished, Carol, I scolded myself. You're too easily distracted.

Still, finding that picture of Jenny and Mark had given me something else to think about. I wondered if he ever married. Mark and Jenny sure would make a good-looking couple. I cheered myself up by imagining the cute grandchildren they could produce if they ever got together.

Maybe Jenny would like to see Mark again. I could drop a few hints in that direction and see what happened. That wasn't really interfering, was it?

Of course it was.

I sighed, told myself to mind my own business and went to answer the kitchen door.

"I'd give you a hug except my hands are full," said Claire, who was balancing several bags with delicious aromas emanating from them, and a small cooler. "Can you take this shopping bag from me?" I was amazed that Claire had arrived so quickly. It showed me how seriously she was taking this situation. Always time-challenged, she'd even been half an hour late for her own wedding.

I grabbed the largest bag, then peered around behind her. "Where are Nancy and Mary Alice? Aren't they with you?"

"I called Nancy on her cell, and she's showing a house to a client. She said she'd be over in about an hour. Mary Alice has some sort of appointment she couldn't break. She was very mysterious about it, too. Said to give you her love and that she'd try to make it over here sometime after lunch. And before you ask me," Claire said, correctly intercepting my next question, "yes, I left a message for Larry both at home and on his cell about the police coming here to question you. I'm sure he'll call you as soon as he can."

Claire put the rest of the food bags and the cooler on the granite countertop. As usual, she had brought enough to feed the entire neighborhood.

"Now, come and give me a hug and tell me how you're doing." She eyed me critically. "From the way you look, I'd say not so great."

My eyes brimmed over. God, was I always this emotional?

I changed the subject before I started to bawl my eyes out. "Does any of this food have to be refrigerated?"

Claire grabbed my arm and pushed me gently into a chair. "Forget the food. It'll keep fine. When Nancy comes, we'll eat it all and won't save any for Mary Alice. Just to teach her she shouldn't keep secrets from us."

She poured a glass of iced tea from a jug she had in the cooler and put it on the table in front of me. "Here. I brewed this for you at home, with extra lemon just the way you like it. Drink up."

I sipped obediently. Delicious.

"That's better. Now, don't try and change the subject. Have you heard from Jim today?"

I told her the whole story, about Sheila Carney's television interview, Jim's phone call, and his ridiculous idea about contacting her to offer his condolences. And to tell her what a great job she'd done in the interview. Ha!

"It's almost like he's deluded himself into thinking that, now that Rhodes is dead and Sheila is apparently taking over the Center, everything will be terrific," I said morosely. "He can take her on as a client and make her a huge media star. Forget the fact that Rhodes's death is suspicious, Jim found the body, and if the police find out why he went to see Rhodes yesterday afternoon, it's sure to make Jim look guilty of something. Then, as if things aren't bad enough already, the police showed up here to ask me some questions."

I slammed my hand down on the kitchen table in frustration.

"And you know what the worst part of this whole mess is, Claire? I don't know exactly what Jim did or didn't say to the police last night, except that he was purposely vague about his relationship with Rhodes. So all the while the police were questioning me, I didn't know if my answers were helping him or hurting him."

Claire nodded her head. "I know what you mean. It seems like men don't share a lot of important things with their wives, doesn't it? Larry can be the same way. Sometimes I think women share too much, and men don't share at all."

I gave Claire the details of my own police interview. "I think I handled myself all right this time, but if they come back to ask more specific questions, I don't know what I'll say. It really helped that Mark Anderson was one of the policeman. He did his best to make me feel at ease. But his partner, Paul Wheeler, is pretty overbearing. I got the feeling he was trying to trip me up with his questions." I shook my head to clear it a little. "I hope I don't have to deal with him ever again."

"It's going to come out that Rhodes died of natural causes," Claire assured me. "Larry was pretty confident about that when he came home last night. He dismissed the fact that Jim was angry at Rhodes for the *Wake Up New England* interview. And he advised Jim to answer the police questions exactly as they were asked, and not to volunteer any extra information. If Larry thought Jim had something to worry about, he'd have told him, believe me. My husband may be an easy-going guy, but he's a very sharp lawyer.

"Now, tell me about Mark. Didn't he have a crush on Jenny back when they were in school?"

"You have a pretty good memory," I answered. "Look what I found in my desk drawer." I pulled out the prom picture of Jenny and Mark from my sweatpants pocket. "They were a cute couple back then, weren't they?"

"They sure were," agreed Claire. "But don't you remember the reason Jenny went to that dance with Mark? Didn't her date with the class heart-throb, Peter Goulet, fall through at the last minute? How come I know this and you've forgotten?"

"The reason you remember and I don't, my friend, is probably because you didn't go through all the mini-romances, crushes, and other assorted crises with Jenny on a daily basis the way I did," I said. "Some weeks there were so many that it was impossible to keep up. There should be a special place in heaven for women who have raised daughters. God, the drama."

Claire laughed. "Raising a son was no bargain either. I don't think I got a solid night's sleep after Kevin got his driver's license. I remember pacing the floor in the family room waiting for him to come home. Praying that he'd come home in one piece. I suppose I was overprotective because he was our only one, but it never seemed to bother Larry. I guess he was in charge of the lawyer-ing and I was in charge of the worrying.

"Speaking of sons," Claire asked, "how's Mike doing down in sunny Florida? Does he know what's going on at home?"

"I haven't said anything to him, and I doubt that Jim has," I answered slowly. "What good would it do to worry him when he's so far away and there's nothing he can do to help? I did get an e-mail from him yesterday, though. He's come up with a new drink recipe for the bar called the Cosmo Girl's Cosmopolitan. It sounded pretty good. Maybe we should all have one for lunch."

"I don't know about drinking this early in the day," said Claire, who always takes things so literally. "But I do know what you mean about protecting your kids from the bad stuff, even when they're adults. I do the same thing. Do you think maybe a part of us still wants to preserve the illusion our kids had when they were little that we were perfect and could accomplish anything?"

I laughed. The idea that anyone in my family thought I was perfect, even for only a millisecond, cheered me up a little. Although it probably wasn't true.

I gave Claire's hand a squeeze.

"I feel better already just having you here to talk to. What do people do who don't have friends like you?"

"Talk to themselves, I guess," said Claire.

"I do some of that, too," I admitted. "More and more lately. But I pretend I'm talking to the dogs.

"Let's talk about something besides Jim and the Davis Rhodes mess for a while," I suggested. "You know we'll just have to go over the whole thing again when Nancy gets here. She hates to miss anything. What do you think is up with Mary Alice? You said she was mysterious on the phone about this lunch meeting of hers. That's not like her at all."

"I was thinking about her on the way over here," said Claire. "And I had a really crazy idea. Do you think she has a lover?"

I choked on my iced tea.

"Good God," I sputtered. "Mary Alice have a lover? What put that idea in your head?"

"It's not as crazy as you think, Carol," said Claire. "She's very attractive, and she's been a widow for over fifteen years. Do you think she joined a convent when Brian died?"

"I don't know. I never thought about it." I frowned a little, trying to think. "She's never mentioned anything about dating to any of us, at least not to me."

At that moment, the kitchen door burst open and Nancy rushed in, carrying more food.

"Who never mentioned anything about dating?" she asked. "Here, Claire, take this bag from me. It's got chocolate ice cream and hot fudge sauce inside and the ice cream is melting. Thanks. So how are you doing, sweetie?" This last was directed at me.

"Have you decided to ditch Jim and start dating? That's an interesting way to deal with all this stress."

"Very funny," I retorted. "We were talking about Mary Alice. She told Claire that she couldn't come for lunch today because she had some appointment that she couldn't break. Claire says she sounded very mysterious."

"I'm dying to speculate about Mary Alice's love life, but before we get to that, can you fill me in on what happened this morning, Carol? Was it awful for you?"

I gave Nancy the highlights of what had happened, including Sheila's television show interview, Jim's phone call, and the police visit. Of course, being Nancy, she kept interrupting me every other minute with questions and observations and suggestions. By the time I was finished, Claire had served up lunch for all of us, courtesy of the heavenly takeout menu of Maria's Trattoria.

One of the many advantages of having friends who know both me and my kitchen so well is that there was no need for me to jump up and help. Claire, Nancy and Mary Alice all know where the silverware is kept, which are the everyday and the "best" dishes, where the good and not-so-good glasses are, as well as which drawer holds my place mats and napkins. They also know where I hide my good jewelry and who are the beneficiaries of Jim's and my estate.

My entire family, including Lucy and Ethel, adore them. So in a pinch, any one of them could just move right in and take over my life without missing a beat.

"It sounds like you handled yourself pretty well, Carol." That was high praise indeed coming from Nancy. "Having Mark Anderson interview you must have made it easier."

"He was really sweet to me," I said, "but his partner scared the daylights out of me. He was a classic example of Short Stature Syndrome. What is it with short men and power trips anyway?"

"Show Nancy the picture you found," Claire suggested. "See if she remembers when it was taken."

I whipped out the picture of Jenny and Mark. "Do you remember that he was sweet on her at one time?"

"You know, I think I do remember." Nancy squinted at the picture. "I bet this was taken when they were going to the eighth-grade prom. I recognize the dress Jenny's wearing."

"You're amazing," I exclaimed. "How in the world do you remember that?"

Nancy shrugged. "Don't give me too much credit. My Terry wore that same dress the following year to her eighth-grade prom. She borrowed it from Jenny. Remember, we used to share good dresses between the girls, because it never made sense to spend a lot of money on something that would only be worn once?"

"Yes, like bridesmaids' dresses," said Claire. "I wish I had a dollar for every wedding I was in where the bride told me I could have the dress altered and wear it again. Never happened.

"So, Nancy," Claire continued, switching conversational gears rapidly, "Carol and I were wondering if you knew anything current about Mark Anderson. Is he dating anyone? Did he ever get married? Is he straight or gay? He and Jenny sure were good friends back in school."

"I think I heard a while ago that Mark was serious about some girl from Westfield." Nancy furrowed her brow in concentration. You could always count on Nancy to have the news. "They were engaged, but they never made it to the altar. I think she ditched him for another guy the week before the wedding. Broke his heart."

"Aha," said Claire. "That's very interesting. Maybe we should all work on a plan to throw him and Jenny together and see what happens."

"Now wait a minute," I protested. "I don't want to manipulate my daughter's love life."

"Yeah, sure," said Nancy. "You think we believe that one? Speaking of a love life, what's this about Mary Alice having a lover? She never said anything to me about it."

"Claire is just speculating, because when she called Mary Alice to come to lunch, she said she couldn't get here until later this afternoon," I explained. "And Claire has jumped to the completely unsubstantiated conclusion that Mary Alice is having a mid-day rendezvous."

"Hmm." Nancy looked thoughtful. "You may not be far from the truth. I confess I've tried to bring up the subject with her a few times. I even tried to fix her up once or twice, remember? She's refused to tell me anything. But she must have some sort of love life. She's still an attractive woman."

"That's exactly what I said," Claire replied triumphantly. "But little Miss Priss here," pointing her finger at me, "refuses to admit the possibility. Face it, Carol, you never were comfortable talking about men and sex, even when we were teenagers and it was practically all we were thinking about."

"That's not true." I tried to defend myself. "I just think that some things are very personal and shouldn't be discussed, even with your closest friends. But that doesn't mean I'm Miss Priss, thank you very much."

"Boy, did the nuns ever do a job on you in high school," said Nancy. "Now, who could Mary Alice be seeing? Oh, I know. I'll bet it's Ron Harrison. His wife died two years ago from breast cancer, and he's certainly attractive. Got quite a bit of money, too. Made a killing in the real estate market, so he'll be set for life. He'd be quite a catch."

"I've got to admit that when it comes to helping me take my mind off my troubles, you two are the best," I said. "But I think gossiping about Mary Alice when she's not here is kind of disloyal."

"Come on, Carol," Nancy shot back at me. "Being interested in one of your best friends' personal life isn't disloyal. We're concerned because we care. Claire, who do you think it is?"

"Well, I was thinking about Ed Whitford."

"Oh, I hope not," Nancy said. "I'm sure he wears a toupee. And a bad one at that. We have to set higher standards for Mary Alice."

"You guys are awful," I said, laughing. "I didn't think anything could make me feel better today, but you've done it.

"There's the doorbell. She's here. Now don't say anything. Just let her sit down and have some iced tea or something before you both start cross-examining her."

Before I could get to the door, Mary Alice had let herself in. We don't stand on ceremony at my house.

"Honey, I'm so sorry I'm late," said Mary Alice, throwing her arms around me and giving me a kiss on the cheek. "You know I would have been here earlier if I could have. I want to hear everything. But first, have I got news for all of you!"

I took a good look at her. Her eyes were shiny and her cheeks were glowing. Claire and Nancy exchanged knowing glances.

"We know what you're going to tell us," Nancy assured her. "We figured it out, you sly devil. Who's the guy? You look like you've just had a fabulous romantic interlude. Come on, give."

Mary Alice threw back her head and laughed so hard she finally had to wipe her eyes.

"You all are a hoot. And you're also dead wrong. There's no guy."

She paused dramatically, then announced, "I've just spent my lunch hour with the human resources person at the hospital. I'm going to retire next month."

I had to admit that, for once in our lives, we were all speechless.

Chapter 14

Re-tir-ing: adjective; drawing back from contact with others, from publicity, etc.; reserved; modest; shy.
— Webster's Dictionary

But we were only quiet for half a second. Then we all started talking at once.

"Mary Alice, my God!" Nancy screamed in her usual restrained way. "You're kidding!"

"I can't believe it," said Claire. "What are you going to live on? Have you talked to a financial planner? Remember that when I retired Larry was still working. We had to plan our finances very carefully once he decided to retire, too."

"Never mind what you're going to live on," I said. "What are you going to do with your time to keep from going nuts?"

Mary Alice held up her hands in mock surrender.

"Ok, ok. I'll tell you everything. But first I want a big dish of chocolate ice cream with extra fudge sauce. I know Nancy must have brought some today. It's one of the basic survival tools for dealing with any crisis we've ever had. And I want to hear what's happening with you and Jim, Carol."

Nancy obediently headed toward the freezer. "I'll get it for you, Mary Alice. But when it's your turn, talk loud. I don't want to miss a word."

Since both Claire and Nancy had heard all the details of Jim, Sheila's television appearance, and my visit from the police, I kept my story short. That was pretty easy, because Nancy wasn't interrupting me all the time.

"I'm very worried about Jim," I admitted, wrapping up my sad tale. "I was so scared when the police came. But maybe they won't be back, and the autopsy will prove that Rhodes died of natural causes. That'll be the end of it. I'm praying that Jim doesn't get fired before all this is straightened out. But there's nothing I can do about saving his job. He's on his own with that mess."

At this point, I was sick and tired of talking about Jim and Davis Rhodes. It was time to change the subject.

"Enough of this. Tell us what's up with you, Mary Alice," I said. "This is a pretty momentous decision you've made."

Mary Alice took a bite from the large dish of ice cream Nancy had set in front of her. "Umm. Yummy. I always think better when I have chocolate."

"Enough of this stalling," Claire said impatiently. "Details. We want details. When we had lunch a few weeks ago, I remember you talked about retiring. But you didn't say you were going to do it now. Are you sure this is a good idea? You're such a terrific nurse."

"That's a typical reaction of yours, Claire," Mary Alice said. "When I decided to go to nursing school, you tried to talk me out of it. You thought I should go to medical school instead."

Claire started to protest, but Mary Alice cut her off. "Don't worry. I forgave you a long time ago. If I hadn't gone into nursing, I wouldn't have met Brian. Marrying him was the best thing that ever happened to me. When he went into private practice, well," her voice trailed off, "it was so wonderful to be his office nurse. We were great partners. Then, he died."

We were all silent, remembering the shock of Brian's death when he was only 43 from a car accident. Life sure was unfair sometimes.

Mary Alice's eyes filled with tears.

Then she composed herself and went on. "Not that I'm feeling sorry for myself. Other people have coped with situations more traumatic than mine, and besides, I had the boys to take care of. I couldn't allow grief to take over my life. Working at the hospital was my salvation during the early years after Brian's death. But now, on top of all the paperwork I seem to spend my entire time doing, the shift schedule at the hospital is always changing. I just hate working nights, and I've had more than my share of them the past year or so. At my age, I'd much rather be vegging out in front of the television at ten o' clock at night than getting into my uniform and heading off to work."

She paused, took another bite of ice cream, and savored it.

"Then, I got the form that Social Security sends out every year. We all get one. It's called 'Your Social Security Statement.' It tells your estimated benefits when you decide to retire, broken down by year. Do you know the one I mean?"

"I always throw those things away," Nancy said. "After all, we're much too young to begin collecting benefits."

"You shouldn't throw those things away," scolded Claire. "It has all your personal information on it. You have to be very careful about identity theft these days. I hope you at least shredded the form first."

Mary Alice jumped in before Nancy could defend herself. "I know it'll be a few years before I'm eligible to apply for benefits, but that form started me thinking. When I really looked at the numbers on the form, I realized that it was financially smart to apply to receive benefits as soon as I could."

"I just hope the country still has Social Security when we're all eligible to collect," Nancy said, wanting to show us that she wasn't completely ignorant about the system. "You never know what the government's going to cut these days to save money. Remember how we all used to joke that we were such fun to be with that we should start a business and be paid just for being us? Maybe sitting back and collecting Social Security is that business."

Mary Alice rolled her eyes at Nancy. "Anyway, that Social Security form inspired me to start crunching some more numbers. I figured out what I need to live on. My mortgage is all paid off, so that's not a problem. I'm not a spendthrift, and the boys are grown and out of the house. They only ask me for money occasionally."

We all laughed. Who couldn't identify with that?

"I finally decided to talk to the hospital human resources people. There's a real shortage of nurses these days, and they don't want to lose me completely. So we've reached an agreement where I'll officially retire from the hospital nursing staff next month. But I'll come back as a part-time consultant, and also teach a few courses at the nursing school. I'll keep all my medical benefits, and I can also do some private-duty nursing. I can finally get back into direct patient care again, which is what I've wanted for a long time.

"My fabulous lunchtime 'romantic' interlude was with the head of human resources at the hospital, where I officially signed my retirement papers. So congratulate me, you guys. I'm starting an exciting new adventure! Who knows where it will lead?"

"I am so jealous," Nancy admitted. "And proud of you for taking the plunge."

"I'll tutor you in Retirement 101," said Claire, "just like I tutored you in conversational French back in sophomore year of high school. Remember, you got an A in that class, thanks to me."

"You both are the best," said Mary Alice. "Thanks for the encouragement and the support. What do you think about this, Carol? You're very quiet, and that's not at all like you."

"I guess I don't know how to react," I said honestly. "On the one hand, I'm thrilled that you've made a decision to do something you obviously want to do. But on the other hand, the word 'retirement' is kind of a dirty word around here these days. And I guess I'm afraid that if I tell Jim about your plans, it'll start him off on his own tangent all over again."

Mary Alice looked hurt at my lack of enthusiasm for her decision. It was obvious she was hoping for 100 percent support from our group. I knew I had to add something positive.

"I'm also a little disappointed, Mary Alice." I waited just a beat before I added, "I was hoping you were having an affair so that we all could share in it vicariously!"

Everyone whooped and yelled over that one.

"But Carol, don't you see?" asked Mary Alice. "Now that I'm going to retire from the hospital, I'll finally have the time to have an affair. I just need to find the man."

Chapter 15

Q: Among retirees what is considered formal attire?
A: Tied shoes.

"I saw Mark Anderson today," I said to Jenny. She had come home from school earlier than usual, probably because she was worried about her father, and the two of us were preparing dinner together. It was a very cozy domestic scene.

"What do you mean, Mom?" Jenny asked. "Didn't Daddy say last night that Mark's a policeman now? What happened?"

"Oh," I answered casually, "he and his partner dropped by this morning to ask me a few questions about Davis Rhodes. Background stuff. You know. It was no big deal." Liar, I thought. You were scared to death.

I gave her a big smile to emphasize my point, but Jenny's look told me she wasn't buying my feeble attempt at false bravado.

I wanted to head her off before she starting asking me more questions I didn't want to answer, so I added, "Mark's certainly grown up to be handsome. He reminded me of Brad Pitt. Down, girls." Lucy and Ethel, sensing the possibility of my dropping a morsel or two from the vegetables I was chopping, were dancing around my legs.

"Mom, don't try to change the subject. Weren't you nervous? Does Dad know the police were here?"

"I haven't talked to your father since early this morning. I didn't see the point of calling him at the office and taking the chance of getting him all upset. He should be home in a little while. I'll tell him then."

"It sure seems like a long time since Davis Rhodes died," Jenny said, "even though it was just last night. So much has happened. I was talking about it at school today with Linda Burns."

"Linda Burns? I hope you didn't tell her about Dad's finding the body."

Jenny patted my hand. "Take it easy, Mom. I'm not that naïve. I'm as anxious as you are to keep Dad's name out of it. It was just a casual conversation, that's all. She was naturally curious, because of the story in the newspaper. She knew that you and Dad had gone to see Rhodes, and she wanted to know what your reaction was to Rhodes's death."

I swallowed hard, and told myself that my daughter was a grown-up now and mature enough to handle sticky situations. And she wasn't a gossip. Her conversation with Linda was perfectly innocent.

But speaking of sticky situations, I decided to take the plunge and bring up another subject before Jim got home. I'd had more than enough of thinking and talking about Davis Rhodes right now. There were a few other things going on in the Andrews family that concerned me. Although I knew they were none of my business.

"Jenny, I've been meaning to ask you about Jeff. You know that Dad and I have both tried very hard to honor your privacy, but have you been in touch with him since you've been home? E-mail, phone, anything?"

"I know you've both been walking on eggshells about Jeff and me." Jenny looked sad, but resigned. "It's been very hard for me to talk about this, but he's finally accepted the fact that our relationship is definitely over. Kaput. *Finis.* It's for the best, at least for me. For all I know, he's already started seeing somebody else."

I started to interrupt her, but she went on, "What I have to figure out is when I can go back to California for the rest of my things. I have a lot of clothes still in the apartment, and some furniture. I'll probably sell the furniture, or see if Jeff wants it, but either way, I'll have to go back there sometime after the summer semester ends. I'm not looking forward to it, though. I tell myself that I can handle it, and that I won't be emotional, but I'm afraid that when I see Jeff, it's going to be too hard for me. I guess I'm not quite as grown up as I'd like to think I am."

I wasn't sure how to respond to this, but being me, I couldn't keep quiet. And I had, after all, introduced the subject in the first place.

"Oh, sweetie, would you feel better if I went along with you? We could make a vacation out of it, maybe combine it with a trip to Hawaii."

"Mom, that's a great offer. Let me think about it, ok?" Jenny patted my cheek. "You really are a doll. You and Dad have made it so easy for me to come back home. But if I decide to stay in Fairport, I'm going to have to get my own place. You understand that, right?"

"Sure I do. But we both really love having you here. And frankly, right now, I'm grateful for your moral support. I hope you don't think that's selfish of me. I'm just so concerned about your father."

The Father-in-Question arrived home from New York about ten minutes later. Fortunately, Jenny and I had moved on to more mundane topics of conversation by that time.

When Jim came through the kitchen door, I gave him a quick hug and whispered in his ear, "How are things?"

He squeezed me back and didn't answer me. Typical. I wasn't sure if he was being difficult or he just hadn't heard me. He's an expert at selective hearing. I fought the urge to cross-examine him, because Jenny was still in the kitchen and I didn't want a confrontation. He'll talk to you in his own time and in his own way, I told myself. But he didn't look like he'd faced a firing squad at work, which was comforting.

"Something smells good," Jim said. "I can tell that you two have been preparing another wonderful feast. What are we having?" He headed toward the stove where Jenny was working and gave her a quick kiss on the cheek. Then he lifted up a pot lid and sniffed the contents.

Two can play at the let's-just-talk-about-trivial-stuff-and-not-what's-really-on-our-minds' game, so I gave him tonight's menu. "Chicken with broccoli, brown rice, and a tossed salad. Oh, and I got an e-mail from

Mike about a new drink he's come up with for the bar. It's called the Cosmo Girl's Cosmopolitan. Do you want to try one before dinner?"

"I'd rather just have a glass of wine, Carol. You know I don't like those fancy drinks. I have some news, most of it good, but I'd rather change out of this suit and tie first. I will tell you both, though, that everything went fine at work today, and that I talked to Sheila Carney."

I started to ask a question, but Jim held up his hand to silence me. "Before you leap to any conclusions, she called me. And I've heard nothing from the police, so I think yesterday's nightmare is over. Thank God."

Oh, boy, I thought. Wait till he hears the police were here to talk to me.

"That's great, Dad," said Jenny, ever the supportive daughter. She flashed me a questioning look and I shook my head slightly.

The phone rang just as Jim was leaving the kitchen to go upstairs and change.

Our caller I.D. announced it was Patrolman Mark Anderson.

Yikes!

"Jim, wait a minute. Mark Anderson is on the phone. Maybe he wants to talk to you."

Jim froze in the doorway, and his expression reminded me of a deer caught in car headlights right before it gets hit.

Jenny stopped tossing the salad.

I cleared my throat and answered the phone, forcing myself to sound cheerful and upbeat.

After the basic preliminaries were out of the way, I put my hand over the receiver and hissed at Jim, "Relax. Mark's calling to talk to Jenny, not you." I handed her the phone. "Why don't you take the call in the family room so you can have some privacy?" I congratulated myself on being so selfless. I was dying of curiosity but I couldn't let Jenny know that.

Jim let out a huge sigh of relief and started to leave the kitchen. I grabbed his arm to stop him. He wasn't getting away from me that easily, and I knew I had to talk fast while Jenny was on the phone.

"Mark and his partner were here to ask me some questions this morning. I didn't call you at the office and upset you, and I tried very hard to give answers about Rhodes that wouldn't put you in a bad light. But that was difficult for me because I wasn't clear about what you told the police last night. Since you haven't bothered to share a lot of it with me." I glared at him.

Jim's face had turned to stone. "You should have called and told me the police had been here. What's the matter with you?"

"What's the matter with me? What's the matter with you? Why won't you tell me what's going on? I'm your wife, for God's sake," I shot back.

"Larry said it wasn't necessary to get specific with anyone, including you, about what the police asked me," Jim answered defensively. "I did give the police truthful answers to their questions, but I didn't mention my doing some P.R. work for Rhodes, or how I'd come to his office yesterday to confront him. I didn't lie to them. I just didn't offer any additional information. By the time Larry got to the Center last night, the police were through with their questions. But when I told him how I framed my answers, Larry said I was right to handle the interview that way. He also instructed me that if it comes out that Rhodes was my client, not the other way around, I should just say I didn't clarify the relationship because I wasn't asked to."

"But Rhodes wasn't really your client. That's part of the problem, don't you see that?"

Jim gave me a sharp look, so I shut up.

"What did the police ask you about, Carol?"

"They wanted to confirm how we met Davis Rhodes," I said. "I tried to give very general answers, but I was nervous. It helped that Mark Anderson was one of the officers who was here, but I sure didn't like his partner. He did everything he could to shake me up."

I grabbed Jim's arm and said, "The only way we're going to get through this mess is to handle it together. We've got to be honest with each other. Please don't try to shield me or hide things from me. I'll go crazy if you do."

"I'm sorry, Carol. It's just hard for me to admit that I'm not in control of this situation."

He smiled. "But at least I still have my job. And the talk with Sheila Carney went well. I'll tell you and Jenny all about it after I change. Thanks for the support, honey. Oh, I tried to call you a few times today on your cell phone. I left you a few messages. Did you get them?"

"I was here all day. In fact, Nancy, Mary Alice and Claire came over for lunch. Why didn't you call me on the home phone?"

"I've told you before that I never know where you are during the day," Jim said impatiently. "You're always out somewhere or other. That's why I got you the cell phone. Didn't you have it on?"

To tell the truth, I didn't have the faintest idea where my cell phone was at that moment. But I certainly wasn't going to admit that. I'd worry about finding it later.

"I didn't think to put the cell phone on, because I was home all day," I replied in an even tone. "You should have tried here first, like you usually do. Next time you need to reach me, leave a message on the home voice mail, too, ok?"

Jim gave me an inpatient look. "I don't have time to leave two messages all the time. I don't see why you can't use your cell phone the way everyone else in the twenty-first century does."

I was not about to fight that battle again. "Why don't you get changed and I'll tell you about my lunch today, dear?" I asked. "I think you'll be interested at the news."

Jenny wandered back into the kitchen, the phone in her hand and a little smile on her face. "Well, that was a surprise. Mark asked me to meet him for coffee tomorrow afternoon. Do you think that counts as a date?"

"I think that counts as two old friends getting together to catch up on their lives," Jim said. "And if you could manage to put in a good word for your old man at the same time, that would be a bonus.

"And now," he announced, "I am really going upstairs to change."

Dinner was pleasant enough, all things considered. I was glad I had cleared the air with Jim, so we could enjoy being together as a family. For once.

Jenny chattered happily about her classes, and appeared to be looking forward to her coffee "date" with Mark Anderson. I filed that thought away to chew on when I was a little less distracted. If I ever were a little less distracted.

She didn't mention our conversation about Jeff, and neither did I.

Naturally, we couldn't entirely avoid talking about the Davis Rhodes situation.

I was burning with curiosity about whether the *Wake Up New England* fiasco had come up at the office, but when I asked Jim about it, he was deliberately vague. "I finessed it, Carol. Everything is fine. The details aren't important."

What the heck did that mean? Women lived for details, and men never wanted to share them. I hoped that Jim's "finessing" hadn't involved more out-and-out lying. I made a conscious decision not to obsess about that. Easier said than done.

My Beloved did deign to share some of the details of his conversation with Sheila Carney with Jenny and me.

"You know, Sheila really was the brains behind the Re-tirement Survival Center, and Rhodes didn't give her any credit at all. She's the one who came up with the whole strategy, and was the book's ghostwriter. But Rhodes told her it would be threatening to men if she appeared to have so much control, and it would be much better if he was the front man for the Center. Because most of their clients are men facing retirement, not women. And men relate better to other men. It made sense to me."

Of course it made sense to you, I thought. You always were a sucker for blondes.

But I didn't buy the story Sheila had told Jim for one minute. After all, now that Rhodes was dead, couldn't Sheila take credit for anything she wanted? Who would be around to dispute her? I made a mental note to go online later, just for the heck of it, and check the Center's web page. I wondered if busy little Sheila had doctored it to promote herself and downplay Rhodes.

"What did she say about the *Wake Up New England* appearance, Dad?" Jenny asked. "Did you ask her about that?"

"She had a perfectly logical explanation. Apparently, before I ever met Rhodes, Sheila had done a mailing of advance copies of the book and a press release to all the major news outlets in the area. The *Wake Up New England* producer called Rhodes, and they set up a date for him to appear on the show. Rhodes never thought to mention it to me. It didn't occur to him that I would see it as a problem."

I thought that sounded like a very weak explanation, but Jim had bought it, hook, line and sinker.

"What about now, Jim?" Since he had finally begun to open up a little, I was bound and determined to weasel as much information out of him as I could. "Did Sheila ask you about continuing your professional relationship with the Center?"

Jim nodded. "She really wants my help in promoting the Re-tirement Survival Center. And before you say anything else, I talked to Mack about it. There'll be a written contract which all parties will sign. With a retainer. It'll all be on the up and up. Sheila said Rhodes felt comfortable cementing deals with just a handshake, but we both agreed a written contract was essential to protect all our interests and prevent any potential misunderstandings."

"I hate to be ghoulish, Dad," said Jenny, "but did you ask Sheila if the police had been around to question her about Rhodes's death? Is she considered his next of kin? How does she think he died?" Way to go, Jenny. Keep those questions coming.

"She did say the police had been around the Center today, but we didn't get into specifics. And we certainly didn't speculate about how he died, since neither one of us has the faintest idea what caused it."

He pushed back his chair from the kitchen table, cutting off the interrogation. Rats. Just when we were getting somewhere.

"If you two have clean-up under control, I'm going to use the computer for a while. And I'm going to bed early tonight. For some reason, I didn't sleep too well last night."

You could have fooled me. I was the one who didn't sleep well. Still, I figured that finding a dead body can wreak havoc with sleep patterns, so I gave him the benefit of the doubt.

Three hours later, when I was lying in bed listening to Jim snoring, I realized I'd never told him about Mary Alice's retirement announcement.

Chapter 16

Q: What's the best time to start thinking about your retirement?
A: Before your boss does.

Both Jim and Jenny left the house early the next morning, so I was on my own with no specific plans for the day. I sent up a silent prayer, asking that the day be less stressful than yesterday, and resolved not to turn on the television or read any newspapers all day.

Instead, I went online to see if the Re-tirement Survival Center web page had changed since Rhodes's death.

"Whoa! Take a look at this," I said to the dogs. Have I mentioned before how computer literate they are?

"The whole site has been reworked. How did Sheila do that so quickly?"

Lucy barked once, but clearly she didn't have the answer any more than I did. Ethel curled herself into ball and went to sleep.

Instead of the picture of Davis Rhodes that had greeted me the first time I'd logged on, now there was a picture of both Rhodes and Sheila on the web site's home page. Although both of them were smiling, it was pretty clear from the body language and the way they were posed that Sheila was the dominant force in the twosome. Hmm. I had heard that photos could be manipulated on the computer somehow. Had that happened here?

There was also a new icon on the home page which read: "Click Here for Details of Davis Rhodes Memorial Service."

Another tap of the computer mouse and I was reading a sanitized synopsis of Rhodes's tragic death (home page's words, not mine), a quote from Sheila concerning the future of the Re-tirement Survival Center which translated to "The show must go on, and it'll be even better with me in charge," and an additional statement from her that a service to honor The Great Man's memory would be held one week from today at 2 p.m. at the Center.

Sheila's statement continued: "This will be a public tribute to Dr. Rhodes, an opportunity for the countless people whose lives he touched to honor him. According to his wishes, there will be no funeral. Anyone interested in participating in the ceremony is asked to e-mail us a brief paragraph summarizing their tribute by this Friday. All tributes will be posted on the Center's web page, and a limited number will be chosen to be read at the service."

"According to his wishes?" I repeated to Lucy. "I doubt that he left Sheila instructions about this." Somehow I couldn't imagine Rhodes taking time out from his clients—to say nothing of his cookie baking—to outline his wishes in the event of his untimely death. The whole thing sounded like a marketing ploy from Sheila to get big publicity for the Center. And herself.

Ohmygod. I suddenly realized that Jim would probably be involved in this memorial service. I wondered if Sheila had already asked him to help organize it. She was wasting no time taking control of the Center. Made her look like a prime suspect to me. I wondered if the police agreed.

Then I mentally scolded myself. You seem to be the only one who's worried about appearances, Carol. If Jim's not concerned about working with Sheila, why should you be?

Because I'm the only one around here with basic common sense? No, that was too harsh.

Because I always see the dark side of every situation? Maybe.

Because I worry so much about everything that goes wrong that Jim doesn't have to?

Yes, that was it. I thought back to when the kids were younger and one of them was late coming home from a party. Who waited up in the dark living room, straining for the sound of a car turning into the driveway?

Not him.

Who made bargains with the Lord? "I swear I'll be more patient, understanding, clean the bathrooms with a smile on my face, whatever You want, if You'll just this once bring my child home safely. And soon. Please, please, please."

That was also me, of course.

All during these crises, where was Jim? He was upstairs doing one of the things he does best—sleeping.

Suddenly, I resented all the sleepless nights I had gone through. I resented being the one who'd willingly shouldered the burden of worry for the entire family for years.

I wasn't going to do it this time. No siree. I was turning over a new leaf.

If Jim was acting like all was hunky dory, so would I. If he thought working with Sheila Carney was a great idea, I did too. If he was going to orchestrate Davis Rhodes's memorial service, that was ok with me. No problemo.

Move along, Carol. It was time for me to focus on my freelance work again. There might even be an editing assignment for me if I took the time to check my e-mail.

Unfortunately, no new job opportunities had magically appeared. Which was probably just as well.

I admitted I wasn't in the right frame of mind to concentrate on work. I'd allowed my professional motivation to go out the window, and it was going to be very tough to get it back again. Depressing, but true.

I sat at the computer and my mind wandered all over the place. I had no plan for how to spend the day. Even worse, I had no plan for my life. I was just drifting along aimlessly.

Mary Alice was probably going to face many times like this after she retired. I wondered how she would cope.

Then, in a flash, I had a brilliant idea. I would do something for Mary Alice to celebrate her retirement. I'd give her a party. A fabulous party. No, not a party. A shower! Where everyone would be encouraged to bring unique gifts to mark this auspicious occasion. At last I had something positive to focus on.

And I knew just who to call to help me plan it. She even had the perfect place to hold the shower.

I got out the phone book and looked up the number for Maria's Trattoria.

"This is a great idea you have for a party, Carol," said Maria. Luckily, when I called, she had an hour to spare that afternoon. We were sitting in a corner booth near the kitchen, and Maria was making some notes in a big three-ring binder while we talked.

"When I retired from teaching," she remembered, "my send-off was in the school cafeteria, with soggy sandwiches and warm sodas. I'd insisted that my students be included in the party, and because of liability issues, the event had to be held on school property. It was a wonderful, meaningful party for me because of the kids. But the food was terrible.

"I want to provide a real feast for Mary Alice's retirement shower. It's a great opportunity for me to show that we can cater private parties, too. Most people don't think of us for that."

I was thrilled at her enthusiasm. And a little surprised, too. While I was driving over to the restaurant, I'd had second thoughts about planning the party with Maria. I remembered that she'd been an excellent teacher, but she ran her classroom like a general on the battlefield. And she didn't tolerate suggestions, which she interpreted as interference, from parents. I wasn't sure I wanted to work with her so closely.

But this was the new Maria Lesco, ready to lend her expertise and creativity to make my shower idea the fabulous party that Mary Alice deserved.

"I don't think I've ever seen the restaurant this quiet," I said, sipping from a glass of chilled Pellegrino water with lemon.

"Three to four o'clock is pretty much down time for us," said Maria. "Too late for lunch and too early for dinner. But about four-thirty, the take-out business starts to pick up, and then we're really busy till around ten o'clock every night." She pointedly looked at her watch. I got the message. I needed to move this conversation along.

"Mary Alice's last official day of work at the hospital is the Friday before Labor Day," I said, "which is about five weeks away. I know that Labor Day weekend may not be the best time to have a party because lots of people are still on vacation, but I'd like to schedule the shower as close as possible to the time when she actually retires."

After discussing a few possible dates, Maria suddenly said, "I've just had a great idea. The restaurant is usually closed on Mondays. How about if we have the shower on Labor Day afternoon? What could be more appropriate than that?"

"I love it!" I exclaimed. "That's absolutely perfect. I'll make some calls to a few close friends and give them a head's up on the date right away. Will you come up with a suggested menu? I'm planning on about thirty people, if some of Mary Alice's co-workers from the hospital are invited. Do you want a deposit?" I reached in my purse for my checkbook.

"No deposit necessary. Don't worry about it. Give me a few days to think about what to serve and then I'll be in touch with you, all right? I've never planned a party like this before, and I'm going to have to do a little research. This is going to be such fun for me."

She rose and walked me to the restaurant door.

"By the way, wasn't that a terrible thing about Davis Rhodes? I couldn't believe it when I read about his death in the paper."

I stiffened. Easy, Carol. Don't overreact. It was an innocent remark.

"It certainly was," I said. "I suppose he must have had a heart attack, poor man."

"From the way he ate every time he came in here, I'd say he wasn't worried about his cholesterol," Maria said. "He loved his red meat and cheese, and never passed up the opportunity for a fattening dessert."

Whoa. New information. I had to find out more.

"Did he come in here often?" I asked, as casually as I could.

I was dying to hear more details. The Miss Lesco I remembered from the kids' school days was no gossip. But maybe the Maria from Maria's Trattoria was. I decided to bait the hook a little more and see how she responded.

I let my eyes fill up just a little (I confess I'm pretty good at that), then said, "You may not know that Jim and I had gone to Rhodes for retirement counseling. His sudden death has been a personal blow to both of us." If she only knew how much of a blow.

Maria looked at her watch again, then said, "You know, I think I have time for a cup of cappuccino. Would you like one, too, on the house?"

I tried not to appear too eager. "I'd love a cup, if you're sure you have the time."

"My pleasure."

We settled down at the corner booth again with two steaming cups of cappuccino, and I waited to hear if she would share more information about Rhodes. I'd read in mystery stories that the police often find silence to be a good method of interrogation, and I decided to try it. I needn't have worried about getting her to talk. Maria needed no prompting from me.

"I know it's not professional to gossip about the customers," she said, leaning toward me and speaking in a low voice. "I'd probably fire one of my staff for talking like this, but Rhodes is dead and who can it hurt now?"

I said nothing. Just looked interested, and took a sip of the cappuccino. Yum. Delicious.

"Rhodes was one of the worst customers we've ever had. He treated all the servers like personal lackeys, and was a stingy tipper to boot. Nothing was ever cooked to his liking. He sent things back to the kitchen all the time. It got so that none of the servers wanted to wait on him. When he'd come in, we'd draw straws to see who would get him. Loser won, if you know what I mean. And it was disgraceful the way he treated that lovely assistant of his. The last time he brought her in here, they had an awful argument."

Maria leaned back in her chair. "You know, it feels good to get this out. I don't ever talk about customers this way, but at least he won't be coming in here any more."

I took a sip of my cappuccino and sent up a silent prayer. "Thank you, God. I know this is You at work. Please don't let me screw this up now by saying the wrong thing." I had to keep her talking.

"Do you remember what the argument was about? I can't imagine Rhodes losing his temper. When Jim and I went to him, he seemed so easy-going. This doesn't sound like the man we knew."

"Hah," retorted Maria. "He had an awful temper. I don't remember specifically what they argued about that time, but you can bet that if he brought someone here for dinner, they'd end up in an argument about something. We used to joke that he'd provoke an argument with the person he was with so he wouldn't have to pay for their food."

A random question popped into my head, and I asked it. "Did he bring in any other women besides Sheila?"

"Well, his wife, of course."

"His wife? What wife?" Now, this was news.

"Well, maybe I should say his ex-wife," Maria said. "I talked to her briefly while she was waiting for him to arrive. She seemed very sweet. And she had gorgeous white hair. Some people go white when they're still young, and it looks fabulous on them, you know?"

I nodded my head encouragingly. Forget the hair. Let's move along here.

"They were apparently in the process of divorcing," Maria said. "You could tell they'd been married a long time. She knew just how to handle him. Wasn't the type to put up with any of his nonsense. That's probably why they were getting divorced."

I hoped my eyes weren't popping out of my head, but I wondered if the police had this information. I decided to probe a little further. I rationalized my nosiness by telling myself I could pass on whatever I found out to Mark Anderson.

"Did you happen to overhear anything they talked about?"

Maria thought for a minute. "They seemed to talk about money quite a bit. I got the feeling that she thought he had hidden some assets so she wouldn't get them as part of her divorce settlement."

"Wow. That could get really nasty."

"It did once or twice during their meal," said Maria. "He only brought her in that one time, about three weeks ago."

She paused for a minute.

"There was one odd thing, though. She didn't call him Davis. She called him Dick. We all had a good laugh in the kitchen about what a perfect name that was for him."

Hmmm.

Chapter 17

Q: What's the first big shock of retirement?
A: When you realize there are no days off.

As soon as I got home, I e-mailed Nancy and Claire about my retirement shower brainstorm. I was pretty sure Claire would think the shower was a fabulous idea and want to help, and Nancy would be annoyed with me for not including her in the preliminary planning. But she'd get over her snit. She always did.

Once I sent the two e-mails, I sat down with my trusty pad and jotted down Maria's comments about Davis Rhodes while they were still fresh in my mind.

I still couldn't get over what she had told me.

At the top of my notes, I wrote: Find Rhodes's wife. I underlined it several times. Then, I realized I had no idea what her name was. Perhaps Maria remembered. But I had to come up with a plausible excuse for my curiosity.

How about if I told her I wanted the name so Jim and I could send a sympathy note to the family? Sounded believable to me. But Maria was no help when I called for the information. "It was several weeks ago," she said in the voice she must have used to strike terror into her students. "You can't expect me to remember back that far with all the customers we've had since then."

Ok. Dead end, pardon the pun.

I remembered that the other curious thing Maria had mentioned was Rhodes's first name. The wife had called him Dick. Was "Davis" not his real name? I had never heard "Dick" used as a nickname for "Davis." And how the heck could I find that out?

Sheila Carney might know the answer. She might also know the wife's name, but I doubted she'd share either one with me.

She might share that information with My Beloved, though. Unless he already knew and hadn't bothered to tell me.

I made another note to myself: Suggest Jim get name of Rhodes's wife from Sheila to invite to memorial service. Ask Jim if the name "Davis Rhodes" could be a pseudonym.

Maria's description of Rhodes's abrasive personality was worth checking out, too. The man she described bore no resemblance to the charismatic retirement counselor Jim and I had met.

If Rhodes had such a short fuse, I thought, it was probably for the best that Jim and he never had a confrontation. Who knows what would have happened?

Then I chided myself for my incredible stupidity. Jim'd found the guy dead, for God's sake. How much worse could a confrontation between the two of them have been than that?

I thought briefly about calling Mark Anderson at police headquarters and giving him the new information I'd gotten from Maria. But I dreaded any conversation with him, and especially his partner, that could lead to their asking me more questions about our involvement with Rhodes.

Besides, maybe I could find out some things on my own.

All of a sudden, I had another brilliant idea. Who knew what was going on in town better than real estate agents? They were incredibly connected, and Rhodes must have used an agent to either lease or buy the building where the Re-tirement Survival Center was located.

And my own very best friend Nancy was a real estate agent.

Quickly, I dialed her cell phone number. She answered on the second ring.

"Nancy, it's Carol. Where are you right now? Can we get together? I really need your help."

"I got your e-mail about the shower for Mary Alice," Nancy said, sounding slightly peeved at me. "I can't believe you started making plans without including Claire and me. I've decided to forgive you, because you'll need our help to pull it off. But the party's not until Labor Day. That's weeks away. What's the emergency about it this afternoon?"

"It's not about Mary Alice's party," I said excitedly. "I found out some information about Davis Rhodes today from Maria Lesco. I need your help tracking down some more information. Can you come over right away?"

Nancy, predictably, rose to the bait. "I just finished showing a house to a new client, and I have to take her back to my office. Can you meet me there? I can close the conference room door so we'll have privacy."

"I'll see you there in fifteen minutes."

"Perfect." She clicked off.

I checked the clock. It was almost 4:00 now. Who knew what time Jim would be home? I hadn't heard from him all day. Unless, of course, he'd left a message on my cell phone, which I still hadn't tried to find.

I decided to take a chance and call him at the office. Better to let him know in advance that dinner might be a little late, not that I'd tell him why.

"Oh, hello, Mrs. Andrews," said Jim's assistant, Deb Brownell. Deb was a sweet young thing, slightly overweight, who read too many romance novels at her desk. We had a good phone relationship, as long as she remembered to give Jim my messages. In between chapters. "Mr. Andrews tried to reach you a little earlier to let you know he's going to be late tonight. Mack asked him to be the agency point man for the Davis Rhodes memorial service, and he's just left for a meeting with Sheila Carney at the Re-tirement Survival Center." She sighed. "What a terrible thing about Dr. Rhodes."

I could tell Deb was dying to get into an in-depth discussion about what had happened, and though she often was a good source of agency gossip that Jim never bothered to share with me, I didn't have time for chit-chat now. I prayed that she didn't know that her dear boss was the one who found the body. It'd be all over the office in five minutes. But Deb had inadvertently given me an important piece of news: the Re-tirement Survival Center was now considered an official agency client, and Jim was the official agency staff person for the account.

"Yes, it was terrible about Davis Rhodes, Deb," I agreed. "I don't want to cut you short, but I'm late for an important appointment now. Thanks for your help. Talk to you soon."

Then I was off to Nancy's office to continue my snooping. I mean, sleuthing.

I needn't have rushed. Nancy was still with her client in the office conference room when I got to Dream Homes Realty ("Where We Make Your Dreams A Reality"), so I had to cool my heels in the frigid reception area for about 45 minutes. After aimlessly flipping through current agency listing sheets, I started to pace back and forth in front of the con-ference room's glass door and make faces through the glass. Nancy was sitting facing the door, and tried not to laugh at me while her client droned on and on about what houses she'd seen today, which ones she liked, which ones she didn't like, and why. Blah blah blah. Honestly, I don't know how Nancy puts up with some of the people she has to deal with.

Finally, the woman stood up and adjusted her shocking pink Lilly Pulitzer sweater, which she had artfully draped around her shoulders.

"I'll expect to hear from you in the next two days with more houses for me to see, Nancy," she said as she left the office.

Nancy smiled and waved her out the door, then came back and col-lapsed into a chair beside me. "Boy, she's a difficult client. I thought she'd never leave. I think she's one of those people who has no intention of ever buying a new house, but just likes to go around and look at what's on the market, especially the expensive ones. What a pain."

She took a good look at my face. "You look like you're about to explode with news. Let's go into the conference room. Just about everybody is gone for the day, but I'll close the door just in case."

When we were comfortably seated, Nancy demanded, "All right, what gives?"

I tried to be as concise as possible with what I'd found out from Maria, but as usual, Nancy kept interrupting me with questions.

"But what about Mary Alice's shower?" she asked. "Are we definitely going to do it at Maria's Trattoria on Labor Day?", zeroing in on what was, beyond any question, a secondary issue.

"Nancy, focus," I said impatiently. "Forget about the shower for just a minute. What do you think about this new Davis Rhodes information? Never mind the fact that he was so rude to the restaurant staff. Apparently his real first name wasn't Davis at all. If this mystery woman was his wife, why would she call him Dick instead of Dave or Davis? Maybe his last name isn't even Rhodes."

"Carol, you focus," replied Nancy crossly. "Why do we care what his name was? Or even if he was married? The guy is dead."

"But Nancy," I said, "Jim found Rhodes's body. The police have termed the death 'suspicious.' They've already questioned Jim, and they even came to the house to question me. Don't you think the more we can find out about Rhodes and his past, the better we can protect Jim? My God, what if they suspect Rhodes was murdered and Jim is accused? Won't you do a little digging to help me?"

"You're letting your imagination run away with you, like you always do. If you're this worried, you should give this information to Larry and let him track it down. He's Jim's lawyer, after all. Or better yet, Mark Anderson."

I started to protest, but she held up her hand to silence me.

"Having said that, we've been best friends forever and you know there's nothing I won't do for you. No matter how crazy. So, what do you want me to do?"

"I know you're right about telling Larry or the police what I found out today," I said slowly. "But everything I just told you is pure unsubstantiated gossip. The kind of thing women know instinctively is true, even if it's not proved yet. So, I thought we could start by finding out if Davis Rhodes was his real name. I also wondered about the Survival Center building. He must have either bought it or leased it, right? And to do any kind of real estate transaction, he had to sign official papers, and he probably had a real estate agent. That's where you come in."

Nancy's eyes widened. "Brilliant, Carol. Absolutely brilliant. I'm glad we're here at the office, because there's computer software here that I don't have at home."

Nancy plugged in the name of "Rhodes" and did a quick search of all real estate transactions over the past year. Nothing came up.

"Let's try this," Nancy said. "We have a huge database of all the local real estate agents. I'll send out a blitz e-mail to everybody and find out if anyone handled the transaction. What's the exact address? And do you have any idea if it's a business property or a residential property? There are agents who specialize in each."

To be on the safe side, Nancy finally decided to e-mail everyone on the database for the property information. "I'm going to ask agents to e-mail me either here or at home, as quickly as possible. I've stressed that this is extremely urgent and highly confidential." She pressed the "Send" icon.

"You know, I have another idea," she said. "It's just possible that Rhodes's wife also saw a real estate agent while she was here about either renting or buying property. It would certainly help if we at least had a first name, though."

"Maria didn't remember," I answered. "And she was kind of annoyed that I called her about it."

"So what?" Nancy shrugged her shoulders. "You're her client now. She needs to be nice to you because she wants your business. Call her again." She held out the phone to me.

"Oh, no," I protested. "I'm not calling her."

"Stop being a jerk, Carol. This is just like the first day of school when you made me go into the classroom first."

Seeing the nervous expression on my face, she relented. "Ok. Give me the phone. I'll call her."

Five minutes later, through the intercession of I don't know what saint, Nancy had a first name for Rhodes's wife.

"Maria actually apologized for being abrupt with you before. I guess she felt bad about that, so she asked the servers who came in to work the dinner shift if anyone remembered the wife's name. Apparently, even though the dinner-in-question happened several weeks ago, Rhodes and his mystery woman made quite an impression on the staff. The waitress who took care of them said Rhodes called the woman Gracie. That made the woman very angry. She kept insisting he call her Grace. Maria also mentioned one other thing which could be important. She said the waitress remembered Rhodes telling the woman that she couldn't stay with him. He was very adamant about it. So she must have just arrived in town. Want me to send another e-mail and see if any of the agents had any business with her? Who knows? Maybe she looked at some property around here."

"That's a great idea," I exclaimed. "Sure, send another e-mail. Let's find out as much as we can. At last I feel like I'm doing something positive, instead of just sitting around waiting. Be sure to mention that she had beautiful white hair."

"Done," said Nancy. She quickly composed another e-mail query and sent it off into cyberspace. Then, she started to laugh.

"What's so funny?"

"You know those ads on television, when a person signs up for a wireless phone plan, and the announcer says, 'No matter where you go, you've got the network'? You, my friend, have the power of the real estate network behind you now. And believe me, there's nothing this network can't find out. Now, let's get out of here. I'll let you know as soon as I hear anything."

When I got home a few minutes later, Jenny was already there. I walked into the kitchen and she was sitting at the kitchen table. She jumped up when she saw me. Her face was white.

"Mom, where have you been? Is Daddy with you? I've been so worried!"

"I was with Nancy. And your father is meeting with Sheila Carney about the Davis Rhodes memorial service. What's the matter? You look terrible."

"I had coffee with Mark Anderson today, remember?"

"Yes, I certainly do. How did it go? Did you have fun?"

Jenny smiled, just a little. "We had a great time, Mom. In the beginning. We talked about school, and old friends. I'd forgotten how easy he is to be with.

"But then he got a call on his cell phone from his partner."

She paused, and her voice got very shaky.

"Mom, a preliminary toxicology report on Davis Rhodes's death came in today. Some sort of drug interaction killed him. The police think he could have been poisoned. I was afraid when I didn't know where you were that Dad had been arrested."

Chapter 18

Q: Why are retirees so slow to clean out the basement, attic, and garage?
A: They know that as soon as they do, one of their adult kids will want to store stuff there.

I've read in all my mysteries that poison is a woman's favorite murder weapon. Less messy than guns or knives. Yuck. There was a least one person in Rhodes's life who had a dandy motive to bump him off. No, make that two: his wife, and dear Sheila. But not My Beloved. No way.

"I don't know if anyone else knows about this yet," Jenny said. "Mark wouldn't have told me anything except, of course, I was sitting right there when he got the call. He reacted so strongly I just knew it was about Rhodes. But he warned me to keep the new information to myself.

"Mark admitted Dad would be questioned again. The police have to examine all the possibilities since it looks like Rhodes was poisoned."

I noticed that Jenny shied away from using the word "murdered." But I knew she was thinking it. Me too.

I decided to share my afternoon's adventure with Jenny. She's tolerated my insatiable curiosity for years, unless I'm snooping into her personal life, of course. "We'll have to tell Dad about this when he gets home.

"In the meantime, let's talk about something else. I've decided to plan a retirement shower for Mary Alice at Maria's Trattoria...."

Jenny held up her hand and stopped me in mid-sentence. "Wait. I think I've missed something here. Mary Alice is leaving the hospital? When did she decide that?"

"With everything else going on around here, I forgot to tell you. Mary Alice is retiring at the end of the summer. But she's going to do private duty nursing and some consulting, so she'll still be connected to the hospital. She made her big announcement the same day that the police came to interview me about Rhodes's death.

"Anyway, I'm planning a party for Mary Alice at the Trattoria, and while I was meeting with Maria Lesco today, I got some real dirt on Davis Rhodes. Maria told me Rhodes was a regular customer at the restaurant, and the staff couldn't stand him. He was unbelievably rude to everyone who worked there.

"Maria also told me that one night he'd brought a woman named Grace to dinner. Their waitress overheard some of their conversation, and figured out that Grace was Rhodes's wife. The waitress told Maria it wasn't a friendly dinner at all. And Grace called Rhodes 'Dick,' not 'Dave' or 'Davis'. How about that?"

"Wow, Mom. I'm impressed that you got Miss Lesco to give you all this info. Way to go. But what does it mean?"

"I know I could be jumping to conclusions," I replied, "but it dawned on me after I talked to Maria that 'Davis Rhodes' may have been an assumed name. I called Nancy to see if Rhodes or his wife had been involved in any local property transactions."

I gave Jenny a moment to be proud of my deductive skills, then filled her in on my trip to Nancy's office, and her e-mails to other local real estate agents. "Nancy says the network is very efficient, and she should have some information soon about both Rhodes and his mysterious wife.

"Oh, I just remembered something else. Maria also told me that Rhodes and his assistant, Sheila Carney, came into the restaurant a few times together, too. She said they had a really bad argument there a few days before he died. Maybe Sheila wanted to take over the Center. She's already changed the web page to feature her picture. She certainly could be involved in Rhodes's death."

I shook my head to clear my muddled brain. It didn't help. Too many possibilities.

"Your father is going to be working very closely with Sheila from now on. He's been officially assigned to the account by the office, and I guess he'll be helping plan Rhodes's memorial service." That is, if he's not in jail by then, I added silently.

Jenny slumped back in her chair. "This is too much for me to take in. When I'm teaching a class, I have an outline of what I want to cover. But there's no outline for anything this crazy. What do we do now? Dad is going to freak."

I had no doubt that Jenny was absolutely right. I also knew from years of experience that there was only one aspect that Jim would zero in on—one thing he would harp on again and again. My Beloved would gloss over the fact that Rhodes had probably been poisoned and that he could be considered a suspect in the murder, ignore the importance of Rhodes's wife, and dismiss the possibility that "Davis Rhodes" could be an assumed name. Only a logical person would be concerned about any of that stuff.

What Jim was bound to zero in on, and harp on over and over, would be the fact that I'd meddled. Interfered. Nosed around. I asked a few innocent questions about a party for Mary Alice and presto. Look what I'd found out. And then, as if that weren't bad enough, I got Nancy and her entire real estate network involved.

As upset as I was about Jim's increasingly vulnerable situation, I was not about to make myself the sacrificial lamb to his all-too-predictable outburst. I'd been down that particular road too many times in the past.

So, I made a snap decision. I wasn't going to tell My Beloved what I'd found out today. At least, not until Nancy had provided some hard facts, like whether "Davis Rhodes" was his real name.

"Jenny," I said, "I have a suggestion. You and I both love your father very much. And we know him very well. I think hitting him with all this as soon as he gets home is a bad idea. You should definitely tell him what happened with Mark and the phone call. He needs to prepare himself in case the police do want to question him again.

"But all I've got to tell him so far is just gossip and speculation. I know he won't react well to that. I think it's best for me to keep quiet and wait to see if Nancy and her real estate buddies can come up with any solid information. I'll tell your father everything once we have something concrete, and I'll pass on what I find out to Mark, too. I certainly don't want to be accused of hiding information from the police. How does that sound?"

My daughter gave me a look that proved she had my number, all right. "I get it, Mom. I used the same technique when I was living with Jeff. Men can only focus on a one issue at a time, and they go a little nuts when they get too much information to process, right? So, only give them a little. After it's been processed, give them a little more. Kind of like spoon-feeding a baby."

I had to laugh. I couldn't have put it better myself.

She gave my hand a little squeeze.

"Try not to worry. I have a feeling that everything's going to work out ok. Of course, I have no clue how that's going to happen."

"It's going to happen because the women in this family are going to make sure that it happens," I responded with more confidence than I felt.

"Now, tell me more about your coffee date with Mark. You said you two were having a good time before that phone call from his partner interrupted it. Did you fill each other in on what you'd been doing over the past ten years?" I'd promised myself I wouldn't ask Jenny any questions about her "date," but, what the heck, it beat worrying about Jim.

Sure, Carol. Like you're not dying of curiosity.

"You're very subtle," said Jenny, laughing. "What you mean is, did we talk about any long-term relationships we'd been in, that kind of personal stuff, right?"

My daughter was getting to be way too smart for me. "Yes, I have to admit that's exactly what I meant. But you know I won't pry." Ha! "If you don't want to talk about it, that's fine with me. But isn't he good-looking now?" Subtle, Carol. When in doubt, stress the superficial.

"Yes, Mark's very good-looking. I never would have expected he'd be so handsome after the skin problem he had when we were in high school. I remember he wore geeky glasses, too. But I suppose I was no beauty back then, either."

"You and Mike were always perfect in every way to Dad and me," I replied loyally. "But let's get back to Mark. I completely lost track of him after high school. Did he stay here in town, go away to college, join the service, what?"

"That's three questions, Mom," said Jenny. "You get seventeen more, according to the rules of the game. But Twenty Questions and then that's it. Yes, Mark went to college in Maine, and graduated with a degree in history. He said he bummed around Europe for a while after graduation trying to figure out what he wanted to do with his life, and finally came back here when his money started to run out. He never intended to stay, but he met a girl and thought she was the woman he wanted to spend the rest of his life with.

"I gather from what he didn't say, though, that his parents were less than thrilled with her and tried hard to discourage the relationship. Anyway, he moved in with her and needed to get a job and earn some money. I think he joined the police force because he thought it would please his parents, especially his father, and take the heat off their objections to his personal life. He's the youngest in the family, which I had forgotten, and I guess his parents have always been more controlling in his life than in his brothers'.

"The relationship ended badly," Jenny continued. "Mark didn't say what happened, and I didn't press him for details. But apparently that was three years ago, and he's been kind of turned off the dating scene since then. I know how he feels."

There was nothing I could say to that, so wisely, for once in my life, I kept my big mouth shut.

"You know, it was so good to be with an old friend today. I think he felt the same way. When you have a shared history, like we do, you can just relax and be friends and not have to get into the role-playing lots of people do these days. I knew I could tell him pretty much anything and it'd be all right. But then his partner called and, well…" Jenny sighed. "I don't know how we can see each other again with Davis Rhodes's death hanging over our heads. Especially if Mark's forced to ask you and Dad more questions. Talk about a weird situation."

"What's a weird situation?" Jim asked. I turned around in surprise. Jenny and I had been so engrossed in our conversation that neither one of us had heard him come home. How much had he heard?

"Hi dear," I said. "How's everything with Sheila and the Center?"

"Don't try and divert me, Carol. I want to know who you and Jenny were talking about. Who could be forced to come back here and ask us more questions? About what? Did something else happen? What's going on?"

"Don't get excited," I said as soothingly as I could.

Jenny interrupted me. "I'll tell him, Mom. It's my story.' '

She turned to her father and said, "Now, Dad, don't get excited."

"God, you sound just like your mother. I am not excited. At least, I wasn't until I got home just now. Who and what are we talking about?"

"I had coffee with Mark Anderson today," explained Jenny.

"A very nice young man," said Jim. "He treated me with the greatest respect the other night at the Center."

"He is a great guy," agreed Jenny. "But while we were together, he got a phone call from his partner with some bad news. It was about the cause of Davis Rhodes's death. I had to worm it out of him, but the bottom line is that according to the preliminary report it looks like Rhodes died from a drug interaction. The police think he may have been poisoned.

"Dad," she said gently, "I'm pretty sure from what Mark said that they're going to want to ask you some more questions."

Jim didn't respond for at least a full minute. The room was so quiet I could hear the grandfather clock ticking in the front hall. Or maybe it was the sound of my heart thudding against my chest.

Then he placed his briefcase, very carefully, on the kitchen counter, and sat down at the table. For a brief moment, I saw his cheeks flush, a sure sign he was under stress. He reached down to give each of the dogs a gentle pat. They responded by licking his hands. Positive reinforcement from our two nonjudgmental canines.

"I want you both to know that I have nothing to hide, and nothing to be ashamed of," Jim told us. "If Mark and his partner want to question me again, fine. Let them. With or without Larry present. This whole thing is absolutely ludicrous."

He sat up very straight in his chair. Jenny and I didn't speak. What was there to say?

Jim cleared his throat. "Now, let me tell you both about my day. That Sheila Carney sure is something."

For the next half hour Jenny and I were regaled with the wonders of Sheila. What was it about long-legged blondes that made men act so stupidly? You would have thought, listening to Jim sing her praises, that she was a combination of Mother Theresa and Princess Diana.

Brother.

According to Jim, Sheila had met Rhodes while she was in graduate school studying for a Master's degree in Psychology. Rhodes was one of the school's guest lecturers. Sheila told Jim that Rhodes was impressed with her intelligence—the actual words Jim quoted were, "He was dazzled by a brilliance far beyond my years"—and convinced her to leave school and come and work with him. That was several years ago, and she had been worshipping at the Rhodes altar ever since.

The concept of the Re-Tirement Survival Center had supposedly been a joint one between Rhodes and Sheila. Jim was slightly hazy on who thought of it first. Perhaps Sheila hadn't made that very clear to him.

But she insisted that Rhodes always intended to acknowledge her contribution to the Center, and together they had planned to tweak the web site and feature a picture of both of them. The fact that the web site had been changed today, immediately after Rhodes's death, was purely a coincidence, or so Sheila said.

The whole thing sounded fishy to me, but the only two people who had been involved in the birth of the Center were Sheila and Davis Rhodes, and he was certainly in no position to contradict anything she said.

"I've really got to admire the way Sheila is dealing with this trauma," Jim said. "Very controlled. Very professional. But I can tell that, underneath, she's really grieving. She and I went over some details for the memorial service next week. But plans won't be finalized until she sees which clients respond to the invitation to pay tribute to Rhodes. Oh, speaking of invitations, Sheila wants me to invite the mayor of Westfield, and the president of the chamber of commerce, and any other local big wigs I can come up with."

Jim stopped to make a few notes to himself. "I guess it's too late to get it on the governor's schedule. Too bad."

I couldn't resist. "Did the governor go to Rhodes for retirement counseling?"

"Don't be ridiculous, Carol."

I was being ridiculous? I wasn't the one who was still in complete denial about being in big trouble. Who did he think he was kidding anyway?

Pardon the pun, but I guess "de Nile" isn't just a river in Egypt.

Chapter 19

Q: Why don't retirees mind being called Seniors?
A: Because it comes with a 10 percent discount.

I was counting on Nancy and her network of real estate agents to come through with information that could get Jim off the hook and put somebody else, preferably Sheila, on it instead. Or even the mystery woman, Grace. Hell, I wasn't picky. Anyone but My Beloved would do just fine.

When I hadn't heard anything from Nancy, by either phone or e-mail, by 10:00 the following morning, I called her cell phone and left a desperate message. She responded within minutes.

"Carol," she whispered into the phone, "don't bug me. I know how upset you are. I'm doing the best I can. I'm at a Realtors' open house right now for a new listing, and one of the agents here thinks she remembers Grace. I'm trying to get her to stay a little longer so I can pump her for more information, but there are ten more houses on the tour today and I can't push her. I'll call you back as soon as I can. Oh, you might want to check today's paper. There's another story about you-know-who on page five."

Another newspaper story? Not good. I poured myself a cup of industrial strength coffee for courage and opened the paper.

Yup, there was the story, on page five, but this time in a more prominent position, "above the fold," as Jim would say.

Foul Play Suspected in Retirement Guru's Death

A spokesman for the Westfield Police Department has confirmed that a preliminary toxicology report on the body of Dr. Davis Rhodes, prominent local retirement coach, has revealed that Rhodes died as a result of a fatal drug interaction. The spokesman refused to speculate as to whether the drug interaction was accidental or the result of foul play. "We are looking at all possibilities, and are ruling nothing out at this stage of the investigation," the spokesman said.

Rhodes was found dead in the kitchen of the Re-tirement Survival Center three days ago by an unidentified client of the Center.

The police spokesman refused further comment at this time.

Oh, boy. Just when I thought things couldn't get any worse, there it was in black and white. The possibility of foul play—read "murder"—in Rhodes's death was now public knowledge. And how much time would it take, I wondered, for "an unidentified client of the Center" to become named as Jim Andrews of Fairport? I didn't see how Jim could trivialize this, but knowing him, he'd accuse me of overreacting again.

I was at a stalemate until I heard from Nancy. After running the dogs in the back yard, I decided to tackle one of the household jobs I hate the most—cleaning the silverware. Not that I was expecting to host a large formal dinner party in the immediate future. Although perhaps when Jim was released from prison, I would.

Stop that, Carol.

The only good thing about cleaning silver is that you can see what you've accomplished. It's extremely satisfying, in a basic kind of way. I was admiring the gleam I'd put on a sterling silver tray we'd received for a wedding present—and never used—when the phone finally rang. It was Nancy.

"Want to take a ride with me?" she asked. "We're going to meet the mystery woman. She's expecting us at one o'clock."

"What? You found out who she is?"

"Of course I did. How could you ever doubt me? That agent I told you about earlier turned out to be a gold mine of information. She rented a house in Westfield to a woman who answered your description of Rhodes's wife. I called the phone number the agent gave me, and the woman couldn't have been nicer. Her name is Grace Retuccio. I'll tell you more when I pick you up. Now, get moving. I'll be there in fifteen minutes. We can pick up lunch on the way."

"I admit it. I am very impressed," I said, talking louder than usual to be heard above the wind blowing me to bits.

Nancy and I were in her red Mercedes convertible with the top down, speeding along Route 15 toward Westfield. She's forever reminding me that one of the perks of being a real estate agent is having a great car, which, conveniently, can also be taken as a tax deduction.

"Who is she, where is she from, and how did you get her to agree to see us?"

"When you're a real estate agent, you can do almost anything," bragged Nancy.

"I gave her a cock and bull story about how real estate agents always want to be sure their clients are happy in their new home. That part is true. When a client buys a house, we always give them a gift. But we never bother to do that with people who rent."

She turned her head and gave me a wicked grin. "That is, until now. I stopped at a florist to get a bouquet for her. I told Grace that her rental agent had asked me to deliver it. That's all it took to get us into the house. After we're inside, you're on your own."

Grace whatever-her-name-was lived in a small Cape Cod style house whose rear yard backed up to the Re-tirement Survival Center. I could actually see the kitchen windows of the Center from the driveway of the rental house. It was a perfect place to keep tabs on someone without that someone knowing about it. I wondered if Davis Rhodes had realized that Grace was living so close to him. Or if he cared.

Maybe that's one of the things they'd argued about at Maria's.

All of a sudden, as Nancy cruised to a stop in front of the house, I realized that visiting this mystery woman on the spur of the moment was a very bad idea. What were Nancy and I doing there anyway? Who the heck did I think I was? I didn't have the faintest idea what to say.

Nancy knows me too well. She could sense I was chickening out.

"Come on, Carol, get out of the car. You have that hesitant look on your face that I absolutely hate. We have to go through with this. She's probably already looked out the window and seen us in the driveway."

Nancy got out of the car and slammed her door. "Come on," she said again. "This was all your idea. Let's go."

Reluctantly, I followed Nancy onto the front porch. She rang the doorbell. I heard some footsteps. Rats. No time to back out now.

The woman who answered the door was short and round. Not a glamour girl, but comfortable-looking. Like everybody's favorite cousin. Her most striking feature was her beautiful white hair, which framed a face with remarkably few lines. Her eyes were slightly rimmed in red. Had she been crying?

We really were intruding.

Unlike me, Nancy never lets anything stop her when she's on a mission. She positioned her body in front of mine and flashed Grace a winning smile.

"Hello, Grace. I'm Nancy Green from Dream Homes Realty. We spoke on the phone a little while ago. And this is my friend Carol Andrews. We've come to welcome you to Westfield, and deliver this bouquet of flowers to you. May we come in?" She thrust the flowers into Grace's hands and ever so slightly inched her way into the foyer.

What else could the poor woman do? She had to invite us inside.

"Of course you can come in. Forgive my manners. This is so kind of you. I'm Grace Retuccio. But of course, you know that already."

She seemed to hesitate for a minute, then made a decision.

"Why don't you follow me into the kitchen and I'll put these flowers in water? The place is still pretty unorganized," Grace said, indicating moving cartons that were scattered around the entryway.

"I've had a death in my family, and..." She paused to dab her eyes with a tissue. "I'm sorry. I don't even know you. And here I am breaking down in front of you."

Nancy and I both rushed to assure Grace that she had nothing to apologize for.

"In fact," said Nancy, "we should probably apologize to you. Barging in here like this and disturbing you. We had no idea." She shot me a look which translated to, "You take it from here."

I felt guilty about taking advantage of the poor woman's grief, but she had given us a golden opportunity to ask her some questions about Rhodes.

"Nancy and I are so sorry for your loss," I said as we sat down at the kitchen table. More than she knew. "Was it someone close to you?"

Grace sipped a little water from a glass Nancy had poured for her.

"It was someone close. But I hadn't seen him for a while."

"A dear friend?" I asked. "Or a family member? It's obviously someone you cared about a great deal."

"I don't know how you'd describe our relationship," said Grace. "Legally, he was family to me. But friend?" She shook her head. "Not a friend. Not lately anyway. He was my husband."

I felt guilty that she was being so open with us. Was this what the police called "entrapment"?

I hesitated, and Nancy jumped in with more questions. "You were separated? How sad. I know more women who have gone through separations. It's such a traumatic thing." She patted Grace's hand. "If it will make you feel better to talk about him, Carol and I would be glad to listen. But if you'd rather we left, we'll do that too. Sometimes, talking to perfect strangers, rather than close family and friends, can be easier at a time like this. At least, that's what Dr. Phil says."

Grace jumped at the chance to talk.

"I've felt so alone," she confessed. "I really don't know anybody here. Except Dick. Our marriage has been unusual, to say the least. Even though we didn't see each other on a regular basis, we were in frequent touch via phone or e-mail. We were involved in a joint business venture which was just about to become very successful."

I nodded at her sympathetically and didn't say anything. As I'd done with Maria. I was finally learning that silence often gets a person to open up.

"Dick and I were involved in the Re-tirement Survival Center. The office is on the next street. Perhaps you've heard of it?"

Nancy gave me a sideways look.

"What an amazing coincidence," I replied. "Yes, I certainly have heard of the Center. In fact, my husband and I went there for retirement counseling recently. We were both very impressed with the services the Center offered. We saw someone named Davis Rhodes, though, not Dick. Your husband mustn't have been there when we had our consultation.

"I'm sorry, I guess I'm a little confused," I continued. "I did read in the newspaper that Rhodes died a few days ago."

Then I put my hand to my mouth in apparent shock. What a bad actress I was.

"Was Davis Rhodes your husband? Oh, my God, I can't believe it. But who's Dick?"

Grace nodded her head. "You must have talked to my husband, then. Dick."

I felt like I was in the classic Abbott and Costello skit, "Who's On First?" I was getting more and more confused, no kidding.

"You see," Grace explained, "Dick's professional name was Davis Rhodes. We both felt the name Dick Retuccio was too ethnic to appeal to a broad number of clients, so Dick used this other name when he was working. He and I are both lifestyle coaches, and I was the one who developed the whole re-tirement strategy for baby boomers. I guess I should say he *was* a coach. I just can't come to grips with the fact that he's dead." She took a paper napkin that was on the table and began shredding it. The poor woman was becoming even more agitated.

"Wow," I said out loud. I used more colorful language to myself, but never mind that.

Jim was never going to believe any of this. I wasn't sure I did. In fact, if Nancy hadn't been sitting right there in the same room, I'd swear I was imagining the whole conversation.

I started to ask Grace another question, but there was no need. She was on a roll now.

"We had an unconventional marriage, but it worked for us. We led separate lives, on two different coasts, but we were still connected. Part of it was our joint work developing the Re-tirement Survival Center, of course. We never bothered to get divorced. There was no need to. And we talked on a fairly regular basis.

"Two months ago, things changed. Dick was not nearly as forthcoming about the clients he was seeing as he had been. I think he began to believe that he didn't need me any more.

"Then he called to tell me he wanted a divorce."

Grace's anger was evident by her completely shredded napkin. The grief we had seen earlier was gone.

"I refused, of course," she said. "I'm sure both of you understand why. I wasn't about to be cast aside after all these years. Especially not now, when my concept, that he was taking complete credit for, was finally becoming successful. No way. I even gave him the recipe for those damn chocolate chip cookies! I was the one who told him to do his preliminary client intake in the kitchen to put people at their ease. He never would have thought of any of that by himself.

"So I hopped on a plane and came east to see for myself what was going on. I counsel most of my clients by phone, so I can work from anywhere."

Grace smiled. This one was not a friendly smile. "Was he ever surprised when I showed up on his doorstep a few weeks ago."

I didn't know what to say. And I could tell that, for once, Nancy didn't either.

"Finding this short-term rental was pure luck." She looked at Nancy. "Your office was so helpful. Thank you so much for coming by with the flowers."

Grace seemed to realize she had told us too much. She stood up, and we followed. It was pretty clear that our little chat was over.

It was also pretty clear that Mrs. Grace Retuccio had a dandy motive for getting rid of her husband.

❦

On the way home, Nancy and I talked of nothing else.

"It's really classic," said Nancy. "The aging wife, who's stood by her man for years, dumped by her Lothario husband when he becomes successful."

"We don't know Rhodes was a Lothario," I pointed out. "Or should I say we don't know if Dick Retuccio was one? This is all so mixed up. Yesterday, Sheila Carney told Jim that she and Rhodes had come up with the Re-tirement Survival Center idea together. It looks like she was lying. Or Grace is. God! Grace seems to have at least two of the necessary ingredients for murder—motive and opportunity. I don't know about the means though."

"How about this?" Nancy suggested. "Maybe Rhodes had a pre-existing medical condition that made a lethal drug interaction easy? His wife would certainly know about that, right?"

"That's good," I said. "Very plausible. So, now that we've found out all this, what are we going to do about it? Should I call the police and have them do some checking on Grace and Rhodes and the whole fantastic story she told us? Is my interfering only going to make things worse for Jim? It sure would be easier to talk to Mark alone than with that horrible partner of his."

I rummaged in the bottomless depths of my purse. "I think I have his card in here somewhere."

Nancy turned the corner onto my street and immediately slammed on the brakes, throwing me forward toward the windshield.

"Hey, watch it," I yelled. "Are you trying to get me killed? What's the matter with you?"

"Carol," Nancy said, "you'd better decide right now what you're going to say. There's a police car parked in front of your house."

Chapter 20

Q: What is the biggest gripe retirees have?
A: There's not enough time to get everything done.

"Ohmygod! I'm not ready to talk to them yet. What am I going to do?"

"Try telling them the truth," said Nancy dryly.

"Very funny," I snapped. "You know what I mean. Can you tell how many people are in the car?"

Nancy craned her neck a little. "I think it's only one person, but I can't be positive. Listen, do you want me to come in the house with you? Maybe it'll be easier for you to deal with the police if you're not alone."

I jumped at Nancy's offer. "What a pal you are. I won't be as nervous if you're there, plus you can hear the questions they ask me. Maybe you'll have something to add. Or subtract. You have my permission to kick me under the table if you think what I'm saying isn't helping Jim."

I took a deep breath. "I'm ready now. Let's drive up to my house before the police wonder why we're spending so much time stopped at the corner."

We pulled partway into the driveway, and I slowly got out of Nancy's car to unlatch the gate. No reason for me to hurry. Be casual, I told myself.

When I turned around, I was face to face with Mark Anderson. Thank the Good Lord he was alone. And very nervous.

"Hi Mrs. Andrews," he said. "I've been waiting for you. I need to talk to you about something important that's come up about the Davis

Rhodes case." He looked pointedly at Nancy, still seated behind the wheel of her car. "Alone."

I pretended I didn't hear him.

"Of course. Mrs. Green and I were about to go into the house for a cup of tea. Why don't you join us?" I hoped nobody I knew was driving by. All I needed were neighborhood gossips speculating about why the police were calling on us yet again.

Lucy and Ethel danced joyously against my legs when I opened the kitchen door, gave Mark a sniff and decided he was a friend, then took off for a quick run in the yard.

Establish friendly connections, Carol, so Mark can't tell Nancy she has to leave.

"Come on in," I said. "Let's get that tea you were dying for on the way home, Nancy. I'm sure whatever questions Mark has he can ask in front of you."

Mark was looking very unhappy at this turn of events, but I ignored him and just kept on babbling. Something I'm very good at.

"You remember Nancy Green, don't you?" I asked him. "She's Terry and Peter's mother. I think they were a few years behind you and Jenny in school.

"Why don't you both sit down and I'll put the kettle on?"

"Mrs. Andrews, with all due respect," Mark said, "this is no tea party. I have something pretty serious to talk to you about, and I want you to sit down and give me your full attention." He nodded at Nancy. "You can stay, Mrs. Green, but you both have to understand that what I'm going to say is extremely confidential. I took a real chance coming to see you today, and I could get in big trouble if my boss finds out I was here.

"But I had to give you a chance to explain, Mrs. Andrews. Heck, you always treated me like a member of your family when I was a kid. I know you're much more comfortable talking to me without my partner." Mark smiled. "Paul watches too many *Law and Order* television shows. He tends to get sort of over the top with his questioning." No argument from me there.

"Now, Mrs. Andrews, I want to know if you can identify this."

He reached in his uniform pocket and pulled out something in a plastic bag.

I took a good look. It was my missing cell phone. I was thrilled.

"Oh, Mark," I exclaimed, stretching out my hand to take the phone from him. "I've been missing this for days. Thank you so much for finding it for me. But how did you get it? And why is it in that plastic bag?"

Mark looked uncomfortable. "Mrs. Andrews, I didn't exactly find your cell phone. Someone sent it to me. And I didn't know it belonged to you until I played the voice mail messages."

I had no idea what he was talking about, but I noticed that Nancy began shifting around in her chair. I wondered if she had to use the powder room. Well, if she did, she certainly knew where it was.

Mark cleared his throat and began again. "Mrs. Andrews, your cell phone was sent to me at police headquarters. There was a note attached to it which said, 'If you want to know who killed Davis Rhodes, check the voice mail messages.' The note was unsigned."

Mark looked really miserable now. Nancy looked like she was going to jump out of her chair. I was having trouble keeping up. What was he getting at?

"I listened to the messages. I had no idea it was your phone until I heard Mr. Andrews's message that he left for you the day Rhodes died. The one where he says he's going over to Rhodes's office to have it out with him. It sounded like a threat, no matter how many times I played it trying to make it sound like something else. Mr. Andrews claims he went to the Center late that afternoon and found Rhodes dead. There are lots of people who won't believe it was supposed to be an innocent meeting after they hear this phone message. There will have to be an official police investigation about this. Do you understand?"

He looked at me pleadingly. "Unless you can give me a good reason why there shouldn't be. I sure hope you can."

I thought I was going to faint. The whole room started spinning. Nancy had gotten up to get me a glass of cola, which normally I never drink. I took a large swig of the soda and rolled it around in my mouth, savoring its sweet, sugary taste.

"Mark," I said. "Come on. You can't believe that Jim had anything to do with Rhodes's death. You've known us since you were a little boy. There's no way he could have done anything like that.

"Sure, he was angry at Rhodes, but not enough to do him any harm. You must know that's the truth."

I then proceeded to tell Mark the whole story. I told him about our first meeting with Rhodes. And Jim's idea of making him a media star, and the *Wake Up New England* interview debacle—everything I could remember. I even told him about the chocolate chip cookies. I didn't mention any suspicions I harbored about Sheila because that's all they were—suspicions.

Then Nancy interrupted me. "I think it's time to tell Mark where we were today. And who we met." She nudged me with her foot.

I looked at her stupidly. Finding my cell phone and its message implicating Jim had knocked everything else out of my head. Then it dawned on me what she was talking about.

"Nancy and I found out some things about Davis Rhodes today that you may not know. I was planning on calling you at police headquarters to tell you as soon as we got home."

Not an outright lie. Just a slight exaggeration.

"Did you know that Davis Rhodes was not his real name?" Mark looked surprised. Very surprised.

I was encouraged by his reaction, so I continued, "Legally, he was Dick Retuccio. He used Davis Rhodes as his professional name. And, he was married to a woman named Grace. She recently moved into a house in

Westfield, which happens to be right around the corner from the Re-tirement Survival Center."

Mark had flipped open his notebook by this time and was taking furious notes.

"Nancy and I met Grace today, and she told us that Rhodes, or Dick, or whatever name you want to call him, had asked her for a divorce and she came east from California to find out why. She was really angry at him, and didn't try to hide it from us, right Nancy?"

Nancy had remained quiet throughout most of this, but I could see she was dying to put in her two cents' worth.

"Mark," she said, "Grace also told us that she and Rhodes came up with the concept of the Re-tirement Survival Center together. She's a lifestyle coach, too, just like her husband was. Apparently, now that the Center has become successful, Rhodes wanted to cut her out of it. That's a pretty strong motive for harming Rhodes, don't you think? And who would know better than his wife if he had any drug allergies?"

"This is all very interesting, ladies," said Mark. "How did you happen upon this Grace Retuccio?"

I told Mark about going to Maria's Trattoria to plan a retirement shower for Mary Alice. I could see his eyes glazing over slightly, so I skipped the shower details and got right to the part where Maria shared information about Rhodes being a regular customer at the restaurant, how he treated the staff, and his bringing in a woman who turned out to be Grace.

Nancy added the piece about tracking down the wife through the Realtors' network.

I hoped Mark was impressed with our detecting. And I desperately hoped this new information would get Jim off the hook.

"I appreciate your telling me all this," Mark said. "We'll certainly follow up on Grace Retuccio."

"Do you have to tell her how you got her name?" Nancy asked. "I don't know if I violated any Realtors' ethics by tracking her down the way I did."

I was annoyed that Nancy could be so concerned about protecting her precious Realtor's reputation when My Beloved was in such hot water, but I kept quiet. I couldn't resist shooting her a dirty look, though.

Mark snapped his notebook shut. "The police don't have to reveal where our information comes from," he said. "I'll try to keep your name out of it. But Mrs. Andrews," he went on, "I still need to talk to your husband. As soon as possible. That cell phone message is pretty damaging."

I must have looked shocked, because Mark added, "Don't worry. We don't use rubber hoses any more. I have to talk to him, if only to eliminate him from a list of people who could have harmed Rhodes."

He looked at his watch. "What time does he usually get home from New York?"

"Jim won't be home tonight until very late," I said. Thank God. "He planned to go to the Re-tirement Survival Center directly from the train. His boss has assigned him to organize the Davis Rhodes memorial service, and Jim's meeting with Sheila Carney about it." Another prime suspect who could have harmed Rhodes, if you asked me.

"Ok," said Mark. "Then I'll head over there and perhaps catch both of them. We wanted to talk to Sheila Carney, too."

I scolded myself for giving Mark too much information. But maybe he'd find something incriminating about Sheila and forget about Jim. I hoped he wasn't susceptible to beautiful blondes the way My Beloved was.

"Does Jim need a lawyer present?" Nancy asked. "Sorry to interfere, but I just remembered that Larry and Claire are in the Berkshires for a few days."

"You're not interfering," I said gratefully. I looked at Mark. "Does Jim need a lawyer?"

"I don't think that's necessary," he assured me. "I'd tell you if I did. Now, no more playing detective, both of you, though I must say I'm grateful for the information you gave me about Grace Retuccio.

"And please don't call and tell Mr. Andrews I'm coming to the Center to talk to him," Mark added. Although he said the last part politely, I got the impression he was giving me an order, not a suggestion. "If he has nothing to hide, he has nothing to be worried about. I'll show myself out."

I reached out to take the cell phone, but he slipped it back into his pocket.

"Say hi to Jenny for me. We had a good time on our coffee date, at least most of it. I'd like to see her again soon."

The kitchen door closed behind him, and he was gone.

Nancy took both my hands and squeezed them, hard. "I know what you're thinking. But you can't go to pieces now. Jim hasn't been charged with anything yet. The police haven't even come out and said the word 'murder.' "

At that, I started to cry.

Nancy handed me a tissue so I could wipe my leaking eyes. "You're not listening to me, Carol. I know that everything is going to be all right and Jim will be completely cleared. Do you want to know how I know?"

I nodded my head.

"I am absolutely, positively sure that Mark will clear Jim, because the last thing he said to us, when he was leaving, was that he wants to see Jenny again. Mark's not going to let anything happen to the father of the girl he wants to date."

I had to admit, she had a good point.

After Nancy left, I decided to switch gears and check my e-mail. Ordinarily, I check it at least five times a day, for no particular reason. I just hate to miss anything. And once I'm online, I can amuse myself for hours by visiting all sorts of web sites.

Scrolling down and deleting all the special offers I'd received during the day, I saw an e-mail from my darling son.

Hey Cosmo Girl!
Just a quick e-mail to let you know that Jenny has been keeping me up to date on what's happening to Dad. I know you haven't said anything to me yourself because you don't want me to worry, but I'm really glad she's kept me in the loop. So, what gives? Is Dad really in big trouble? Should I come home? I can certainly find someone to watch over the bar if you need me there. Let me know. Please. Love you. The Florida Branch of the Family

What a doll that Mike was. I know all moms think their kids are terrific, but in my case, it certainly was the truth. I was glad that Jenny had e-mailed him about what was going on up here, although I hated to have him worry long-distance. It was nice to know that the siblings were communicating, and I was selfishly relieved that the burden of explaining the whole mess to him had been taken on by Jenny.

I started to dash off a quick reply to assure him that things were under control when I heard the front door open.

"Hi, Mom," Jenny called from the front hall. "I had some car trouble at school. That's why I'm late."

"Oh, Jenny, I'm so glad you're home. You won't believe what happened today. Nancy and I..." I stopped myself in mid-sentence because Jenny interrupted me.

"But I was so lucky that Linda Burns came along to help me. She was nice enough to follow me home, to be sure I got here all right."

"Hi, Carol," said Linda, following Jenny into my office. "I was glad to help Jenny out. How are you doing? I haven't seen you since we met at the hair salon." She gave me a quick once-over. Probably checking to see if my roots were showing already.

I was trapped. What could I do but be polite to her? I quickly closed the lid of my laptop so she couldn't read my e-mail.

"Thank you so much for helping Jenny get home." I was trying extra hard to be gracious, mainly because I had no choice. "Where did she go?" I looked around, but my daughter had disappeared.

"I think she went to change," Linda replied. "Do you mind if I use your powder room before I leave? I got some grease on my hands fiddling with Jenny's car. I can find it myself. Thanks." She was up the hallway before I had a chance to reply.

Be nice, Carol. She helped Jenny out of a tight spot, and she won't stay long. I hope.

Linda came back into my office, drying her hands on one of my good guest towels. You know the ones I mean—we all put them out just for show and nobody ever uses them. Some nerve.

She handed the damp towel to me and settled herself into the sofa for a cozy chat. Great. Just what I needed. I had to get rid of her before Jim came home.

I rose from my desk chair and stood over her, hoping she would take the not-so-subtle hint.

"It was so nice of you to help Jenny today," I said again with as much warmth as I could muster. "I don't want to keep you. I'm sure you're in a rush to get home."

"Don't worry about it," Linda said with a laugh. "I called Bruce and told him I'd be a little late because I was stopping off here." Too bad you didn't call me, too, I thought uncharitably. I would've found someplace else to be.

Linda looked around my office. "This is really a nice setup. I don't think I've ever been in here before. In fact, I don't think I've ever been inside your home before."

Oh, please God, don't let her ask for a tour of the house, I prayed, remembering the unmade bed in the master bedroom and the wet towels hanging over the side of the bathtub.

"Now, Carol," Linda continued, motioning me to sit beside her on my sofa just like we were best girlfriends, "I heard from Jenny that you're planning a retirement shower for Mary Alice. You know she is absolutely one of my dearest friends."

Really, I thought. Does Mary Alice know that?

"I want to organize it with you. I'm excellent at party-planning. In fact, I don't want to brag, but Bruce's boss is always pestering me for ideas about parties at the office. He says if I ever decide to leave teaching, I could have a whole new career as an event planner." She gave me a big insincere smile.

At that point, I would have promised her almost anything just to get her out of my house. I knew Nancy would kill me, but I heard myself saying, "That's so generous of you, Linda. We'd love to have your help. The party's planned for Labor Day at Maria's Trattoria. I've already been in touch with Maria, and she's going to come up with some menu suggestions and get back to me in the next few days."

I stood up and looked down on her—I mean, at her. "Why don't I give you a call when I hear from Maria, and you and I and Nancy and Claire can all get together and talk about the party. Ok?"

At that point, Lucy and Ethel, who had been snoozing in a sunny spot on the kitchen floor, came bounding into my office and began to give Linda some serious sniffing in rather personal parts of her body.

"Oh, dear," Linda said, shooing the dogs away and getting up from the sofa in a flash. "I'd forgotten I have to stop and pick up some food at the supermarket on the way home. I'll wait for your call. Tell Jenny goodbye for me, and a big hello to Jim."

When I heard the front door close behind Linda, I took the dogs into the kitchen and rewarded them for their bad behavior with three dog biscuits apiece.

Chapter 21

Q: What is the common term for someone who enjoys work and refuses to retire?
A: Nuts!

"Sorry to leave you alone with Linda Burns," said Jenny, walking into the office with her wet hair wrapped in a towel. "I know she's not one of your all-time favorite people. But I was desperate to take a quick shower after fiddling around with my car. It's a good thing Linda came along when she did and helped me. I was clueless when I couldn't get it started."

She took a hard look at me. "Something's up with you, and it's a lot more serious than my stupid car problems. Or your having to deal with Linda Burns for a little while."

I poured out the whole story of my day to Jenny, starting with the good news: Nancy's finding Grace Retuccio, our visit to her, and all the amazing things we found out from Grace about Davis Rhodes. And how much Grace hated him for asking her for a divorce now, when the Center was becoming successful.

Jenny was impressed at my sleuthing. And excited at my progress.

"God, Mom, you've got to tell Mark right away. This might let Dad off the hook, and it sure gives Grace a good motive for Rhodes's death."

"I told Mark already. Unfortunately, when Nancy and I got back from Westfield, he was waiting for me. He wanted to ask me more questions about Dad's and my relationship with Davis Rhodes. And unfortunately, none of this lets Dad off the hook."

When Jenny heard about my cell phone arriving at police headquarters under such mysterious circumstances, together with the note about checking the voice mail messages, she realized why I was so upset. "This could be damaging, but it doesn't have to be," my sensible daughter pointed out. "Somebody, obviously not you, sent the phone to the police. Can't they check the package for fingerprints or something, and find out who did it?"

"I never thought to suggest that to Mark," I admitted. "I'm sure that's done automatically. At least, it is in all the mystery books I read."

I was beginning to realize how little a real life murder investigation resembled those books I'd read over the years. One would think that all that reading would have given me tips on investigating a crime, but sadly, it hadn't. Where were my little gray cells when I needed them? They probably self-destructed due to hot flash overload.

"Mark left here a little while before you came home with Linda," I said. "He was on his way to the Center to question your father and Sheila Carney. He warned me not to call there and let your father know that he was coming. I feel like such a traitor. But I'm glad that Mark is on the case. I have to believe he'll do everything he can to get this mess cleared up and find the person who was responsible for Rhodes's death."

"He better," said Jenny, "or the next time he calls me for a coffee date, I'll slam the phone down right in his ear."

Jim came home from the Center two hours later, very subdued and upset. I think the reality of his situation was finally beginning to sink in.

He tried to put up his usual brave front when Jenny was around, but when she went upstairs to do some work on her computer, he took out his anxiety on the handiest person—me.

"I can't believe you didn't call and warn me that the police were coming to question me, Carol. Do you enjoy seeing me in trouble? Mark had that odious partner of his with him, which made things even worse. He kept threatening to take me downtown if I didn't cooperate. Damn it, I was cooperating! And I couldn't reach Larry, either. Where the hell is everybody when I need them?"

"I wanted to call you," I answered in my defense, "but Mark told me not to. Ordered me, in fact. Nancy was here, and she'll tell you the same thing. Larry and Claire have gone to the Berkshires for a few days, but I'm sure he's reachable on his cell phone." Oops. Probably shouldn't have mentioned the words "cell phone" to Jim.

"That's another thing. Where did you lose your blasted cell phone? How could you be so careless? And why didn't you erase my voice mail message as soon as you heard it?"

Jim ran his fingers through what was left of his hair. "God, with family support like this, I'll probably end up in prison."

I knew My Beloved was frantic, but that didn't make being the convenient scapegoat for his tirade any easier for me. I felt miserable enough about the cell phone debacle without his rubbing it in.

"I don't remember where I lost it," I snapped back. "If I knew where I'd lost it, I would have found it, right?" Well, that logic made sense to me. "What I'd like to know is, who did find it and turned it into the police anonymously. Who would want to cause us so much grief?"

I crossed the room and put my arms around him. "Honey, I love you. I do." We held each other tight, just for a minute. "I would never, ever, deliberately do anything to cause you pain. I only want what's best for you. Please, believe me. We are in this together, and we'll get out of it together."

Hell, truth be told, I didn't trust Jim to get himself out of this mess on his own. He seemed to be getting in deeper and deeper. I conveniently ignored the part my own carelessness had played in his plight. Couldn't dwell on that now.

It looked like Mark Anderson was on our side, but I wasn't so sure how much help he could be without jeopardizing his job. I was positive he would do the best he could, because he wanted to stay in our (that is, Jenny's) good graces. But the bottom line was, Mark was one of the policemen assigned to this case. Hmm. That did have its plus side, because he would be privy to inside information, if I could just get him to share it with me.

Think positive, Carol. You can do this. I just had to be sure that Jim didn't know what I was up to, because I was positive that he would tell me not to interfere.

I decided it was time Jim knew what Nancy and I had found out about his precious Davis Rhodes.

"Sit down a minute," I said. "I have some things to tell you. Just hear me out, and maybe you'll decide that things aren't as bleak as they seem."

I held out a kitchen chair for him and repeated, "Sit."

"Who do you think I am, Lucy or Ethel?" Jim said, with just a trace of his old humor. "I hope it's not a long story. I have to reach Larry tonight before it gets too late."

I tried not to be annoyed. Jim had already decided that what I was going to tell him wasn't important.

I started with my visit to Maria's Trattoria to plan the retirement shower for Mary Alice, and some of the information I got from her about Davis Rhodes.

Jim immediately interrupted me. "When did Mary Alice decide to retire? You never told me that."

"I forgot to tell you with everything else that's been going on. But don't concentrate on that right now. You have to hear what I found out about Davis Rhodes."

Then I told him about Nancy and her Realtors' network, and how we managed to track down and talk to Davis Rhodes's wife. Jim was not impressed when I informed him that Grace had come up with so much of the concept for the Re-tirement Survival Center.

"She could have been exaggerating how important her contribution was, Carol."

"But, don't you see, it was when Rhodes asked her for a divorce that she decided to come east and confront him. She didn't want to take a chance on losing her share of the Center's profits." That made perfect sense to me.

I decided to skip the part about "Davis Rhodes" being the professional name of Dick Retuccio. Jim's eyes were looking a little glassy already at all the information I was throwing at him. But I could tell he thought what Nancy and I had uncovered was helpful.

"You two are quite the detectives. Did you tell the police about the scorned wife?"

"Of course I did. I told Mark all about her when he was here this afternoon. He was very grateful, and said he was going to check her out. She seems to have a very strong motive for wanting Rhodes out of the way, don't you think? More of a motive than you."

"I didn't have a motive for wanting Rhodes out of the way," Jim countered. "Hell, I just wanted to promote the guy and his retirement concept. Like I'd do for any client. It's not my fault things worked out the way they did."

Jim was starting to get angry again. Not that I blamed him.

"I know you better than anybody," My Beloved said, glaring at me. "I'm willing to bet you believe that you, and only you, can straighten out this whole thing. Am I right? Be honest with me, Carol. Come on, admit it."

I looked right back at him. This was a classic husband-wife standoff. Who would blink first?

"I know you don't like me to meddle, but this time, I can really help," I responded with more assurance than I felt. "Please let me. I promise that anything I find out, or Nancy finds out, or Claire or Mary Alice, we'll bring it right to Mark Anderson." As long as what we find out will help you, not make things worse for you, I added silently.

"Well, call me crazy, but I don't see how you could make things much worse," Jim grudgingly admitted. "I already know I shouldn't have gone to the Re-tirement Survival Center to see Sheila Carney about Rhodes's memorial service. Even if the agency did assign me to the job, I should have delegated that assignment to someone else on the staff. That twit Paul made it clear he found our working together so soon after Rhodes's death very suspicious. Mark walked me to my car after he finished questioning Sheila and me, and he suggested strongly that I not do any work on the Center account for the time being. He wants me to find somebody else to help Sheila organize the memorial ceremony.

"I thought about what he said all the way home and realized I have to do what Mark suggested. I have no choice. I thought about who I could get to take over for me, and I've come up with the perfect person. She's someone Sheila already knows, and even better than that, she's someone who could make Sheila open up about her relationship with Rhodes. Who knows? Maybe Sheila did want to take over the Center. That's a pretty good motive for wanting him dead."

"That's fabulous," I said. "Who is it?"

My Beloved looked me straight in the eye again and said, "You, Carol."

I have to admit, that time he made me blink first.

Chapter 22

Q: Name another perk of retirement.
A: You can sit around and watch the sunset—
if you can stay up that late.

The next morning, I was up and in the shower very early. I wanted a chance to talk to Jim again about how to deal with Sheila. I'd come up with a brilliant plan, naturally, but I figured I'd better run my idea by My Beloved before he headed off to the train, just to be sure we were both on the same wavelength.

It was not to be.

Just as I was rinsing the shampoo out of my hair, I heard Jim talking to me through the shower door. I couldn't understand a word he was saying because the running water was louder than the sound of his voice. Risking getting shampoo in my eyes, I turned off the shower and stuck my head out the door.

"Jim, Jim, don't leave yet," I screamed. "I want to talk to you about Sheila."

I heard the side door slam and his car start up. I had to laugh at the irony of the situation. Usually, I spend a lot of time not telling Jim things. Like major clothing purchases—"What? Don't you remember this old thing? I wore it out to dinner in New York last month." Most wives know that drill.

This time, I wanted to talk to Jim, and he was off to work before I had the chance. I wondered if he'd tell his boss he'd delegated the planning of the Davis Rhodes memorial to me.

I had an official job to do, and I was confident (ok, maybe more hopeful than confident) that I was up to the challenge. As I was toweling myself dry, I allowed myself another fantasy. In this one, Jim was actually on trial, and it wasn't looking good for him at all. At the very last minute, right before the jury was certain to find him guilty, I rushed into the courtroom, followed closely by Nancy, Claire and Mary Alice—my "associates"—and dramatically announced to the judge, "Release this prisoner, Your Honor. I have irrefutable evidence that Mr. Andrews did not commit any crime."

Jim burst into tears. Of course. "Honey, I knew you'd save me!"

In this fantasy, by the way, I was a perfect size 6 with long, lush blonde hair and I was wearing a chic black designer suit and stiletto heels. Think of Reese Witherspoon wowing the jury in *Legally Blonde.* Hell, this was my fantasy and I could imagine anything I wanted.

My reverie was interrupted by Jenny, who'd overheard me on her way downstairs to have some breakfast.

"Mom? Do you know you're talking to yourself?"

I jumped. "You scared me."

"Mom, you scared me. What the heck were you saying, anyway? And don't deny it. I heard you."

"Ok," I confessed, slightly chagrined, "you caught me. I admit I've been known to talk to myself, although usually I'm talking to Lucy and Ethel. This time, I was practicing defending your father in case we end up in court." I saw her stricken look and caught myself. "Not that I think we will end up in court, honey. But I was having this great fantasy about being the one who saves the day. I guess you must think I'm a little crazy."

"No more than usual," Jenny said with a grin, giving me a peck on the cheek. "Come on, let's go get some coffee and you can tell me all about your fantasy to save Dad."

Fortunately, Jenny had a little extra time to spare before leaving that morning.

"What about your car?" I asked her while I rummaged in the refrigerator for some milk. "With everything that happened here last night, I never asked you what was wrong with it. Are you going to have our mechanic check it?"

"I'll see how the car is this morning," Jenny said, "but apparently what happened was no big deal. Linda Burns took a look at it yesterday afternoon and said it was some sort of fluky thing that probably would never happen again. I was lucky she happened to be in the parking lot when I couldn't get the car started. I guess I panicked when I couldn't start it, and kept trying and trying but the darn engine just refused to turn over. Linda fiddled around with a few things under the hood and then told me to try to start it again, and it worked like a charm. She insisted on following me home just in case I had another problem, though."

So now dear Linda was an automotive expert, too?

Jenny gave me a knowing look. "I know she's not one of your all-time favorite people. But I think she has a good heart, and she's been terrific to me at school.

"Anyway, I'm going to drive the car today and see what happens. I'll have my cell phone in case I have a problem."

I stiffened.

"Sorry," Jenny said. "I should know that mentioning 'cell phone' to you is a no-no. I wasn't thinking."

"No problem, sweetie," I said, pouring some granola into a cereal bowl for her. "You know, driving your father's old car to school every day, with more than one-hundred-thousand miles on it, was a breakdown waiting to happen. It was so nice of Linda to help you, and be sure you got home safely." Though she did use one of my good guest towels, I reminded myself.

"Since you started teaching at Fairport College with her, you've shown me a side of Linda I never knew existed," I said magnanimously. "Maybe she's not as self-centered as I always thought she was. She even offered to help me arrange the retirement shower for Mary Alice. I never knew she and Mary Alice were that close, but she certainly seemed sincere. And who knows? She could have some good ideas."

So there. I could turn the other cheek when pushed hard enough.

I poured us both a little more coffee. I know I was stalling for time. It's hard to admit to your child that you've screwed up, big time.

"As far as my cell phone is concerned," I went on, my voice getting a little shaky, "if I'd paid more attention to where the heck I left it, your father wouldn't be in so much trouble. I'll never forgive myself for not erasing his voice mail message. Who knew it could sound so incriminating? I'd love to get my hands on the person who found it and turned it in to the police."

"Can't go back and take a do-over on it," said Jenny, giving my hand a squeeze. "You always told me not to look back, just keep moving forward, if you want to solve a problem. So, what's your grand plan to get Dad off the hook? And what's he going to say when he finds out what you're up to?"

"Well, Miss Smart Aleck, as a matter of fact, I'm doing this with your father's blessing. In fact, it was his idea."

Jenny looked skeptical. "That doesn't compute. Mike and I were always amazed at some of the things you'd pull on Dad, and he was never the wiser. Like the time you hired a cleaning woman, remember? He never caught on that the reason the house started looking so good was not that you were working so hard on it, but that you had someone come in once a week to spiff it up."

My goodness. What a terrible example I had been giving to my children all these years.

"Well, I'm turning over a new leaf," I proclaimed. "And before I forget, I got an e-mail from Mike last night. He said you've been keeping him up to date on what's going on here."

"Well, he's part of this family too. I hope you're not mad at me, but I thought he had a right to know."

"I'm not mad, sweetie. I'm glad that you've been telling him about the latest family crisis. I haven't had a chance to respond to him yet. I want to think a little about how to word it. If you should happen to e-mail him today, will you please assure him that it's not necessary for him to get on the next plane and come home? Maybe I should call him instead of e-mailing him. I don't want him to feel like he's not involved."

"I'll e-mail him for you, Mom. But there is a way he can help, even though he's in Florida. If there's anything at all you want checked out on the web that might help Dad, ask Mike to do it. You wouldn't believe how computer savvy he is. He's found out some amazing stuff for me that I've been able to use when I'm teaching. Give him a job to do."

I hadn't thought of doing research on the web. I wondered if Mike could check out Grace and Dick Retuccio, to see if the story she told Nancy and me was on the level. I filed that idea away to think about later. And hoped I'd remember it. Just to be sure, I scribbled a note to myself on a paper towel.

Jenny looked at her watch. "I have to go in a few minutes. Are you going to tell me what Dad asked you to do?"

"He needs someone to work with Sheila Carney and help organize Davis Rhodes's memorial service. Mark suggested to him last night that Dad's being closely involved with the Center so soon after Rhodes's death was not a good idea. Of course, I told him that too, but your father didn't listen to my advice."

"Ok, Mom. So…?"

"So, Dad said he thought I would be the perfect person to help Sheila. After all, she already knows me, and he said—and these are his exact words—that she may open up to me if I ask her a few questions about her relationship with Rhodes."

"Wow, Mom. Just what you've always wanted. Permission to snoop."

She gave me a quick hug. "I've got to leave now. Keep me posted if you can. Good luck with Sheila."

Once again, I had the house to myself. Correction: Lucy and Ethel and I had the house to ourselves. I sat down at the kitchen table to contemplate how exactly I was going to win Sheila's confidence. What would I say to her when I called her? What if she didn't want me to be involved at all?

That's stupid, Carol. She has to organize this memorial service, if only to make herself look good, and Jim can't help her. He's asked you to help her. Or rather, help him by helping her.

I had a ridiculous thought. We could invite Dan and Marni and put the entire service on *Wake Up New England.* Now I was really losing it. I needed help.

"All right, girls," I said to the dogs. "What do we need to do first? Call Nancy or Mary Alice and brainstorm about my organizing the memorial service? Call Sheila and set up a meeting? Wait for Jim to call me and tell me he's talked to Sheila and she's eagerly waiting for my call?"

Once again, the dogs looked supportive, but I wasn't getting any clear advice from either of them as to how to proceed. Just as a test, however, I mentioned Sheila's name and there was no response at all. Then I mentioned Nancy's name and they both wagged their tails enthusiastically. They love Nancy.

"Good choice," I said. "We'll call Nancy first."

I had my hand on the phone when it rang. Unfortunately for me, it was Mark Anderson. I had picked up the phone right away, but I was so nervous when I heard his voice that I dropped it on the kitchen floor. I could hear him faintly, saying "Hello. Hello? Mrs. Andrews? Jenny?"

"Hi, Mark," I said. "Sorry about that. My hands were slippery. I just washed them and they were still wet." Shut up, Carol. He doesn't care about that.

"So what can I do for you this morning?" I paused and let him get a word in. I was babbling again, but I couldn't seem to stop myself.

"I was hoping to catch Jenny before she left, Mrs. Andrews. Did I call early enough?"

Relief flooded over me. He didn't want me or Jim. This was a social call.

"You missed her by about fifteen minutes," I said. "She usually leaves by eight-forty-five so she can get some work done in the library before her classes start. Do you have her cell number?"

Mark laughed, a little nervously I thought.

"Funny you mentioned a cell phone, Mrs. Andrews. Under the circumstances, I mean."

He'd put me on the defensive. I ignored his reference to my cell phone debacle and continued with information about Jenny. "She had car trouble yesterday, Mark. I'm glad she has her phone with her today in case she has another problem. She was lucky it wasn't very serious, and one of the professors at the college, Linda Burns, helped her get it started."

What is it about men and cars, anyway? Mark immediately wanted to know all the details of Jenny's car problem. "She can call me anytime and I'd be glad to come and help her if I'm not on duty. I know quite a bit about fixing cars," he announced proudly.

"That would be a big relief to me. I hate to think of her getting stuck somewhere." I proceeded to give him Jenny's cell number, then decided to get a little nosy since Mark and I seemed to be getting along so well.

"I suppose you're not at liberty to discuss the case," I began. "But I wondered if you'd had a chance to interview Grace Retuccio yet."

"My partner and I are seeing her later this morning," Mark answered. "I really appreciated that tip, by the way. But you know I can't tell you what we find out.

"I hope you understand, Mrs. Andrews, how difficult a position I'm in right now. It's very hard for me to be objective about Mr. Andrews because I've known your family for so many years, but the fact is, he did threaten Davis Rhodes, and that's very serious. Plus, he deliberately misled us about his relationship with Rhodes."

I gave a nervous laugh. "I guess I did too, Mark. But you know I didn't mean to."

"That doesn't make it any less serious," he answered stiffly.

Oh, dear. I wondered how Mark would react if he knew that I was going to help Sheila Carney organize Rhodes's memorial service.

Impulsively, I said, "Before you hang up, there's something I want to run by you. I don't want to be accused of withholding more information from the police, and I hope you don't think this is inappropriate." I paused.

"Mrs. Andrews, what are you up to?"

"You know that the public relations agency my husband works for has taken on the Re-tirement Survival Center as a client, right? And that Jim had been assigned the job of organizing the memorial service for Rhodes. Since he won't be doing that job, at your suggestion, the agency has asked me to take over in his place." I know that was stretching the truth a little, but hell, Jim worked for the agency, and he'd asked me to do it. It was all the same, wasn't it?

I gave Mark a minute to process what I'd told him. Then, before he had a chance to tell me not to do it, I added, "You know, this could really be helpful to you in figuring out what happened to Rhodes. After all, Sheila Carney must be on your short list of suspects, and I'll be working very closely with her on the memorial service. I promise I'll pass anything she tells me right along to you." As long as it's helpful to Jim, I added silently.

"Now, Mrs. Andrews, we don't like private citizens interfering with police business."

"But I won't be interfering," I hastened to reassure him. "I'm going to be involved in planning the memorial service anyway. If I find out anything while I'm doing what Jim's agency asked me to do, I'll tell you. Unless you don't want me to give you any additional information," I added as a little dig.

"I didn't say not to tell me. Oh, hell. I know you're going to ask questions no matter what I say. Just don't get into trouble."

I assured him I would behave myself. I couldn't help but smile, despite everything. I not only had Jim's permission to snoop. Now, I had an unofficial blessing from the police, too.

Chapter 23

Whether a man ends up with a goose egg or a nest egg when he retires depends a lot on the kind of chick he marries.

"We've got to swing into high gear," I said to Lucy and Ethel. "I'm now officially on the staff of Jim's P.R. agency and the local police department. Aren't you proud of me?" Both the dogs looked at me reproachfully. They can always tell when I'm exaggerating. "Ok, maybe I'm on their staffs unofficially. But at least I'm not going to get criticized this time for sticking my nose in where it doesn't belong."

Talking out loud had bolstered my confidence. A little. I knew that the sooner I contacted Sheila, the better. Once we started working together on the memorial service, maybe I could get her to open up to me. Especially since I had adopted my new mantra: keep quiet and let others do the talking.

I finally worked up my nerve and called her, after rehearsing what I was going to say over and over to the dogs so I would get the tone just right. I was completely bowled over when Sheila told me that My Beloved had already called and convinced her that I was an expert at organizing all sorts of special events. That was stretching the truth more than even I would dare, since my main special events expertise came from orchestrating our children's birthday parties. But Sheila bought it completely. In fact, she seemed surprisingly grateful for my help.

"I'm pretty new in Westfield and don't have too many local contacts, much less friends," Sheila confided to me. "Jim tells me you're an absolute whiz with organizing and producing this kind of thing. I can't wait to meet with you and get your ideas about the memorial service. I see it as a tremendous marketing tool for the Center."

Interesting take on the situation, I thought. Sheila certainly was expert at hiding her grief.

Then, as if reading my thoughts, she added unconvincingly, "This is such a sad occasion for me. I need all the support I can get."

Yeah, right.

🐾

I decided it wasn't smart to meet with Sheila by myself. I wanted another set of eyes and ears to go along with me to pick up on things I might miss, as well provide me with moral support. I was very nervous about living up to the big build-up Jim had given me. If Sheila was as smart as I thought she was, she'd see through my act in a flash.

Nancy was with clients for most of the day. I knew Claire was still away in the Berkshires with Larry. "Besides," I said to the dogs, "Larry would kill her if he found out she was snooping with me. Especially since he's Jim's lawyer. He'd worry about the appearance of conflict of interest or something.

"I wonder if I can talk Mary Alice into coming with me." The dogs danced around at the mention of Mary Alice's name. Another one of their favorite humans.

I agreed with their decision. In fact, the more I thought about bringing Mary Alice along, the more I liked the idea. True, she was the most serious member of our group, and always had been. But she was full of the devil, as my mother used to say, when she was in the right frame of mind.

The most perfect part of all was that Mary Alice really was retiring soon, and I could introduce her to Sheila as a potential client for the Center.

Carol, you are so clever!

Unfortunately when I called Mary Alice with my proposition, I woke her up. And she was grumpy.

"I just got to bed after working the night shift," Mary Alice said crossly. "I feel like I've only been asleep for ten minutes, and then you call and wake me up. What do you want and why can't it wait till later?"

"I didn't remember that you're working the night shift for the next two weeks. I'm really sorry I woke you. But this is important and could help Jim. He's in big trouble. A lot has happened since I last talked to you, and none of it is good."

I knew I had her attention now. Mary Alice is a sucker for helping people. That's why she's such a good nurse.

When I finished bringing her up to date, she agreed (reluctantly) to meet me around the corner from the Re-tirement Survival Center at 3:30 that afternoon. "I'll do anything you say, as long as I can get a few hours' sleep." Then she banged the phone down in my ear.

I just hoped she'd remember to show up.

I needn't have worried about Mary Alice. She was actually five minutes early, fully made up, perfectly coiffed, and raring to go. "This is exciting, Carol," she said. "I'm sorry about being crabby when you called me. Being sleep-deprived has that effect on me. But I got a few hours of quality rest, and I had the craziest dream. I was the star witness in a murder trial, and my testimony saved the accused from being convicted for a crime he didn't commit. Isn't that something? Must have been my subconscious working overtime. So, what do you want me to do?"

Stop having my dream for starters, I thought. I'm the one who's going to save Jim. Then I mentally slapped myself. Who cared how many of my friends had delusions about being the one who exonerated my husband? Hell, Mary Alice had been one of the bridesmaids in our wedding. She had a stake in this, too.

"Just be yourself and follow my lead," I told her. "I'm going to introduce you to Sheila as a friend of mine who's getting ready to retire. But don't tell her you already have a retirement strategy mapped out for yourself. We need her to think you're a potential client of the Center, and see how she responds."

"Got it," Mary Alice said. "Gosh. I've never done anything like this before. It's kind of like working undercover for the CIA, isn't it?"

"Don't be silly," I snapped. "We have a perfect right to see Sheila. I'm there to help her plan the memorial service, and you're there for retirement help. We're not spies, for heaven's sake. And don't forget, Jim's asked me to do this. We'll take both cars so you can go right home from the Center. Let's go."

There were no other cars in the Center's parking lot when we pulled into the driveway. Perhaps Sheila wasn't taking on any new clients until after the memorial service. I was willing to bet, though, that once the word was official that Rhodes had been murdered, business would really pick up. Some people can't resist being at the scene of a crime.

I shrugged off the thought that maybe I was one of those people and raised my hand to ring the doorbell. I needn't have bothered. Sheila must have been watching for me out the window, because the door flew open and a blonde vision greeted us. Sheila was wearing a classic black Chanel suit with three-quarter-length sleeves, medium-heeled black pumps, black leather gloves, and a pillbox hat with a heavy veil.

I had the urge to genuflect and kiss her ring, but managed to control myself just in time.

I could sense Mary Alice's reaction behind me. She sounded like she was trying not to giggle.

Sheila reached forward, grasped both of my hands in hers, and put out her cheek for a kiss. Jeez! I'd only met the woman once!

I settled for squeezing both of her hands and offered my condolences.

Sheila, playing the role of widow to the hilt, graciously ushered us in. Remembering my manners, I introduced Mary Alice as a dear friend of mine who was thinking about retirement, and who occasionally helped me in my event planning, which was not a complete lie. (She did lend me some games for Mike's fifth birthday party.)

Once again, I was back in that lovely living room. I could see out of the corner of my eye that Mary Alice was impressed by the decor. Hey, it was gorgeous by anybody's standards. Mary Alice and I sat side by side on the plush camelback sofa, and Sheila sat opposite us in an equally plush wing chair.

I coughed nervously.

"Sheila, I know this must be so difficult for you," I began.

She raised a lace hanky to her eyes. "You have no idea how difficult," she said. "Dave and I were very close. Closer than most people realized."

I wondered if she were close enough to "Dave" to know that his real name was Dick Retuccio, and that he was married to a woman named Grace, but decided I wouldn't get anywhere if I asked her those questions.

"I feel I should explain why I'm dressed this way," she went on. "This is what I was planning on wearing to the memorial service. I wanted your opinion. Do you think it strikes the right note of classic grief? I really feel I must be a role model for all the clients whose lives Dave touched, who are undoubtedly devastated by his death."

Was she kidding? How in the world did I warm to this woman the first time I was here? She was as phony as a three-dollar bill.

"Well," I said cautiously, "it is a classic look. It reminds me of someone. I can't quite think of who."

She leaned forward eagerly in her chair. "Do you think it's reminiscent of what Jackie wore to JFK's funeral?"

I couldn't look at Mary Alice. I knew I'd start to laugh if I did, and this was serious business.

Mary Alice spoke for the first time. "I don't know. With your blonde hair, Sheila, you remind me more of Princess Grace."

Sheila beamed. "How kind of you. I know we're going to be great friends."

I cleared my throat. "Now, Sheila, let's talk a little bit about the memorial service itself. I'm not sure how far you and Jim had gotten in the planning. Do you have a guest list in mind? How many people are you thinking of? Will you want food served? A tasteful buffet after the tributes are over, perhaps? And flowers? Any favorites? Music? Oh, and..." I gave a little laugh. "Do you have a budget for the event?"

Forty-five minutes later it was clear to me that Sheila would have invited the Pope himself if he happened to be touring the United States next week. She wanted the governor invited, our two U.S. senators, the entire Connecticut congressional delegation, any prominent local legislators, the mayor, the list went on and on. And she wanted media coverage. Lots and lots of media coverage. It sounded more like a political rally than a memorial service.

I was writing furiously while she was talking. So far Mary Alice hadn't said another word. I think she was in shock. Or perhaps she was thinking hard about how we could really imitate JFK's funeral and where we could find a few horses for the procession.

I snapped my notebook shut. "I think I have a good idea of what you're thinking of for the service. Of course, if everyone we invite shows up, we'll have to put up a tent in the garden. Maybe two tents."

I paused. I wasn't too sure how much more I could say about Rhodes's memorial service. This was a little more complicated than ordering a clown to show up at a birthday party and juggle a few balls for the kids.

Sheila tapped her foot impatiently.

"I know our office has addresses for the people you want invited," I said. "It's important to get the invitations out immediately, because we have such a short lead time." Lead time. Now that was an official word I'd heard Jim use many times. I never thought I'd hear it coming out of my mouth.

I decided it was high time I switched from my role as official events consultant to womanly confidante and see how far I could get.

"Sheila," I said as sincerely as I could, "both Mary Alice and I want to support you in your hour of grief. I hope you'll think of us both as your friends."

Mary Alice nodded her head in complete agreement. And then she surprised me.

She leaned forward and took Sheila's hand. "I know we've just met," Mary Alice said, "but you and I have much more in common than you realize. I lost my husband several years ago, and I've never completely gotten over it. I don't think Carol can empathize with what you're going through, but believe me, I can."

Sheila's eyes spilled over. I was impressed that she could whip up tears so quickly.

"I'm also a nurse," Mary Alice went on. "In my job I deal with lots of families going through the grieving process. Everyone does it differently. Losing your husband is a profound thing. After listening to your plan for your husband's memorial service, I want you to know that I think it's wonderful that you want to pay tribute to him this way."

Huh? This wasn't in the scenario I'd envisioned. Mary Alice and Sheila were bonding over their "widowhood," and I was the odd woman out.

"That's so kind of you to say," said Sheila. "But I want to clarify something. Dave and I were kindred spirits as well as colleagues. We were also very much in love. But unfortunately, we weren't married. We planned to be, very soon, but something got in our way. Or should I say, someone."

I leaned forward on the sofa. Now we were getting to the good stuff.

"You see, Mary Alice," Sheila said, completely ignoring me, "Dave wasn't legally divorced from his first wife."

Her eyes narrowed. "That woman, Grace, had the nerve to show up here a few weeks ago and tell him so. I was livid. I thought he'd lied to me. And after all I'd done for him, working with him for all these years to start up the Re-tirement Survival Center. I wasn't going to take the chance he'd dump me and go back to her. No way."

Ooh, this was a good motive for bumping him off. Hell hath no fury and all that stuff.

"And then he died. He died before I had a chance to tell him I forgave him, that I'd stick with him no matter what. And that I loved him and knew he'd never deliberately deceive me." Sheila was crying in earnest now.

"That's the last time I saw him alive. I feel so guilty. That's why I want this memorial to be so perfect. I want to make it up to him, somehow."

Brother. This was a little hard to swallow.

But Mary Alice had exactly the right answer for Sheila. "You have survivor's guilt," she said. "You're alive, and he's dead, and you never had the chance to say you were sorry. Believe me, I know about that too. The day Brian died, we had a big fight over something stupid. I don't even remember what it was about. He left the house angry, and an hour later he was dead."

What? This was news to me. You go, Mary Alice! Sounds good.

We left soon after that revelation. What else was there to say? To her credit, though, Mary Alice promised to keep in touch with the still weeping Sheila.

I waited until we were safely in the parking lot and then said, "Mary Alice, you were amazing in there. That phony story about you and Brian really made Sheila open up. I need to get home right away and get in touch with Mark Anderson. He's going to want to question her."

Mary Alice got into her car and slammed the door. "I'm not proud of this, but it wasn't a phony story. I just never told anyone about it before."

She turned the key, pressed her foot down on the accelerator, and sped down the block, leaving me standing on the curb with my mouth hanging open.

Chapter 24

Q: What's the downside of doing nothing?
A: You don't know when you're done.

All the way home, I stewed over Mary Alice's unexpected revelation. There were so many times over the years that Jim and I would have harsh words over trivial things, and then he'd storm out to catch his train, leaving the matter unresolved until that evening. I'd always taken it for granted that he would come home, and that we would (eventually) talk things over and reach an agreement on such earthshaking subjects as what brand of paper towels to buy, how many friends Jenny was allowed to invite over for her next sleepover, if Mike could have a girl over for a study date, and whether he could keep his bedroom door closed when she was here. That last one caused a lot of arguments, because I always feared the worst (naturally) and Jim was of the "boys will be boys" mentality.

I resolved to take Mary Alice's lesson seriously, and become kinder and gentler toward my husband.

At least, I would try.

After I got home and let the dogs out for a quick run in the yard, I reviewed my options for the rest of the afternoon.

I really wanted to talk to Mark Anderson, but after our phone conversation earlier today, that didn't seem like a very good idea. Then I noticed the red light on my phone was blinking. The message was from

Jenny, who'd had still another car problem and, when she couldn't reach me, had called Mark on his cell phone. Luckily for her, he was able to come to her rescue and was following her to our mechanic's, where she'd drop off her car. They were going to have an early dinner together and then she'd be home.

Well, that was certainly interesting. Two "dates" in such a short period of time. It sure would be funny if they got together after all these years, I thought. I wondered if Mark spent any time complaining to Jenny about what a nosy mother she had. Or if he discussed any part of the Rhodes case with her.

Nah, I thought. Not likely. Mark was obviously trying to impress Jenny, and criticizing her mother would not be helpful. Besides, Jenny already knew I was nosy. Discussing the pros and cons of her father as a murder suspect wouldn't win him many brownie points either.

I decided the most productive use of my precious time before Jim came home from the office was to go over the notes I'd taken about the memorial service. Dinner could wait. Maybe we'd even get takeout for a change—Chinese or a pizza.

I was so deep in concentration trying to decipher my chicken scratch handwriting that I didn't realize My Beloved was standing over me.

And he had a bouquet of flowers in his hand. What was going on? The last time he'd brought me flowers was when Mike was born.

"You startled me, Jim. How long have you been standing there?"

He thrust the flowers at me, slightly embarrassed. "Here. These are for you. I just want you to know how much I appreciate your helping me."

I started to protest that flowers weren't necessary, but then Jim said, a little impatiently, "Don't make a big deal out of this. I got the flowers from one of the vendors outside Grand Central. It's not like I went to a florist or anything."

Typical, Carol. Jim does something nice for you, and you put him on the defensive for doing it. What's the matter with you?

"That's so sweet of you, honey. Thank you."

He pulled me up from my chair and gave me a quick peck on the cheek. "It's the least I could do for my best girl. Now, why don't you fill me in on what happened today. Did you see Sheila? How did it go? And before you ask me, no, I haven't heard anything more from the police. Which I assume is a good thing." That bit of news reassured me that perhaps we could have a "normal" evening at home, whatever that meant under the current circumstances.

Knowing that the way to My Beloved's heart was through his stomach, I announced that before I brought him up to date, we were going to order a takeout meal. His choice: Italian or Chinese. And we were going to shoot the budget tonight and pay the extra money to have the meal delivered. Jim started to argue that he could easily go and pick up the order. I knew what he was really thinking—bringing me flowers should have been enough. Paying a delivery charge was way over the top. But I stuck to my guns and after just a little more bickering, we agreed on a Chinese feast from The Lotus Blossom, a scant two miles away. Jim grudgingly called and placed our order, warning the woman that if the meal were delivered cold, there would be no tip for the driver. Ordinarily, I would have commented on that, but I let it go. A kinder, gentler Carol, that was the new me.

"Now," I said, "do you want to sit down and get comfortable? I have such a lot to tell you. I know that sometimes you think I go on and on without getting to the point, or skip from one subject to another, and that drives you nuts.

"I have an even better idea," I said, not giving the poor man a chance to get a word in. "If you want to go upstairs and change and wash up first, go ahead. I'll make up an agenda for all my news. How's that?"

I've found that making up an agenda for a discussion with My Beloved can be quite helpful. This may not work for everybody, but it's prevented several serious arguments for us over the years. For one thing, it forces both of us to focus on the same thing at the same time. A novelty in marriage.

I fired up my computer and, before doing my agenda, sent off a quick e-mail to Mike, assuring him that his father was not about to be fitted for an orange prison jumpsuit and promising to keep him posted on what was going on up north. Then I remembered Jenny's suggestion about Mike's Internet expertise, so I added:

May want to use your sleuthing skills long-distance. Can you track down people on the web if I just give you names, not addresses? That could be a great help. Love from your Geriatric Cosmo Girl.

I could hear the sound of the shower running upstairs. Good, I thought. Hopefully that would relax Jim and put him in a receptive frame of mind for all I had to tell him.

First on the agenda, the purpose of the meeting. That was an easy one—to keep Jim from getting arrested. But I didn't think he'd react favorably to that wording, so instead I wrote: To share information on anything pertaining to Davis Rhodes investigation. I hoped that was broad enough. There have been times that one or the other of us has abused the meeting agenda and branched out into other things that were bugging us. Not fair.

I kept the agenda topics loose:

Report on Gibson Gillespie/Re-tirement Survival Center client relationship: Jim

Report on Davis Rhodes personal data: Carol

Report on meeting with Sheila Carney: Carol

Report on conversation with Mark Anderson: Carol

Next Steps: Carol (with some input from Jim)

Next Meeting Date

I put a time limit for discussion by each of the agenda items. It didn't mean a thing as far as I was concerned, but that tactic pleased Jim immensely. He believes all meetings should be kept to an hour, maximum. After that, he says, you're just wasting time.

When I read what I had written, I realized that I had given most of the agenda to myself. Oh, well. I knew Jim would interrupt me whenever he felt the urge, which was allowed according to our own unique interpretation of Robert's Rules of Order. At least, this gave us a place to begin an orderly conversation.

I made sure there was plenty of room between each agenda item for notes. Then I printed out two copies and put them on the dining room table. In my opinion, serious discussion means an upgrade of locale from the usual kitchen hangout to the formal dining room.

Just in time. The front doorbell rang and I rushed to let in the deliveryman before Jim could come downstairs and check over the bill. He's never figured out that there's a direct relationship between how long it takes him to ponder over the bill before paying it and the temperature of the food when we finally get to eat it. The more bill pondering, the colder the food.

I needn't have worried about his checking this one, though. It was written entirely in Chinese.

I gave the deliveryman a generous tip and sent him on his way.

By the time my freshly showered husband came downstairs, I had set the table and put his flowers in a vase to use as the table centerpiece. The steaming Chinese food was ready to serve, and smelled delicious. There was an agenda at each of our places. I was set to start my dinner meeting.

"What's the occasion?" asked Jim when he walked into the dining room. "We never eat in here." He looked at me and raised one eyebrow. "What are you up to?"

"I might ask you the same question," I retorted. "You never bring me flowers. What are you up to?"

"*Touché*," said Jim. "You're right. We have to start treating ourselves, and each other, better. If there's one thing this whole Rhodes fiasco has taught me, it's that no one can predict what's going to happen in life. We should enjoy each day."

Huh? Was this my cynical husband talking? Maybe some good would come out of this mess after all.

"Where's Jenny tonight?" asked Jim as he dug into one of his favorite Chinese dishes, Chef's Special Flavor Chicken. "This is so good. What a treat."

"She had more car trouble today." I watched My Beloved's reaction as I added, "She called Mark Anderson to help her. He followed her to the mechanic's and then they're having dinner together."

Jim didn't even react when I mentioned Mark's name. He was too busy eating.

"You realize that Mark will be bringing her home, right?" I asked. "He may come in to say a quick hello. Just so you're prepared."

"It'll be fine. Don't worry. He's always treated me respectfully. I wish I could say the same for that partner of his, though. Hopefully, this whole nightmare will be over soon and we can all get back to our normal lives."

"Amen to that," I said fervently.

I tapped my glass with a spoon.

"This meeting is now called to order."

Since most of the agenda items were mine, naturally I monopolized most of the conversation for the next hour.

The only piece of information that Jim was willing to share with me about his office situation was, "I'm handling it. It's not a problem." So much for My Beloved being forthcoming. Oh, well.

Jim was amazed to learn that "Davis Rhodes" was really Dick Retuccio. "That's incredible. So he was using an assumed name. I wonder why. That story about the name Retuccio being a turnoff to clients doesn't sound plausible. I wonder if someone from his past had it in for him."

"Someone like his wife Grace," I said. "I think she's a prime suspect. Plus, she rented a house right around the corner from the Center. Pretty convenient if you wanted to bump somebody off, I'd say."

I ticked off items on my fingers. "She had motive and opportunity. And if Rhodes—I can't stop calling him that—had any kind of drug allergy or medical condition, who'd know that better than his wife?

"Now, let's move on to Sheila." My favorite suspect.

I filled Jim in as succinctly as I could on my meeting. He approved of my taking Mary Alice along with me. "Always good to have someone else with you, Carol. Especially in a tricky situation like this."

When I got to the part about Sheila's suggestions for the memorial service guest list, Jim started to laugh. "She didn't mention most of these people to me when we last talked. Does she seriously think the entire Connecticut congressional delegation is going to come to this?"

This was the first time I'd heard Jim say anything negative about Sheila. Instead of tossing off one of my wisecrack answers, I opened my fortune cookie. "A problem clearly stated is a problem half solved," it read. That was encouraging. At least someone thought I was on the right track.

"The agency has all these V.I.P.s on our master e-mail list," Jim said. "I guess it won't hurt to send them an electronic invitation. Maybe also suggest that if they're not able to attend, perhaps they could e-mail back a tribute to Rhodes to be read at the service. I'll have the office do that first thing tomorrow morning. We'll see if any of the big shots respond. Did Sheila mention whether she'd gotten any tributes from clients?"

"She didn't say a word about that," I replied, pushing away my plate. "She seemed more fixated on the guest list. And playing the role of the broken-hearted lover. She admitted to Mary Alice and me that she and Rhodes had a personal relationship."

Jim raised his eyebrow again. He seemed surprised at that revelation. And I was equally surprised that he hadn't figured that out for himself. Men don't have the radar that women have, I guess.

I refrained from describing Sheila's Jackie Kennedy-like outfit. I knew Jim would think that was petty of me. Or, more likely, the analogy would go right over his head.

"I told Sheila I'd take care of ordering any food she wanted. She wants to have a buffet luncheon for the guests after the memorial service. But I can't actually order anything until we know how many people will be coming. I thought I'd call Maria Lesco and see what she'd suggest. She's supposed to be coming up with a menu for Mary Alice's retirement shower, so I can check in with her about that, too. Maybe if she's doing two events for me, she'll give me a better price."

Jim nodded his approval. Anything I could do to save some money was always great with him. Even if he wasn't paying for it.

"Now, one more thing on the agenda before we get to next steps for both of us," I said. "I want to tell you about my conversation with Mark Anderson this morning."

At that exact moment, I heard a key turn in the front door. "Hello? Anybody home?" It was Jenny, back from her "dinner date" with Mark.

"Mark is with me. He's not feeling well. I think he ate something at that new Mexican place that didn't agree with him." Jenny noticed us at the dining room table for the first time. "Oh, there you both are. In the dining room, no less. Pretty fancy."

Mark was right behind her. His face was sweaty and pasty white. "Sorry to disturb you both," he said. "But I wondered if you had some bicarbonate of soda or Alka-Seltzer or something I could take to settle my stomach. I need to take something or I'll never make it home. I don't understand what's wrong with me but I feel pretty awful. I guess the food I ate was too spicy."

I immediately became the solicitous mother. "Mark, I think there's some Alka-Seltzer in the master bathroom medicine cabinet. Do you want me to get it for you?"

"That's ok, Mrs. Andrews," Mark said. "You don't have to. If you don't mind my going upstairs to help myself, that is. I remember where your bathroom is." It occurred to me that Mark might have other uses for the bathroom and needed some privacy, so I just waved my hand and said, "Help yourself. Give us a shout if you can't find it."

Jenny started to help me clear the remnants of the Chinese dinner off the table. Jim hastily folded up our agendas and shoved them in his pocket. So far, he hadn't said anything, and I know he felt as uncomfortable as I did having Mark here. But we were both trying to put a good face on it, especially for Jenny's sake.

Less than two minutes later, Mark was back downstairs. He looked even worse now than he had before, and he was holding something wrapped in a handkerchief.

"Mr. Andrews, Mrs. Andrews, I'm afraid I have to ask you some more questions. This is very difficult for me." Mark opened the handkerchief and revealed a little blue prescription pill bottle.

"Can you tell me where and under what circumstances you acquired this?"

We all squinted at the label. It was something called Enalapril. "I don't think I've ever seen that before," I said. "Nobody in this house is on that medication. What's it used for?"

"It's a heart medication," Mark said, "and we suspect it's the drug that caused Davis Rhodes's death."

Chapter 25

Q: What is a wife's common reaction to her husband's retirement?
A: She realizes she never gave his secretary enough sympathy.

Jim, Jenny and I started talking at the same time. Even Lucy and Ethel got into the act, adding their yips of moral support.

Mark finally pulled out a dining room chair and gestured for us to sit down. "All right, everybody. We're all friends here. At least, I hope you still think of me as a friend. Let's sit down and take a deep breath and see what we can figure out. I'm not officially on duty now, so think of this as a brainstorming session. Ok?"

Jenny offered to make a pot of fresh coffee, and disappeared into the kitchen. Jim sat down at the head of the table and put his head in his hands. I sincerely hoped he wasn't crying, but I couldn't blame him if he was. I looked down at my hands and realized they were shaking.

Mark looked at me. I noticed his color was better now. It looked like his upset stomach had improved. My stomach was doing flip-flops, and it definitely wasn't from the Chinese food.

"Mrs. Andrews, you're first. I told you this morning that I wasn't happy about you asking any more questions, though I didn't see how I could stop you. No, let me finish," he said as I started to defend myself. "I realize that you and your friends are in a unique position to help clear up this mess. So, I want you to go over everything you've discovered, and everyone you've talked to, in the last few days, about the Davis Rhodes case. But before you start, I want you to know that I don't believe for one minute that you, Mr. Andrews, are responsible for Davis Rhodes's death. I think you just were in the wrong place at the wrong time."

We breathed a collective sigh of relief.

"However," Mark went on, "someone did cause his death, and I believe that same person is setting you up, Mr. Andrews. Unfortunately, my colleagues down at police headquarters don't share my view of the case. If they had their way, you'd be hauled in for more questioning, or maybe even held as a material witness. I've had a real tough time keeping that from happening, and I'm not sure how much longer I can keep stonewalling them. My partner is really on my back about it, especially after the cell phone arrived.

"This is a very frustrating case. And I want to come up with the truth. But I'm not going to risk losing my job."

Jenny poured the freshly brewed coffee into everyone's cups. I couldn't help but notice that she served Mark first, and that she also knew exactly how he took his coffee. A little cream and two sugars.

Mark looked at me again, and said, "From the top, please. And don't leave anything out."

Being me, of course, I couldn't just tell the story from the top. Not with what Mark had just admitted.

"It's so scary that you think someone is setting Jim up. But I have to say that's the first thing I've heard about this nightmare that makes any sense. Thank you, from the bottom of my heart, for believing in him. None of us want to see you lose your job. I didn't realize how much pressure you were under at work because of this case."

"It's in everyone's best interests to resolve this as soon as possible," said Mark. He appeared to be slightly embarrassed. Perhaps he thought he'd said too much about his personal situation.

"While you were talking, Mark, I realized that Jim and Davis Rhodes had a terrific relationship. That was obvious to me at our first consultation." I refrained from adding the part about the chocolate chip cookies.

Jim nodded his head vigorously. "That's right. Rhodes and I worked very well together and I really admired him. It wasn't until the actual day he died that we had any problems. And I'm sure they could have been cleared up if we'd had a chance to talk."

"Mark, don't you think the person who was responsible for Rhodes's death had to have planned it well in advance?" Jenny asked. "After all, if it was some kind of drug interaction, and some of these heart pills were planted for Rhodes to take, who knew when he would actually take them? Is that what happened, some of this Enalapril was planted among some of his regular medication?"

Mark looked at Jenny in admiration. "You'd make a good detective. That's exactly what we think must have happened. But so far we have no idea who could have done it. And of course, there's the matter of proving it, too."

I cleared my throat. "I've thought of something else. I've been wondering why this blue bottle looks familiar. This isn't an ordinary prescription bottle, like you'd get at a pharmacy. This is the kind of bottle veterinarians use for animals. I have one in the kitchen cabinet right now that has pills in it for Lucy's thyroid condition. I think vets use blue bottles so they can't be confused with medicine for humans."

We all pondered that piece of trivial information for a minute. I, for one, was clueless as to what that fact could mean, but I felt that somehow I had added an important piece to the puzzle. Nobody else seemed to share that opinion.

Mark looked at me again. "Ok, go over everything for me and please, don't leave anything out, even if you think it's not important."

I started my story with meeting Maria at the Trattoria to plan Mary Alice's retirement shower. For the first time I added Maria's comments about how badly Rhodes had treated the restaurant wait staff. I talked about Grace Retuccio, and Sheila, and how each of them had eaten dinner with Rhodes at the restaurant. I threw in the part about Grace calling Rhodes "Dick." Then I told Mark how Nancy and her real estate network had tracked down Grace, and our subsequent meeting with her. I finished with the meeting Mary Alice and I had with Sheila about organizing the memorial service for Rhodes. I spared no details. I probably went on for a good twenty minutes.

Mark took copious notes in a little wire-bound notebook.

I took a sip of my coffee and realized it was now stone cold. What the heck. I drank it anyway.

Jenny and Jim said nothing after I was through. Somehow, I didn't think they were both speechless with admiration for all I'd accomplished, but who knows?

Mark asked me again about my cell phone.

"I wish more than anything that I could remember where I lost it," I said helplessly. "But I use the damn thing so seldom that I never missed it."

I glared at Jim. "I told you I never wanted one in the first place. But you insisted." Then I realized how cruel that sounded. How could I scold My Beloved when he was suspected of murder?

"Jim, I'm sorry. I wasn't thinking."

My husband gave me a tight-lipped smile.

"Let's stick to the point here," Mark said. "I want you all to think very hard. Is there anyone who's been in this house since Davis Rhodes's death who could have planted that pill bottle in your medicine cabinet?"

"Nancy, Claire, and Mary Alice have all been here," I said. "And you and your partner, of course." Now there was an interesting thought. Wouldn't it be great if Mark's pain-in-the-ass partner planted the pill bottle?

Stupid, Carol. Move along.

"We did get a Fed Ex delivery a few days ago, but the deliveryman didn't come inside. Oh, and there were two college students selling magazine subscriptions, but they didn't come inside either. That's it."

Jenny opened her mouth to say something, and all of a sudden I realized I had left out one person on my list of recent visitors, Linda Burns.

But what possible motive could she have to implicate Jim? I shook my head slightly at Jenny, and she got the hint and didn't speak. I was not about to mention Linda, and have the police question her, until I figured out a few more things. And I knew just how I was going to start. As soon as Mark left, I was going to e-mail Mike and have him do an Internet search on her.

Jim said, "Mark, I feel better knowing you believe in me, but I'm going to call my lawyer now and bring him up to date on what's happened tonight." He stood up and shook Mark's hand. "It's good to have you in my corner. Thanks."

Mark asked Jenny for a plastic bag to put the pill bottle in. Then he said, "I hope you understand that I have to turn this bottle in to headquarters, even though I believe Mr. Andrews is innocent. It's evidence in a murder. I'll do what I can to convince the powers-that-be of my theory, but you may have to come down to the station tomorrow for questioning, Mr. Andrews. Also, I've done my best to keep your name out of any newspaper stories, but I'm not sure how much longer I can do that."

Jim nodded his head and left the room to call Larry.

Jenny walked Mark to the door and I could hear murmured talking.

I didn't even bother to try to overhear what they were talking about. I had more important things to do than eavesdrop on my daughter and her perhaps-boyfriend.

I e-mailed Mike in Florida and asked him to find out anything he could about Linda Burns. Then, I had another brainstorm, and asked him to find out about Dick Retuccio, too. And I told him it was an emergency.

I just prayed he'd check his e-mail tonight.

Jenny and I had a quick conference in the kitchen before we both went upstairs to bed.

"Mom, why didn't you tell Mark that Linda Burns was here yesterday, and went upstairs to wash her hands? Come to think of it, that's kind odd. We have a perfectly good powder room downstairs. But I definitely heard her go upstairs."

"I didn't think it was smart to mention Linda's name to Mark yet. It could just be a coincidence that Linda used that bathroom. And I'd never hear the end of it from her if the police questioned her because I suggested it. She'd probably sue me for slander. Or libel. I never could keep those two things straight. Anyway, I just e-mailed Mike and asked him to do an Internet search on Linda Burns. And while I was at it, I also asked him to check on Dick Retuccio."

"Good plan, Mom. I hope Mike responds quickly. In the meantime, what else can we do to help Dad?"

"Well," I said slowly, "it might be good to give Mike some more information about Linda. For instance, do you know where she got her degrees from?"

Jenny laughed. "That's easy. You go into her office and the whole wall is full of her diplomas. It's really weird, because most of the other professors don't display them, the way doctors and lawyers do. She got her undergraduate degree from Papermill University, just outside of Los Angeles. I'm not sure what year, though, but I can certainly check tomorrow when I go to school. And I think she got her graduate degrees from Athena University, which is a really top-notch school. It's somewhere in the state of Washington." She yawned.

I was immediately the doting mother. "Sweetie, you need your sleep. I'm just going to send Mike another quick e-mail with the new information you gave me about Linda, and then I'll be up, too." I gave her a quick squeeze. "We both know Dad's innocent. It won't be long before the police know that, too."

Now if I could just tell myself to stop worrying. Yeah. Right.

Chapter 26

On anniversaries, the wise husband always forgets the past, but never the present.

Thursday morning snuck up on me far too soon. I lay there in bed, feeling groggy. Probably because I had tossed and turned for most of the night. I was debating whether to roll over and give sleep another try when I heard the comforting sounds of Jenny moving around in the kitchen. I inhaled and smelled the heavenly aroma of perking coffee.

Being a caffeine junkie, there was no contest. I just made sure not to look at my haggard face in the mirror when I brushed my teeth. Too scary. And depressing.

It was wonderful to have Jenny home for a while, I thought for the hundredth time. I knew I'd better not get too used to it, though. She'd already made it clear that if she stayed, she'd want a place of her own. No more mooching off Mom and Dad.

I threw on a sweat suit and went downstairs to enjoy a leisurely breakfast with my daughter before she left for school. It was also a good opportunity to continue our brainstorming about Linda Burns.

Imagine my surprise when I walked into the kitchen and found My Beloved there instead of Jenny. Being someone who always jumped to the worst possible scenario, I panicked. I was sure something horrible had happened that I didn't know about. Yet.

"Easy, Carol," Jim said, correctly reading my mood for once. "Larry and I had a short conversation last night, and we decided it was important for us to get together this morning and come up with some sort of defense strategy." He saw the stricken look on my face and hastened to explain. "Not a defense strategy as in a court-defense strategy. Larry is looking for an angle to take me off the police's suspect list. Permanently. He agrees with Mark's theory that someone is trying to frame me. I'm meeting him for breakfast, and then I'll take a later train into New York. I've already called the office and said I'd be late today.

"You know," he added, "I feel so much better knowing that Mark believes in my innocence. Oh, by the way, Jenny has no car today, remember? She had to leave for school extra early because she was hitching a ride with another instructor. She said she'll call you later and let you know what she finds out. Am I supposed to know what that means?"

I was dying to tell Jim my theory about Linda Burns, but muzzled myself. I needed some proof, something that tied her and Davis Rhodes together, before I dared voice my idea to Jim. He'd tell me I was crazy. And, of course, he could be right. So I ignored his question and distracted him by holding out a coffee cup for him to fill.

"If I retire soon, I'll make the coffee for you every morning," Jim said. "Wouldn't you like that?"

Ouch. No, I wouldn't like that.

With all that had been going on, I'd lost track of the reason why this whole mess had started in the first place. Or, to put the proper spin on the situation, why I had started what turned into an unholy mess. I didn't want the traditional husband-wife roles mixed up. Hell, I didn't want my turf invaded. There, I'd finally admitted to myself that what Nancy had accused me of so many weeks ago was true. I knew I'd have to find a way to deal with these feelings when Jim did actually retire, but right now, I had other things to accomplish.

I managed a weak smile and said, "That's a great idea. It's something for me to look forward to when you retire. In the future."

Jim laughed. "It's not going to happen today, honey. I'm leaving now to meet Larry. I'll check in with you later today."

I walked him to the door, gave him a quick smooch, and sent him on his way. Then I settled back with the morning papers to enjoy my delicious cup of coffee. I had to give the guy credit—he did make better coffee than I did.

I ignored the little blue plastic bag with the *New York Times* inside, in favor of our local paper. I wasn't feeling smart enough yet to digest the *Times*.

Whoa! What was this story at the bottom of page one?

Break-In Reported at Local Retirement Center

The Re-tirement Survival Center, recent scene of the death of its founder, Davis Rhodes, was broken into sometime Wednesday night, a Westfield police spokesperson said. Entry was gained through a window at the rear of the structure. "It's too soon to determine whether anything was taken," said the spokesperson, who also refused to speculate about any connection between the break-in and the suspicious death of Davis Rhodes.

I couldn't believe it. I sat down at the kitchen table with the paper in my hand and read the story again. Who would have wanted to break into the Center? Why? And where were all the juicy details a story like this should have?

Even though the police spokesperson had refused to speculate about any connection between the break-in and Rhodes's death, it was clear to me that the two events had to be related. It didn't make sense any other way. I was sure the police had come to the same conclusion and didn't want to release that fact to the press.

But the murderer—I finally was able to use that word, if only to myself—the murderer had to have a powerful motive to return to the scene of the crime and risk getting caught. Unless...unless it was someone who had a perfectly reasonable explanation for being there, like Sheila. No, that wouldn't work. Sheila was there every day. If she wanted to look for something, she had all day, every day, to do it. There was no need for her to break in.

Then there was Grace. Hmm. That one needed some more thought. But I just couldn't picture her as a burglar.

I knew I needed to find Jim and Larry right away and tell them about the break-in, in case they hadn't seen the news article in today's paper. I started to punch in Jim's cell number. Then, my hand froze.

It suddenly occurred to me that this break-in was, pardon the pun, a lucky break for us. If everyone agreed that the same person who was responsible for Rhodes's death was also the person who broke into the Center, then My Beloved was 100 percent in the clear. Because while the break-in was happening, Jim and Jenny and I were sitting at our dining room table with one of the policemen on the case. Jim had an iron-clad alibi for this one.

I couldn't wait to share the good news with Jim. I tried his cell phone but he had his voice mail on. I decided not to leave any message, remembering the trouble a voice mail message had caused on my own cell phone. That was another loose end I needed to figure out. Where the hell did I lose my cell phone, and who'd found it and sent it to the police?

Priorities, Carol, priorities. First, find Jim. Then, think about the cell phone.

I quickly dialed Claire. We hadn't spoken since she and Larry had gotten back from the Berkshires.

"I have so much to tell you," I said, cutting her off before she could barrage me with questions. "But I have to reach Larry right away. I know he's with Jim. It's really important. Did you see this morning's paper?" I took a deep breath and then asked, "Am I babbling again? I'm sorry. But I have to reach them right now. Then I'll call you back and bring you up to date. Promise."

Claire laughed. "We've been friends since before puberty. I'm used to your babbling, although you don't do it nearly as much as Nancy does.

Anyway, Larry was going to meet Jim at the Marathon Diner, because it's close to the train station. He always keeps his cell on. Call him, and then, for God's sake, call me back and tell me what's going on." She rattled off the number and I'm embarrassed to admit that I didn't even say thank you to her. I just hung up and immediately dialed Larry.

As luck would have it, both Jim and Larry had just read the article about the break-in at the Center.

"I agree with you, Carol," Larry said. "The chances of the two incidents not being connected to each other are pretty slim. It's lucky for Jim that Mark Anderson was at your house last night, although finding that pill bottle in your medicine cabinet doesn't look so good." He put his hand over the receiver for a minute, then came back on the line. "Jim wants to talk to you for a second. Here he is."

"Jim, isn't this great news?" I asked excitedly.

"I suppose so," Jim said. "But it would be even better if I could figure out who's behind all this. I want you to call Sheila this morning, maybe even go over to the Center, to see if she needs some moral support, all right? I wouldn't be surprised if the break-in will put the timing of the memorial service back a week or two, but that's up to her. Or rather, it's up to the police. I have to admit, though, that things seem to be looking up for me. I just don't want to get over confident. I'll call you from the office. My train's coming. I have to go."

I hung up and practically danced around the kitchen. Finally, there was just a glimmer of light at the end of a very dark tunnel. I hadn't felt this upbeat in quite a while.

Ok. Calm down, Carol. The nightmare wasn't over yet. And there were several important things on my to-do list for today.

Let's see. Well, I absolutely had to figure out what had happened to my blasted cell phone. If I could figure out where I left it, or even the last time I'd used it, that could lead me to the person who'd anonymously mailed it to the police.

Jim was right. I had a dandy excuse to snoop around the Center today. Not that he put it that way, of course. In my official role as coordinator of Rhodes's memorial service, I had to find out whether the e-mail invitations should still go out today. And I could see if Sheila had any idea what, if anything, had been taken.

But I had to call Claire back first. Knowing her, she was probably sitting right by the phone and willing it to ring. Maybe I could even talk her into coming with me today. As long as Larry didn't find out, of course. As much as I liked him, he could be a stuffed shirt at times.

I smiled to myself. If only husbands knew how much we wives keep from them. For their own good. Of course.

Claire didn't take a whole lot of convincing to come with me to the Center. Once I'd brought her up to speed on everything she'd missed while she was in the Berkshires, she was raring to go. She also loved the idea of the retirement shower for Mary Alice.

"A shower is a great idea. We're going to have such fun putting it together. And Mary Alice will be so surprised. But how in the world did Linda Burns end up helping us organize it? I didn't know she was such a good friend of Mary Alice's. How can we get out of it? Just forget to call her?"

"I already thought of that, but I don't think that'll work," I replied. "Linda was pretty definite about wanting to help. She gave me some story about how she's a party planner extraordinaire. She bragged that Bruce's boss consults her all the time when his office is planning any kind of bash. If we don't call her, believe me, she'll call us." For the moment, I decided to keep quiet about my Linda Burns - Davis Rhodes theory. I'd share them if Mike turned up any solid evidence from his Internet sleuthing.

"I'm waiting for Maria Lesco to get back to me. She was going to come up with some possible themes and menus for the shower. Right now, I'm much more concerned with seeing what I can do to clear Jim's name once and for all. So, are you game? Do you want to come to the Re-tirement Survival Center with me and talk to Sheila Carney?"

"I have another suggestion. How about if we meet for an early lunch at Maria's Trattoria? Maybe she's come up with a few ideas for Mary Alice's party. And we have to eat, anyway. Then we can also figure out if we should just show up at the Center or call first. You know, it's possible that the police have the whole area cordoned off because of the break-in. Sheila may not even be there."

"I hate it when you make such good sense," I said. "Of course, you're absolutely right. I'll see you at the restaurant at eleven-thirty."

Perfect. That gave me at least two hours to shower and dress, and then force myself to concentrate on solving the riddle of my missing cell phone.

I put myself together as quickly as I could. No time for meditating in the shower today. Luckily, I found a pair of khaki pants and a white polo shirt that were freshly ironed. Probably too casual, but adding a blazer brought the outfit up a notch. I wasn't out to make a professional impression on anyone today.

I didn't even bother to blow my hair dry. When you have short hair like I do, you can sometimes get away with letting it dry naturally, and then add a little gel to it for some body and shape. I frowned at myself in the bathroom mirror. Were those new wrinkles on my face? Yuck. And no cover-up cream could mask the bags under my eyes. Double yuck.

My hair looked a little too spiky for my taste. And I couldn't get it to behave without taking another shower. My hairdresser, Deanna, would never approve. How could she run her hands through my hair and make it look great, and when I tried to do the exact same thing, it looked like I was suffering the after-effects of an electrical shock?

I shrugged. It was the best I could do and it would have to be good enough.

Looking at myself in the bathroom mirror and fooling with my hair started me on a chain of thoughts that seemed to come out of nowhere.

My hair. Deanna. The hair salon. Mary Alice in the chair. Nancy coming into the hair salon announcing to everyone that Davis Rhodes was going to be on *Wake Up New England* the following day. Linda Burns being rude to me and leaving. And my cell phone ringing. Jim was on the phone. I remembered that I didn't answer that call because at that moment, I didn't want to talk to Jim.

And then, I went into the changing room at the salon to listen to the voice mail message in private. I could visualize myself sitting on the hamper of used smocks, listening to Jim talk. Telling me how angry he was at Rhodes for making arrangements about *Wake Up New England* behind his back, and saying he was going over to the Center to have it out with him.

Was that the last time I used my cell phone? Had I lost it at the hair salon? Did it fall on the floor, or maybe fall inside the hamper? Had Deanna found it and...what? Sent it to the police anonymously, to get Jim into trouble? Why? That made no sense at all. Linda Burns was at the hair salon that day, I reminded myself. But she left before Jim called. As much as I liked Linda in the role of First Murderer, that part didn't fit either.

But what about Deanna? I thought she was my friend, but how well did I really know her? Yes, she'd been doing my hair, and the hair of my three best friends, for at least five years now. Yes, we exchanged gossip and harmless secrets and laughs every time I had an appointment. But, come to think about it, I was doing most of the confiding and Deanna was doing most of the listening.

Was it possible she was a blackmailer, or even a murderer? What did I know about her life before she came to Fairport? Oh, get a grip, Carol. You're getting way out of control here.

Well, there was only one way to find out. I had an hour to kill before I was supposed to meet Claire at the Trattoria. And my hair looked like hell.

I was going to get myself over to the hair salon and see if Deanna could fit me in for a quick styling. And maybe, if I was very clever, I could get her to answer some of those troubling questions, too.

"This is hysterical," I said when I walked into Crimpers. "Why didn't you tell me you were coming here first before you met me at Maria's?"

Claire sat in Deanna's styling chair, her hair covered with noxious smelling glop. "You should have figured it out yourself. You knew I'd been away for more than a week. And you were the one who commented the last time I saw you, that my white roots were showing."

"True. But I said it with love." I leaned down and gave Claire a quick peck on the cheek, being careful not to disturb her hair. "I've missed you. Welcome back." I studied myself in the mirror under the harsh fluorescent lights. "Boy, I thought I looked bad at home. Under these lights I look like I'm a hundred years old. I need a quick hair fix. Where's Deanna?"

I looked around the hair salon and saw two of the hair dryers were occupied. "Who else is here?" I asked Claire. "Anyone we know?"

"Deanna's in the back mixing up a color treatment for a client, the one who's under the dryer on the right," answered Claire. "I don't know who she is, but she's here for a glazing, whatever that means. And the other woman looks a little familiar, maybe from church, but I don't know her name. Unfortunately, that happens to me a lot these days. Forgetting people's names, I mean. I don't think either of them can hear you right now. Those dryers are loud. And they both look like they're absorbed in their magazines."

I headed to the back of the shop to find Deanna and throw myself on her mercy. I didn't need to explain my problem to her. She took one look at me and said, "What on earth have you done to your hair?" She surveyed me critically. "It's all spiked up like someone in a rock band."

"Deanna, I hate to ask you this," I pleaded, "but I have an important dinner tonight and I just can't get my hair to look right. No one else can make it look as good as you do. Do you have time to just give me a little tweaking? The dinner's with Jim's boss. I really need to look good." I wasn't proud of myself, but I was getting better and better at lying. My mother used to say that practice made perfect, though I doubt this is what she was encouraging me to practice.

"That's one of the things I'm best at, dealing with emergencies for favorite clients like you," said Deanna. "You sure know how to make me feel needed. I'll just spritz you down with some water and re-do you. Won't take a sec. But you may have to wait a little while. I'm sort of backed up." She gestured around to the other clients. "I hired a new shampoo girl last week, and she called in sick today. On top of everything else. I guess I have to think about hiring another stylist, too. I'm getting too popular."

"It's a good problem to have," I said, making myself comfortable in the chair next to Claire's. "I was meeting Claire for lunch today at Maria's Trattoria. Since we're both here now, we'll leave together. Works out perfectly."

I picked up the latest issue of *People* magazine. "Don't mind me. I'll just sit here and get caught up on all the gossip until you can fix me." I pretended to glance through the magazine while I tried to figure out how to introduce the subject of my cell phone.

"So, have things calmed down at all at your house?" Deanna asked me. "The last time you were here, you seemed pretty upset about your husband and Davis Rhodes, remember? And then, that night, Rhodes was found dead. I couldn't believe it when I read about it in the paper the next day. It must have been awful for you."

A timer rang, and Deanna motioned Claire to follow her to the sink, where the gunk would be rinsed off her hair. I followed them both, so we could continue the conversation.

"It was very scary," I admitted. "Poor Jim. He was so upset. That whole day and night are like a blur to me. As a matter of fact," I continued, "ever since that day, I haven't been able to find my cell phone anywhere. Could I have left it here? I'm lost without it, and I don't want to have to buy a new one."

"Why, Carol, didn't you get it back?" Deanna asked me. "I found a cell phone in the used smocks hamper in the changing room the morning after you were here. I figured it must be yours, because I remembered you'd gone in there to hear a private message from Jim. You must have accidentally dropped it inside the hamper and didn't realize it." She furrowed her brow. "But I'm sure I gave it to someone to return to you the next day. That's why I didn't call you. I thought it was all taken care of."

It took every ounce of self-control I could muster not to scream at Deanna, "Who did you give it to? Don't you realize how important this is?" Instead, I waited for Deanna to continue. My new interrogation style.

"You need to sit under the dryer for ten minutes, Claire," Deanna said. She checked her other two customers and, satisfied that they were doing fine, beckoned me to her styling chair. She started to mist my hair down so she could re-style it.

"It's kind of hard to remember that far back. So many people come in and out of here. And sometimes, the days just seem to run together. Of course, that day was different, because everyone who came in was talking about Rhodes's death."

Deanna stopped misting my hair for a minute and was deep in thought. "There were a few people in that morning who knew you. I think one of them was Maria Lesco, from the Trattoria."

This was news. "Did you give her my cell phone?"

Deanna shook her head. "No. I was going to, because she said it was no problem for her to drop it off at your house. But then..." She snapped her fingers. "I remember now. Linda Burns came in to buy some hair conditioner and overheard our conversation. She said that your daughter was teaching at the college now, and she was going to see her that afternoon.

"I gave Linda the phone to return to you."

Chapter 27

Q: What's another definition of retirement?
A: Twice as much husband on half as much money.

"You're jumping to conclusions again," Claire said. "Just because Deanna gave Linda your cell phone to return doesn't prove that Linda's the person who mailed it to the police."

It had turned out to be a beautiful day with low humidity—rare in Connecticut during the summer—and Claire and I had decided to leave our cars in the salon parking lot and walk the five blocks to Maria's Trattoria. Though lots of other people were out enjoying the beautiful day, nobody paid us the slightest attention. One of the perks of being card-carrying members of the AARP generation.

"You've been living with Larry too long," I said. "That business about being innocent until proven guilty doesn't apply here. I'm sure Linda's the one who sent the phone to the police. And she also has to be the person who planted those Enalapril pills in our medicine cabinet. The big question is, why? What does she have against Jim and me? What did she have against Davis Rhodes? Do you think I should call Mark Anderson and let him know what I've figured out?"

Claire stopped dead in her tracks and I nearly tripped over her. "So far, this is just a series of coincidences," she said.

I started to protest that these were more than coincidences but Claire continued unfazed. "As far as we both know for certain," she emphasized the last three words, then repeated them to be sure I understood her point, "know for certain, this is just a series of unfounded, unproven coincidences."

"But don't you think I'm right, Claire? You do, don't you?" I was practically jumping up and down on the sidewalk in front of her.

"Whether I think you're right or not isn't the issue. It's much too soon to call Mark. We have to find the link between Linda and Davis Rhodes. And then we have to figure out what Linda's motive for harming Rhodes could possibly be. That's the only way we're going to convince Mark."

I was encouraged, at least, that she'd used the words "we have to find the link." That meant she was willing to help.

"Here we are at Maria's," I said. "And I'm starving. I don't think we should talk about this inside. You never know who'll overhear conversations in a place like this." Like Maria, overhearing Davis Rhodes, for instance. "If either of us gets a bright idea, let's write it down so we don't forget it. My short term memory isn't what it used to be."

"I have a better idea," responded Claire, as she opened the door to the noisy restaurant. "It looks like we'll have to wait for a table. Why don't we get takeout and eat it on the way to the Center. Here." She handed me her phone. "Call Sheila now and see if she's there. Tell her you're on your way over. I'll take care of ordering our lunch."

Sheila was apparently screening calls and didn't recognize Claire's cell phone number. I started to leave a message on the voice mail, but as soon as I identified myself, she came on the line. Gone was her pseudo Jackie Kennedy persona. This time she sounded more like a real human being.

"Carol, thank God you called. Please tell me you haven't sent out the e-mail invitations to the memorial service yet."

She paused and I heard a hiccup. Had she been drinking? Or was she crying? Either way, she sounded desperate. I briefly wondered if she'd parlay this latest incident into another television appearance, then chided myself. For the time being, Sheila and I were allies. She had information that I needed. So I willed myself to be well behaved.

"Don't worry," I replied, trying to be soothing as well as professional. "When I heard about the break-in, I had the office put a hold on the invitations." Only a technical fib, because I knew Jim would have done that first thing when he got to the office, and we were a team, right? "Are the police still at the Center?"

I didn't give her a single second to answer. Just plunge ahead, Carol. "Do you need any help cleaning up? My friend Claire and I can both be there in less than half an hour."

Sheila seemed to welcome my offer of help. Just to be on the safe side, though, in case she changed her mind once we got there, we added extra desserts to our lunch order. No chocolate chip cookies, though.

"Dollar for your thoughts, Carol." Claire's voice broke into my food-induced reverie.

"A dollar?" I asked. "What happened to a penny?"

"Inflation," Claire responded. "Everything's going up. So, what's the drill when we get to the Re-tirement Survival Center? We're almost there."

"I don't worry about you," I said, wiping my hands with a napkin. "You weren't a psychology major for nothing. You're always good at feeling people out and making them open up to you. Besides, Sheila's a real talker. I don't think we'll have any trouble getting information out of her."

"Well, I hope you're right because we're here." Claire eased her car into the Center parking lot and shut off the motor. "You go first. It's more natural that way. I'm just a friend who happened to have lunch with you, ok?"

Claire slammed the car door shut and looked around. "I don't know what I was expecting, but this sure isn't it. Looks like a fancy home, not an office."

"Wait till you see the inside," I said. "The living room is to die for."

I rang the bell and Grace Retuccio opened the door.

She peered out at me and said, "Do I know you?"

I stood there like a complete idiot for about half a second, then realized I had to say something or she'd shut the door in my face.

"Grace, hi," I said. Brilliant, Carol. Keep going.

I stuck out my hand. "I'm Carol Andrews. We met a few days ago when Nancy Green from the real estate office dropped off some flowers to you."

Ignoring her lack of response, I peered around her into the Center's hallway. "Is Sheila here? She's expecting me. I'm helping her organize the memorial service for Davis Rhodes. I mean, Dick Retuccio. I brought my friend Claire McGee along with me."

I hoped I wasn't babbling again. I also hoped, fervently, that Grace had not put two and two together and realized the coincidence of Nancy's and my visit to her home and the subsequent arrival of the police to question her.

I heard Sheila call out from inside, "Carol, is that you? I'm in the office. Close the door and come on back. You're letting hot air in."

I could hear Claire snort behind me, and I knew she was thinking that I was the hot air. Fortunately, she didn't say it out loud.

We followed Grace down the hallway toward the back part of the building. So far, it didn't look like anything had been disturbed. But when we reached the office, which was right off the kitchen, it looked like a bomb had hit it. There were papers, files, and books strewn all over the place.

Sheila, wearing a shocking pink sweat suit, was sitting on the floor in the middle of the chaos. She waved her arm around the room. "Isn't this awful? What a mess. It'll take days to get it all straightened out. And the police expect me to tell them right away if anything is missing. How the hell am I supposed to know?"

She rose to her feet in one fluid movement. I tried hard not to hate her, but I knew I would have had to roll over onto my hands and knees in order to get up from that position. And I certainly could never do it gracefully.

Sheila looked quizzically at Claire, and I hurried to introduce them. "I'm glad you brought extra help, Carol." She sighed dramatically. "I wish I could figure out what the burglar was looking for."

Claire, always Ms. Perfect Manners, expressed her condolences about Rhodes's death. "I never met him," she said, "but Jim and Carol spoke so glowingly about him. It sounds like he was a wonderful man. His death is such a tragedy, and now this." She gestured around the office, indicating the shambles all around us.

"He was quite a guy, all right," said Grace. "I never realized until very recently what a busy guy he really was." She turned to me. "I'll bet you didn't expect me to open the door." I guess she remembered me after all.

I wasn't sure how to respond. I couldn't understand how Sheila would allow Grace inside the Center, especially since she blamed Grace for keeping her and Rhodes apart. But since it was totally out of character for me to remain silent for long, I heard myself saying, "You're right, I was very surprised. Under the circumstances. After what you said to Nancy and me the other day." Boy, this was awkward.

"Sheila called this morning and asked me to come over," Grace said. "To say I was flabbergasted would be a major understatement. I almost hung up."

"You did hang up the first time I called, remember?" Sheila interjected. "I called you back again. I can be very persistent when I want to be."

"I finally decided we should clear the air between us, Sheila," Grace said. "I know you and Dick had a relationship. Of course, he was 'Dave' to you. For the sake of simplification, I suppose we should call him 'Dave.' "

Grace hesitated. "I came over today because I want to find out who's responsible for his death. I want to see that person punished for it. As I see it, the best way for that to happen is for you and me to work together. Unless you did it, of course."

Ignoring Sheila's expression of fury, Grace went on, "I also want to see the Re-tirement Survival Center succeed. I have a financial stake in it, too, in case you didn't know that."

Sheila's eyes opened wide. Clearly, this was news to her.

Claire and I said nothing. We just listened.

Sheila slowly nodded her head in agreement, then realized Claire and I were hanging on every word. "I hope you understand that the memorial service will have to be placed on hold until the police give us the go-ahead, Carol. The first thing I have to do is get this place cleaned up."

"The memorial service can easily be postponed." Especially since I'd done absolutely nothing about it so far. I looked around the office. "This looks like my son Mike's room when he was in high school," I said, with a feeble attempt at humor. "If there's one thing I'm really good at, it's making order out of chaos. Years of practice with the kids. Just tell us where you want us to start, and Claire and I will get to work."

"Why don't you two start shelving the books, and Grace and I can sort through the papers?" Sheila suggested.

"At least the certificates on the walls weren't touched," said Claire, bending down to pick up a few text books. "Otherwise, we'd have to sweep up broken glass before we could do anything else."

"Umm," I responded. I was concentrating on trying to read the diplomas on the wall behind the desk without my glasses. They were an impressive group, and I said so to Claire.

Grace overheard us and started to laugh. "They're not real diplomas, Carol," she said.

I looked at her stupidly. "Not real? You mean Dave never went to any of these schools?"

"They're not exactly phony, either," Grace went on. "They're 'enhanced.' Do you know what I mean by that?"

"I haven't a clue."

Sheila jumped in to explain. "Dave did go to some of these schools. Of course, his name wasn't Davis Rhodes then, so he had to change the name on the diplomas. And while he was at it, he also changed the degrees he earned. He never graduated 'magna cum laude,' and he never was valedictorian of his class. He never got a Ph.D. from Harvard either. It's amazing what you can do with a computer and a good laser printer these days."

To me, there was a very fine line between "enhanced" and phony. Wait until I told Jim about this.

"So where did he get his undergraduate degree from, Sheila?" Claire asked.

"Dave used to kid about the name of that college. Called it P. U. But that wasn't the real name, of course. It was some place in California, right Grace?"

Grace started to answer, but before she could, Claire pulled a yearbook out of the pile of books on the floor. "Is this his? From Papermill University? Class of 1973?" She rummaged around on the floor. "There are some other yearbooks here from the same college, 1972 and 1975."

"That's odd," said Grace. "He graduated in 1974. If he kept all the other yearbooks, why wouldn't he keep the one from his own class?"

"Maybe he did," I said slowly. There was an idea percolating in my mind that was so outrageous I was hesitant to voice it.

I remembered hearing about Papermill University last night from Jenny. Supposedly, it was Linda Burns's alma mater too.

Another coincidence? I didn't think so.

"I bet Davis kept his own class yearbook on a bookshelf with all the others," I said slowly. "That's what the burglar broke in to steal."

Sheila looked at me like I was crazy. "Come on. Why would anyone want an old college yearbook? Because his picture was terrible?"

I realized I shouldn't say any more. Not to Sheila and Grace. Claire and I could hash this over—and over—on the way home.

"Don't tell me this is a coincidence, too," I said as soon as Claire and I were safely back in her car. "I knew there had to be a connection between Linda Burns and Davis Rhodes, and I finally found it. They went to college together."

"Don't go off half-cocked about this," Claire replied, immediately throwing cold water on my carefully thought-out theory. "You think Linda went to the same college. You're guessing they were in the same class and graduated at the same time. You're supposing that's the link between them. But once again, there's no proof. And even if there were proof, what's Linda's motive for getting rid of Rhodes? Since when is being college classmates a motive for murder?"

I sucked in my breath and considered what Claire was saying. She did make some good points. But I had a strong hunch that I was right. This was the link between Linda Burns and Davis Rhodes I'd been looking for, and once I had verified their class and graduation dates, I was going to keep right on digging until I proved that Linda had a motive to eliminate Rhodes. And then I'd call Mark Anderson and tell him what I'd discovered. Boy, would he be impressed.

But Claire wasn't finished with me quite yet. "Something else occurred to me about Linda Burns." She glanced sideways at me to be sure she had my attention. "This is going to sound harsh, and I don't mean to hurt your feelings, but I wonder how objective you're being about her. What I mean is, how would you react if you suspected me, or Nancy, or Mary Alice of causing Rhodes's death and framing Jim, instead of Linda? Would you go to these lengths to get evidence on any of us?"

"That's a ridiculous thing to say," I responded heatedly. "You're my dearest friends, and I love you all. I'd never believe that any of you would do those awful things. That's just crazy."

"My point exactly. We're your friends. Linda isn't. Face it, you've never liked her. Ok, I admit that none of us have ever liked her. But in all fairness, I'm just pointing out that you're being a lot quicker to think the worst about Linda than you would be if you suspected any of us. You're not being objective about her at all.

"Be very careful, Carol. In case you're wrong."

I had no smart aleck response for Claire. She was accusing me of unfairly suspecting Linda, and of doing everything I could to find evidence against her.

Some friend.

I was so hurt at what she'd said to me that I didn't respond at all. I just clamped my lips together tightly; we rode the rest of the way back in complete silence.

Chapter 28

It's sad, but true, that when some people decide to retire, nobody knows the difference.

When Claire dropped me off, she reached over and gave my hand a little pat. Wisely, she said nothing more. She could tell I was upset and would have to work through her criticisms on my own. She also knew that being honest with each other is one of the most valuable things about a friendship like ours, and whatever happened, we would still be close. Even if I thought her comments were completely out of line and unfair.

I wouldn't say I slammed Claire's car door when I got out. But I didn't make any effort to be gentle closing it, either. Ok, call me childish.

When I finally got into the blessed coolness of my air-conditioned house, Lucy and Ethel raced up to greet me, vying with each other as to which would be the first to jump up and give me those wonderful sloppy doggy kisses. That's the great thing about dogs. They're totally non-judgmental. Who could resist a relationship like that, so full of unconditional love?

While the dogs went for a quick run around the yard, I stewed over Claire's accusation. One of the personality traits I hate the most about myself is that I absolutely, positively, cannot take criticism of any kind. I brood about it, worry about it, and as a result I become paralyzed with inactivity and filled with self-pity and self-doubt. Pretty pathetic, right? I could feel myself starting down that road, and I decided that I was not going to allow myself to go there.

So, when my favorite two canine therapists came back into the house, I bribed them with a doggy treat and sat them both down in front of me. "Listen, girls, you'll never believe what our friend Claire said to me this afternoon." I described the entire scenario, trying hard to be objective about it so as not to prejudice their opinion. I ended with, "What do you think, kids? Am I trying to get incriminating information about Linda Burns just because I don't like her?"

The two dogs looked at me with sorrowful eyes, and clearly communicated their feelings to me. "How can anyone accuse you of something that is so completely untrue? You are the most unbiased, loving human we know. You just keep right on snooping and find out everything you can about Linda Burns. We're sure you're on the right track. Claire, as much as we love her, is way off base here."

Swear to God, that's what they told me.

I felt a little better, but not my usual energetic self. I was still brooding over Claire's accusation when the dogs began barking, announcing the arrival of the mailman.

Right on the top of the pile of bills and junk mail was a reminder from our vet, Dr. Karen Ross.

Dear Lucy and Ethel: We know you don't like to get shots, but your rabies and distemper boosters are due this month. Please have your human call our office for an appointment. And don't worry! The shots won't hurt a bit!

Your Friend, Dr. Karen

"All right, I'm going to call the vet's office right now and make the appointment for your shots," I informed the dogs. "And don't start sulking the way you always do when you hear the word 'vet.'" True to form, the dogs had begun backing away from me and heading for the safety of the family room.

"You can run but you can't hide," I told them both. "And just for that, I won't tell you in advance when your appointment is. It'll be a complete surprise."

Fortunately, when I called, I wasn't put on hold, for once. And my favorite receptionist, Patty, answered the phone. In no time at all, once she determined there was no canine emergency—we've had our share of those over the years—she cheerfully scheduled the dogs' shots for the following Tuesday morning. Then she asked, "Does Lucy need any more pills for her thyroid, Mrs. Andrews, or do you have enough for now?"

While I assured her that we had plenty of pills for Lucy, I suddenly remembered that little blue bottle of Enalapril that Mark Anderson had found tucked away in our medicine cabinet. Who better to ask about that than Patty? And who better to tell me if Linda Burns had taken her critically ill dog to Dr. Karen for treatment?

"Patty, just one more question before I go." I laughed a little. "Have you ever heard of Enalapril?"

"Of course," she replied. "It's prescribed for high blood pressure. We use it often to treat dogs with heart problems. Why?"

I pretended I didn't hear her ask me why I wanted to know about Enalpril and plunged ahead.

"I was kidding when I said I had only one more question, Patty. I really have a few more. If you have the time. Do all vets fill prescriptions in little blue bottles these days? I know Lucy's thyroid medicine is in a blue bottle, and I wondered if that was common practice among vets?"

"You're piquing my curiosity, Mrs. Andrews. Yes, we do fill all our prescriptions in blue bottles. Why do you want to know?"

All of a sudden, I could hear that pesky beep on my phone line, indicating another caller was trying to get through. I couldn't take the chance that Patty might hang up, so I ignored it.

"My daughter Jenny is doing a research paper on drugs," I lied, "and she asked me to find out for her.

"I'm wondering how far back you keep your client records," I continued. I could hear other phone lines ringing in the background. I felt guilty about taking up so much of Patty's time, but I wasn't giving up now.

"We keep our client records in a database that goes back five years," she answered. "When an animal dies, their records go into an inactive file, but we still keep them for five years. Personally, I think it's ridiculous to keep them that long, but that's the way Karen wants it. And she's the boss."

"Patty, you've been so helpful. I can't thank you enough," I gushed. "You know, all my friends use your office for their pets. I always recommend you. Whether you realize it or not, Claire McGee, Nancy Green, Mary Alice Brennan, Linda Burns, all of them came to you on my say-so. I'm your number one salesperson."

I held my breath. Would she say something about Linda? Or was I wrong? Maybe Linda had used a completely different vet three years ago when her dog was so sick.

Patty took the bait. "That was such a sad thing. We try hard not to get involved personally with our clients, but in this case, it was just heartbreaking." She paused, just long enough for me to know that she was dying to tell me more if I asked her to.

"Do you mean Linda Burns's dog?" I inquired as innocently as I could. "I know she died very young, and I heard Linda did everything possible to save her."

"She did," confirmed Patty. "We all did. But Muffin's heart just gave out, poor little thing. Even with the special diet and the drugs she was on." She paused. "It's funny you should be asking about Enalapril, Mrs. Andrews. I remember that's one of the drugs Muffin was taking."

So, I'd found out that Linda Burns had access to the drug Enalapril. I speculated that when her dog died, it was very possible that there were unused pills left over, and Linda didn't throw them away. Instead, she probably put the bottle away and forgot about it. Until recently. When she found another use for those pills, eliminating Davis Rhodes. Linda could have easily put the bottle in our medicine cabinet when she went upstairs to wash her hands a few nights ago. This was pure conjecture on my part, but it made sense. Sounded like a strong case against Linda to me.

No one in our family, canine or human, had ever been prescribed that drug. That could be proved by physician and veterinary records. One point for our side.

I sighed. I hated to admit it, but Claire was right. My so-called "case" against Linda was based completely on guesses and suppositions, with a few stray facts thrown in just for the heck of it. Circumstantial evidence.

Before anyone would take me seriously, I had to confirm the possible link, that they were college classmates. Did I also need to prove that Linda had seen Rhodes when he moved into the area? And discover a motive for her eliminating Rhodes? No, this last part was definitely a job for the police. After all, I had to leave something for them to do.

Means, motive, opportunity. The big three in every mystery story I'd ever read.

I thought back to my visit to the Re-tirement Survival Center earlier this afternoon. The new alliance between Sheila and Grace was certainly peculiar. And surprising. Had they suddenly banded together to cover up for each other? Or had they been working together all along? Could Grace have killed Rhodes and Sheila was blackmailing her? Or the other way around? Both of them appeared to have motives. Each of them had admitted arguing with Rhodes before he died. And they certainly had opportunity.

I couldn't ignore the fact that both of them would have intimate knowledge of any medication Rhodes was already taking. With easy access to the Internet, anyone could figure out what drug could cause a fatal interaction with current medication. I wasn't sure about their access to Enalapril, but it was not impossible.

My head was starting to hurt.

Ok, here was another theory, even more far-fetched than the others. What if Linda, Grace, and Sheila were all in this together? Wasn't there an Agatha Christie mystery about something like that, where more than one person was the murderer? Oh, Carol, you are really losing it now. Talk about a vivid imagination.

I had pretty convincing proof (to me, anyway) that Linda had anonymously given the police my cell phone, had access to the drug that killed Rhodes, and planted the drug in my medicine cabinet. Why would she go to all that trouble if she weren't involved in Rhodes's death?

Means, motive and opportunity.

I wondered if I should just quit investigating right now. Mark Anderson was convinced that Jim was being set up by someone. Hopefully, he'd managed to convince the powers-that-be at police headquarters of the same thing. And that should be the end of it, right? My family would be safe, and we could resume our normal lives again. It wasn't up to me to solve the case. That was a job for the police.

Then I remembered someone had tried to call me while I was talking to the vet's office. It was Jenny.

"Mom," she whispered on the voice mail, "the degree I saw isn't on her office wall any more. But I know I saw it there just a few days ago. I can't figure out why that one is missing when all the other diplomas and awards are still there. And it looks like she's starting to do some major redecorating. Gotta go."

I sat down on the sofa in the office and thought about Jenny's message. Why was Linda redecorating her office? Had she been officially appointed chair of the history department and was celebrating by sprucing up her digs at the college?

What about the disappearing diploma? In light of what I'd learned today about Davis Rhodes's "enhanced" degrees, was it possible that Linda's degrees were "enhanced" too? Was she afraid that Rhodes would recognize her and know that she wasn't part of the 1974 Papermill graduating class? Maybe he did, and he was blackmailing her. I was no expert on academic protocol, but I was willing to bet that if Fairport College found out that her degree was a phony, it would be grounds for immediate dismissal.

Yes, that was a pretty impressive motive, all right. Even Claire would have to agree with that. I was being objective. Could I help it if the facts kept pointing more and more toward Linda?

I had to ask Mike to check on Papermill University's class of 1974 right away, to determine once and for all if Linda Burns had been a member of that class.

"Time to fire up the computer," I told the dogs. "I think we're on a roll."

Lucy and Ethel obligingly rolled over for a tummy pat.

"No, not that kind of a roll." I laughed at them even though I had to step over their prone bodies to get to the computer.

Scanning my e-mail, I saw one from Mike.

Rhodes/Retuccio, 74- Burns, 0.

Hey Cosmo Girl!

It's your faithful research assistant reporting from sunny South Beach. Was able to find some things about Dick Retuccio/a.k.a.Davis Rhodes. His official bio on the Center's web site doesn't match what I found out from my other research. ????? I can send you everything I found out as an attachment, if you want details. But briefly, he's originally from La La land—I mean, Los Angeles—and got his undergraduate degree from Papermill University, which is in one of the many L.A. suburbs. Graduated in 1974 with degree in history. Then went on to grad school at a variety of places, and finally got Master's and Ph.D. degree through Las Vegas U. in Lifestyle Management. Whatever that means. His career really took off in the late '80s, and you know the rest about his Re-tirement theory. Married Grace Baker in 1983. No children. Struck a blank wall about Linda Burns until 1979, when she came to Fairport and started teaching at the college. Couldn't get any early bio or educational info about her at all. Tried all my usual websites and came up empty. Do you have any specific leads on her you want me to check out?? How's Dad??????? Is he wearing prison stripes yet? Ha, ha!

So far, what Mike had, or rather hadn't, found out about Linda, confirmed my suspicions even more. I hoped that Papermill University's alumni records were available on the college website. I didn't know if that was common practice these days, but with all the websites I've seen popping up all over the Internet advertising how to find lost classmates, I figured maybe Papermill provided that service gratis for graduates.

I hoped Mike was online now, and instant messaged him. To my delight, he responded right away that he would try to get that information and to stay tuned. Ah, the age of instant communication!

Within fifteen minutes, I had another message from Mike.

Burns, Zip. The Plot Thickens?
Papermill U. doesn't have a very friendly website and doesn't offer alumni information online. I took a chance and called the college alumni office on my cell phone. What the heck. Told the woman who answered that I was Dick Retuccio, a member of the class of 1974, and was trying to track down a fellow classmate. I was lucky that news of his death hadn't reached the West Coast yet, right? Anyway, she was very helpful, and checked the alumni records for me. She found no record of Linda Burns graduating from there in 1974, or in any other year, for that matter. She assured me the college keeps very accurate alumni records because of fundraising requests. Fortunately, before she could get into any more specific questions with me, she had to take another call and put me on hold, so I hung up. Now what?

Good question. I had no idea. But I didn't want to leave Mike hanging, so I quickly e-mailed him back.

Now What Indeed?
Thanks for the detective work, sweetie. I think you've uncovered something very important. By not uncovering anything, if you see what I mean. Jenny was positive that Linda went to Papermill U and had a degree from there hanging on her

office wall. Your dear sister, also working as a private eye for dear old Mom and Dad, has just reported in that the diploma is no longer in Linda's office. Will be back in touch as soon as I can. Dad is doing better. Things are looking a little brighter here in the Nutmeg State. More details later. Love you. Mom

I logged off the computer and did a quick time check. Almost 5:30 p.m. Jim and Jenny would probably both be home soon. And ravenous, especially Jim. I was still pretty full from my lunch at Maria's Trattoria. But I had to put something on the table for dinner. Time to put my detecting on temporary hold. And not a minute too soon. My head was swimming with everything I'd found out today.

I checked the refrigerator and, as I suspected, there were no leftovers. Alas. But then, that was no surprise, because I hadn't cooked a full meal in days. No cooking, no leftovers.

Preparing a home-cooked meal was not an option. Not enough time, even if I had the inclination, which, after the day I'd had, I quite honestly did not.

Quickly, I dialed Seafood Sandy's, a local restaurant that specializes in the most delicious seafood on this part of the Connecticut shoreline. Plus, they delivered. At least, for me, they did. Sandy guaranteed me that my order would be at my door in thirty minutes. Or it would be free. Can't argue with service like that.

Then, just so my family wouldn't think my snooping had completely interfered with my ability to cook, I decided to whip up a batch of ice cream bread. That's right, bread. This is the simplest recipe known to man, and when Jenny and Mike were little, they used to love to help me make it.

Hmm. Come to think of it, Mark Anderson used to love my ice cream bread, too.

And just like that, because I'm impulsive to a fault, I made a snap decision. I wanted to brainstorm with Mark about all I'd found out. Right now. So I decided to call Mark and invite him over for supper.

I ignored the warning voice in my head that told me this wasn't a good idea, and punched in Mark's number. His outgoing message indicated he was working the 10 a.m.-6 p.m. shift today. I left him a cheery invitation. "Hi, Mark. It's Carol Andrews. I know this is very short notice, but I'm calling to invite you for supper tonight if you're free. It's nothing fancy. I'm making ice cream bread for dessert, and I suddenly remembered how much you used to love that when you were a kid. Hope to see you any time after six tonight. You don't have to bother calling me back, unless you can't make it. Hope to see you later."

There. How could anyone refuse an invitation like that?

Chapter 29

Too many folks want to retire before they actually start working.

Mark showed up on my doorstep at 6:30 sharp. The dogs greeted him suspiciously, sniffed him thoroughly, then curled up over the air conditioner vent to take a nap.

Mark looked as nervous as I felt. "Mrs. Andrews, you may not want me to stay when you hear what I have to tell you. Finding that pill bottle was pretty conclusive as far as my boss was concerned. There's a warrant being issued for Mr. Andrews on a charge of murder. He'll probably be arrested tomorrow morning. I'm sorry, but there's nothing I can do."

Oh, God. Mark had completely blindsided me. Suddenly, my attempts at sleuthing appeared pretty pathetic. And those ridiculous fantasies I'd had about rushing in and saving the day were just that—ridiculous.

I took a few deep breaths to calm myself. "I know you've done your best," I said, all the while thinking that he could have tried a lot harder to help Jim. "I still want you to stay for dinner. There are a few things I've discovered that I want to share with you. Maybe they'll convince you to change your mind." They probably wouldn't. Still, I had to try, didn't I?

"Can we keep this warrant business just between us for now?" I pleaded. "At least until you hear what I have to say?"

Jenny arrived home next, interrupting our conversation. She must have recognized Mark's car in our driveway, because she came into the kitchen all smiles. Fortunately, he'd come in his own car this time and not a police cruiser. Our neighbors had enough to talk about as it is.

"Hi, Mark. Mom, don't tell me you're making ice cream bread? We haven't had that since my fourteenth birthday party!"

Fortunately, she was so happy Mark was here that she didn't notice how terrible I looked. Ignoring her teasing, I gave her cutlery with orders to set the kitchen table. No eating in the dining room tonight.

Jenny and Mark put out the place mats, plates and silver. It was quite a domestic scene. And the condemned man will eat a hearty meal?

By the time My Beloved came home, the takeout meal had arrived and was ready to serve. And the ice cream bread was cooling on a rack beside the stove.

"Carol, there's a strange car..." Jim stopped as he realized that Mark was sitting at the kitchen table next to Jenny. For just a second, he appeared panicked, then recovered himself. He looked at me and telegraphed silently, "What's he doing here?"

I gave Jim a quick peck on the cheek. "Do you want to sit down right away? Or go up and change first? I invited Mark to supper on the spur of the moment and he was able to come. Isn't that nice?" I telegraphed back to Jim, "Just play along." I hoped he got the message, but with men you never know.

"Is that food from Seafood Sandy's I smell?" Jim asked as he pulled out a kitchen chair. "You know me, I'm salivating already. I just want to sit down and eat. Nice to see you here, Mark."

Ha. If only he knew.

"Mom made ice cream bread for dessert, Dad," Jenny added. "Chocolate. Your favorite."

We all busied ourselves piling our plates high with the crispy fish and chips.

I tried to eat, but everything seemed to stick in my throat. I wondered briefly what kind of food Jim would get in jail. Then I mentally slapped myself.

Maybe that mental slap lodged something loose in my brain, because I suddenly realized that I had overlooked something very important about Linda Burns. How stupid I was. When she was at Papermill University, she wasn't married, so her last name wasn't Burns. Oh, God, no wonder Mike hadn't been able to confirm she'd graduated from there. My whole "case" was about to blow up in my face because I had given him the wrong name to check.

I had to get Mike on the phone right away. So I started to cough. I mean, I really coughed, like I was choking on a piece of fish. I grabbed my throat dramatically and jumped up. "Bathroom," I whispered. "Not feeling too well."

I snatched the cordless phone on my way through the family room, headed for the downstairs bathroom and locked myself in. I turned the water on, just for effect, and kept on coughing.

Jim banged on the door. "Honey. Are you all right?"

"Just give me a little time alone. I feel dizzy from all this coughing. I'll be ok in a few minutes. I'm drinking some water."

I sighed with relief as I heard Jim walk away from the bathroom door. Now, if I could just remember Linda's "maiden name," an archaic term if I ever heard one. Nobody had "maiden names" any more. Desperately, I dialed Nancy, Claire and Mary Alice, but all I got were their voice mails. I don't curse a lot, but allowed myself to whisper "shit" ever so softly. That made me feel a little better. So I said it again.

I massaged my forehead. Sometimes that helped me focus. I realized I was hyperventilating. I also realized I was screwed. And so was Jim. Except he didn't know it yet.

I couldn't stay in the bathroom forever. Unfortunately. I had no choice but to go back and give Mark my skimpy information. And the quicker the better. Sort of like taking a band aid off a cut. Just get it over with, Carol. And, for God's sake, don't show everyone how scared you are.

Both dogs raced up to greet me when I came back into the kitchen. The three humans jumped up too, but I waved everybody away. "I'm really fine now," I fibbed. I stared down at my unappetizing fish dinner, which had congealed into a cold greasy mess on my plate.

Stop stalling, I told myself. All I needed to do was to give Mark enough information to convince him that arresting Jim tomorrow morning would be a big mistake. There were other suspects for the police to investigate.

I topped off Mark's iced tea glass, then plunged right in with my story.

"You know that I've talked to some people about the Davis Rhodes case," I said, looking directly at him. "I know you didn't want me to, but I've found some more information the police may not have. For instance, did you know that Grace Retuccio and Sheila Carney have become allies? Are they both still on your suspect list?" I stopped and waited to see what Mark's response would be. It was predictable.

"Mrs. Andrews, you know I can't answer that. It's part of our ongoing investigation." Hmm. So, even though the police were planning on arresting Jim tomorrow morning, the investigation was still "ongoing." Maybe there was hope after all.

I rapidly switched gears.

"I respect that you need to keep the official investigation confidential. But Jenny and I believe we have a pretty good idea who's been giving you false information about Jim. And as of this afternoon, I may even know why."

I looked at Jenny and she nodded her head. "We didn't say anything last night, because the person we suspect is someone we know, and we didn't want to accuse her until we had concrete information. But from what we've been able to piece together today, there's definitely something fishy going on with her."

I took a deep breath. It was now or never. Oh, well, if I were wrong, we could always sell our house and go into the Witness Protection Program.

"The person we suspect is Linda Burns."

Jim, who until now had been very quiet, sat up very straight in his chair and let me have it with both barrels. "Are you crazy? We've known Linda and Bruce Burns for years. Bruce has been commuting with me every day since I started working in New York. What the hell are you talking about?"

I knew I had to be very organized about how I presented my case. No emotion. Just the facts.

"Fact Number One. Davis Rhodes, then known as Dick Retuccio, graduated from Papermill University in California in 1974. That's been confirmed by the university. Last night, as you know, his office was broken into. The only thing that Sheila Carney can determine was taken is his 1974 college yearbook."

"What the hell does that have to do with anything?" Trust My Beloved to be argumentative at a time like this.

I held up my hands. "Just wait. Please. Fact Number Two. Jenny recently saw a diploma from Papermill University on Linda Burns's office wall at the college. The diploma said that Linda was also a member of the class of 1974. That's the same graduating class as Davis Rhodes. Isn't that a remarkable coincidence?

"And what's more," I paused dramatically, "Jenny says that as of this afternoon, that diploma is no longer in Linda's office, right Jenny?" I looked at my daughter and she nodded her head again.

So far, Mark had said nothing. But at least he appeared to be listening.

"I decided that was a little fishy, so I asked our son, Mike…"

"Carol, did you get everyone we know involved in this?" Jim's sarcasm usually stopped me cold, but not this time.

I sent him The Look. Jim knew better than to try and interrupt. He contented himself with raising his eyes heavenward.

"I asked our son, Mike," I repeated with great deliberation, "to do some Internet research on Linda Burns's educational background. He's found out there's no record of anyone with that name graduating from Papermill University, in 1974 or any other year. She could have been a student there, but didn't finish." I paused. Time to offhandedly throw in the "maiden name" problem. I decided to stretch the truth, just a little. "Mike's also checking out graduate records under Linda's maiden name." Well, he would, as soon as I gave it to him. "So far, he hasn't come up with anything. But he's going to keep on digging."

"You're being completely ridiculous. What are you talking about, checking under Linda's maiden name?" Jim demanded.

"Hey, I'm trying to keep you out of jail. What do you mean, I'm being ridiculous?"

"Carol, your memory is going. Not that I blame you, with all this stress. You know as well as I do that Linda Burns never changed her last name when she married Bruce. His last name was Linden, but she didn't like it. She convinced him to legally change his name to hers. When you found out about that a few years ago, you carried on about it for weeks."

I stared at Jim like the idiot I was. He was absolutely right. And, praise the Lord, that meant that I was, too. I had a case against Linda after all.

Then Mark said, "Mrs. Andrews, with all due respect, who cares? What does this have to do with Davis Rhodes's death?"

Jenny responded for me. "Mark, if Linda Burns had a phony diploma on her office wall, that amounts to faking her academic credentials. I heard the other day that Linda's being named chairman of the college history department. That's very prestigious. If the college administration suspected she'd faked her credentials, she not only wouldn't get promoted, she'd lose her job, tenure or not."

I jumped right in to reinforce Jenny. "For all we know, Rhodes did recognize her from his college days and was blackmailing her. Don't you see, Linda couldn't take the chance that Rhodes would publicly identify her as a fraud. Well," I glared at Jim, who was shaking his head in disbelief, "it's possible. She had to eliminate him. And I think she broke into the Re-tirement Survival Center last night and stole that college yearbook. Because her picture wasn't in it as a member of that graduating class."

"This is pretty lame, Mrs. Andrews. But just for the sake of continuing this fascinating discussion, how did she set up Mr. Andrews?" I ignored Mark's sarcasm. At least he was still listening.

"I finally figured out this morning that I'd lost my cell phone at Crimpers, the hair salon I go to," I answered excitedly. "Deanna, my hair stylist, remembers that she asked Linda Burns to return the phone to me. Instead of doing that, Linda must have mailed it to the police anonymously to incriminate Jim with that voice mail message."

I looked triumphant at my brilliant reasoning.

"What about planting the Enalapril in your medicine cabinet?"

Jenny answered that one. "Linda gave me a ride home when I couldn't get my car started the other day. When she dropped me off, she asked to use the bathroom to wash her hands. Mom and I both remember that she used the bathroom upstairs, not the one downstairs. She could have planted the medicine bottle then.

"Maybe Linda even did something to my car so she'd have an excuse to take me home."

I interrupted to add that Linda's dog had been on Enalapril before it passed away three years ago. Fact Number Five. Or Six. I'd lost count by this time.

"Way to go, Mom," said Jenny. "I was wondering how Linda could have gotten hold of the drug."

"This is the most preposterous thing I've ever heard. Why would Linda want to incriminate me?" My Beloved demanded.

"I think you were just convenient, honey," I answered. "She knew you were doing some work for Rhodes. So there was already a handy connection between you two that she could exploit to her advantage."

"You've made some interesting points, Mrs. Andrews. But I'm still not convinced," Mark said. "This information is all hypothetical and circumstantial. There's no proof that Linda Burns and Davis Rhodes knew each other in college, or that they saw each other after he moved to the area and set up the Re-tirement Survival Center. Or that he recognized her. Or that she had the opportunity to plant the drug that killed him.

"I need a concrete reason to question her. You haven't given me one."

I slumped back in my chair. I'd given it my best shot. Sadly, it wasn't enough.

"Oh, my God," Jim said suddenly. "Maybe there's no proof connecting Rhodes and Linda, but I referred Bruce Burns to Rhodes for counseling. And I know Bruce went, because I saw him coming out of the Center a few weeks ago. "

Jim looked at me. "You remember, Carol, that he's been out of work for the last six months."

"What are you talking about?" I exclaimed. "Bruce takes the train into the city with you every morning."

"I know I told you about Bruce's situation months ago, and asked you to keep it to yourself," Jim insisted firmly. "He's still commuting into New York every day. But he's not going to a job. He's going to his outplacement agency."

"You never told me!" I retorted.

Jim sighed patiently. "I did tell you," he repeated. "And you say I never hear what you say to me. You never listen to me either. "

"Ok, ok," I admitted. "Maybe you did tell me and I forgot. This bickering isn't getting us anywhere. Go on."

"Bruce kept his job loss as quiet as possible," Jim continued. "I'm sure he and Linda expected he'd land another job right away, so nobody would ever have to know he'd been out of work. I always thought Bruce was a pompous bore, but he certainly has my sympathy for what he's been going through. I imagine their income has taken a pretty severe hit, with Bruce being unemployed for so long."

I looked at Mark and continued my scenario. "I'll bet Bruce saw the diploma from Papermill University on Rhodes's office wall when he went to the Center for counseling. He recognized the connection with Linda and her phony diploma."

"He must have been pretty desperate by that time," Jenny speculated. "He couldn't afford to take the chance that Linda's fake credentials would be discovered and she'd lose her job."

"Bruce switched Rhodes's blood pressure pills for the Enalapril, knowing that it would be fatal to Rhodes. And Linda's been covering up for her husband's crime by implicating Jim," I finished triumphantly. It all fit, didn't it?

"How would either of them know what drug to use to poison Rhodes?" Mark objected.

I smiled at him sweetly. "I haven't the faintest idea, Mark. But I know you and the rest of the police will figure that part out. And until you do, arresting someone else would certainly be premature, wouldn't it?"

I immediately switched from being Carol Andrews Super Sleuth into my Perfect Hostess role. "Now that we've figured all that out, anyone for ice cream bread?"

Chapter 30

The guy who can't figure out what to do with a Sunday afternoon is usually the same one who can't wait to retire.

After laborious police work to confirm my wild theory, Linda Burns and her husband Bruce were arrested and charged with the murder of Davis Rhodes. I heard an unconfirmed rumor that Linda was taken out of her classroom in handcuffs, and she was so angry she tried to bite one of the policemen.

Naturally, Mark wasn't able to tell us much about the hard evidence the police had accumulated against Linda and Bruce, despite all my pleading, but he did say that Rhodes had suffered all his life from very low blood pressure, a condition confirmed by both Grace and Sheila. The police theory is that Linda knew about this condition from their college days, when she and Rhodes dated briefly, and Bruce (with Linda egging him on) switched the pills Rhodes was on to treat his low blood pressure with Enalapril, which is prescribed to control high blood pressure. Then, they sat back and waited for Rhodes to have a heart attack.

One brilliant reporter got the idea of dubbing Linda and Bruce "Mr. and Mrs. Macbeth," after the Shakespeare play. Get it? They'll be standing trial in November.

My crack investigative team, of course, got absolutely no credit whatsoever for solving the case, which was just fine with me. The less that people in town knew about our contributions, the better.

Mary Alice's retirement shower was a huge success, largely thanks to Maria Lesco, whose obvious flair for putting on private parties is certain to give her a whole new list of clients.

Mark and Jenny see each other regularly. They seem to be quite enamored of each other, and I am doing my best not to nurture (that is, interfere in) the budding romance.

Jenny never went back to California to pick up the rest of her things. As she pointed out to me, she was starting a whole new chapter in her life. Out with the old, in with the new.

Nancy is up to her ears in real estate transactions. If the housing bubble has burst, nobody's told her.

Mary Alice is happily adjusting to her new life as a nursing instructor and private duty nurse. She has given the word "retirement" a whole new meaning.

Claire and Larry are thinking of becoming "snowbirds" and buying a condo in Florida. They've assured us they would only use the condo during the winter months, so they won't be moving away for good. And, of course, they would be near Mike, so they could keep an eye on him for Jim and me. Not that I would ever admit that to Mike, of course.

As for Jim and me, My Beloved did decide to retire. He was offered an excellent package from Gibson Gillespie, and he took it.

It's funny, but when he told me his decision, I wasn't as upset about it as I thought I'd be. After all, the man almost went to jail for a crime he didn't commit. Having him around on a regular basis is a blessing, compared to what could have happened.

But Jim wasn't one to sit at home for very long. Just when I started to wave travel brochures in his face, he announced he'd taken a part-time job as a columnist on our local paper. He's dubbed himself the paper's "curmudgeon-in-residence." He writes a weekly opinion piece, "State of the Town," in which he gets to criticize and comment on anything and everything. It's absolutely perfect for Jim since he thinks he's an expert on everything, and it also gets him out of the house.

Life was good. Maybe, too good.

And then one morning, over a leisurely second cup of coffee (which Jim had made), My Beloved said, "Carol, I think we should consider downsizing. Maybe selling this house and moving to one of those active adult communities. What do you think?"

I could think of a million come-back responses to that idea, all of them negative.

But that's another story.

Questions For Discussion

Carol Andrews would have saved herself and her family a lot of trouble if she'd been honest with Her Beloved about her fears. Don't make the same mistake she did. If Your Beloved is facing retirement, here are some questions Davis Rhodes suggests couples use to start a discussion about the next phase of your life.

1. How do you adjust to change?
2. How do you measure self-worth?
3. What is your idea of time well-spent?
4. What is your definition of success?
5. How/where do you see yourself in the next ten years?
6. On a scale of one-to-ten, with one being the highest, rank the following as being important in your life: financial security, a solid family life, social interaction, giving back to the community, professional satisfaction, living independently, good health, spousal interaction, being in charge of a situation, positive feedback.
7. If you could choose one thing to do every day, what would it be? Why?
8. What are your relationship expectations post-retirement? Do you visualize doing more things as a couple? Less? The same amount? Which activities, and why?

Good Luck!

Ice Cream Bread Recipe

From Agnes Seiwell

Prep time: 5 minutes.

Ingredients:

1 pint (2 cups) ice cream, softened. Flavor: your choice.

1 ½ cups self-rising flour.

Stir together ice cream and flour just enough so that flour is thoroughly moistened. Spoon batter into a greased and floured 8x4 inch loaf pan. Bake at 350 for 40 to 45 minutes or until a wooden toothpick inserted in center of bread comes out clean. Remove from pan and cool on a wire rack.

This two-ingredient bread is great any time of day. It can be served as a dessert topped with some whipped cream and chocolate or other flavored sauce, or toasted and used as a side dish to a meal.

Enjoy!

To Learn More About ***Retirement Can Be Murder***

WEBSITE Please visit our website, babyboomermysteries.com, for a schedule of author events, book signings, general news or to send us your questions and comments. If you have tips about dealing with retirement, or stories to share, we'd love to hear them.

ATTENTION BOOK CLUBS If you have made *Retirement Can Be Murder* your book club selection and would like to have Susan Santangelo discuss the book with your group after you've finished reading it, please go to the website and send us an e-mail. Due to scheduling constraints, not all book club meeting requests can be satisfied, so please reserve your date well in advance.

About the Author

An early member of the baby boomer generation, Susan Santangelo has been a feature writer, drama critic and editor for daily and weekly newspapers and magazines in the New York metropolitan area, including a stint at *Cosmopolitan.* A seasoned public relations and marketing professional, she produced special events for Carnegie Hall's centennial. Susan is a member of Sisters in Crime and The Cape Cod Writers' Center, and divides her time between the Connecticut shoreline and Cape Cod, MA. She shares her life with Her Personal Beloved, husband Joe, and three English Cockers: Tillie, Tucker and Lucy.

A portion of the sales from *Retirement Can Be Murder* will be donated to the Breast Cancer Survival Center (breastcancersurvival.org), a non-profit organization Susan founded in 1999 after being diagnosed with cancer herself.

Susan loves to hear from readers. Contact her at ssantangelo@aol.com. E-mail her and share your retirement stories.

Moving *Can Be* Murder

A Carol and Jim Andrews Baby Boomer Mystery

By Susan Santangelo

My Beloved had finally worn me down. I'd agreed to sell our beautiful antique home in Fairport, Connecticut, and downsize to a nearby "active adult" community.

The moving truck had come today, and all of our cherished possessions had gone into storage. Our new home wouldn't be ready to move into for two more months. I wanted to postpone the closing, but Jim, not wanting to lose the buyer—God forbid—opted to move us and our two English cocker spaniels, Lucy and Ethel, into a furnished one-bedroom apartment temporarily. It was quite a comedown—trading a five-bedroom home for a space smaller than our old master bedroom suite.

Within a month after his retirement, Jim had signed on as a columnist for our weekly newspaper, which kept him busy and out of my hair most of the time.

That is, he was out of my hair in a five-bedroom house. How that would translate to our temporary cramped digs remained to be seen.

I'd tried to put a brave face on when we walked out the kitchen door and locked it for the last time. But I felt like something I truly loved had died.

Coming in 2010